ALSO BY MATTHEW SHARPE

Stories from the Tube

NOthing is terrible

NOTHING IS TERRIBLE

a novel

Matthew Sharpe

VILLARD ❦ NEW YORK

VILLARD BOOKS and colophon are registered trademarks of Random House, Inc.

Grateful acknowledgment is made to Random House, Inc.,
for permission to reprint an excerpt from "If I Could Tell You"
from *W. H. Auden: Collected Poems,* edited by Edward Mendelson.
Copyright © 1945 by W. H. Auden.
Reprinted by permission of Random House, Inc.

Library of Congress Cataloging-in-Publication Data

Sharpe, Matthew.
    Nothing is terrible: a novel / Matthew Sharpe.
      p.   cm.
  ISBN 978-0-812-99227-4
    I. Title.
  PS3569.H3444N68   2000
  813'.54—dc21   99-39236

Random House website address: www.atrandom.com
Printed in the United States of America on acid-free paper

Book design by Jo Anne Metsch

146484122

FOR AMY

Contents

NOthing is terrible

I Die   A PROLOGUE

"THAT GIRL IS not normal, and neither is the boy," I overheard my uncle say to my aunt late one summer night a month after my parents had been killed in a car accident on the way home from a wedding. My twin brother Paul and I were ten years old at the time, and we were the children my childless uncle was talking about. "The boy is sickly, that much we know," he went on. "The girl—hard to say what the trouble is there."

This remark of my uncle's seems like as good a place as any to begin. If you'll stay with me here for a few moments, I think I can show you that what happened that night gave rise to a series of events that turn out to be the fabulous little story I call, for want of a better expression, my life.

My uncle was not kidding, by the way. He calls them as he sees them. Who once said it takes a mean man to tell the truth about others and a melancholy man to tell the truth about himself? No, I'm asking because I really can't remember who said it. There's so much to forget, my dear reader, and a lot of it will be forgotten here by me, your kind, happy interlocutor, the adult woman whom the little girl of our tale is astonished to find she has become. Ah, but enough about the person who is writing this autobiography. Let's return to the person who is living it.

"Paul!" I called out in a whisper to my brother. We were lying in the dark in our new bedroom. The air was hot and thick, and sound traveled well in that little house.

"Yes, Paul?" Paul replied. The name our parents had given me was Mary, and you may call me that if you wish, but at the time we saw no reason to honor their conventions, now that they had done the most irresponsible thing a pair of parents could do. Besides, we felt "Paul" suited me better, describing the person I was as well as it described my twin brother, just as the word *cleave* means both *to adhere* and *to split in two*.

"Paul," I said, "I don't feel like staying in bed tonight. Can you think of something for us to do?"

"Let's go down the street to the golf course," he said, and explained what he thought we ought to do when we got there. If a boy who had little hope for life and could do nothing well but think can be said to have a beautiful mind, then that was what Paul had, whereas I was a fine physical specimen of a girl, if a little wifty in the thinking department. The two of us had a division of labor whereby he thought up things for us to do and I did them.

The night we strolled out the front door of the small suburban house of our uncle the unlucky electronics repairman and his almost mute wife was a warm and clear and starry night. Coming from the city, we had not seen stars, and now that we were seeing them we agreed that we didn't like them. To us they were so many blemishes in an otherwise smooth sky. We knew that everyone was supposed to like stars. We'd heard nothing but good things said about stars, and we didn't care. Sorrow makes its own principles, which are not necessarily shared by the unsorrowful; I hope you will bear this in mind as you read on.

We walked on the wet grass of the fairway in short pajamas. I carried the shovel. Thousands of invisible crickets rubbed their legs together. Our naked feet were wet and cool, and cut blades of grass stuck to them in the dark. Far away on the narrow road we came from, a solitary car passed.

We were two pale, thin children with curly black hair. Paul's paleness was embellished by a spiderweb of red veins spread out just under his skin. These you could see anywhere you chose to look on the surface of his body. I imagined that the function of the veins was to make his skin that much more sensitive than other people's skin. I imagined the discomfort of being housed in that body, and when I had a physical sensation that I wished to experience more sharply, I tried to feel how Paul would feel it. The soft breeze on his arms and legs that night, I believed, felt like an ongoing swath of fine sandpaper moving across them. Paul walked ahead, navigating in near darkness with his fine abstract sense of space and time. I walked behind with a flashlight, idly investigating the two narrow strings of muscle that connected his torso to the back of his head.

We arrived at the first green and he removed the flag from

the hole and commanded me to expand the tiny golf-ball hole into a hole that the bodies of two small children could fit into. I bent my back and began to dig while he stood tall above me, head tilted back, nostrils aflare, holding the flag erect at arm's length like the white explorer claiming some wild land that I the dark native beneath him was busy getting in touch with. I dug and dug and dug and dug, or so it seems from the vantage of memory. And while I dug, my poor little twin brother, who shimmers now on the shared border of consciousness and oblivion, began another round of a game he referred to as the Philosophical Conundrum.

"All right, Paul," said Paul, "let's say your twin-engine Cessna has crashed in the middle of the Sahara Desert, and your millionaire boyfriend lover died in the crash and it's just you alive in the middle of the desert. And then a guy comes along giving you a choice."

"Where's the guy come from if I'm in the middle of—"

"It doesn't matter. He's just a guy, like a guy in a suit. And he comes down out of somewhere to give you a choice. And the choice is you can have a big diamond worth a hundred million dollars or you can have enough glasses of cold milk to last you till you get out of the desert. Which do you choose?"

"But I already have the rich boyfriend."

"But he's dead."

"But he leaves me all his money because he loves me so much."

"No he doesn't. He's just in it for the sex."

"No, it's more than sex. He loves me."

"Okay, he loves you, but he just met you like a month ago and he didn't have time to change his will yet."

"Who'd he leave the money to, before me?"

"His ex-wife, and she's a bitch and she hates you."

"The diamond."

"What?"

"I choose the diamond. From the guy."

"Okay. Fine. The diamond. Now. Poof, the guy's gone. Now it's just you and the diamond and a hundred thousand miles to the nearest water."

"No. There's water."

"Where?"

"Right over the hill."

"But the hill is a hundred thousand miles long."

"How come it has to be?"

"Because I'm the one making this up."

"You can't make stuff up *after* I choose."

"Your optimism is gonna get you killed one day."

"No it isn't."

"Shut up and dig."

I was bent over down inside the hole I had created thus far. Paul put his bare foot on my back, which, given the depth of the hole, was nearly level with the ground. I had taken off my pajama shirt for digging, and some of the blades of grass from his bare foot went onto my back and made infinitesimal bloodless cuts in the skin, and the sweat went into the cuts and my back started to itch and hurt. I laughed. I had to stop digging because Paul was making me laugh so much by having his foot on my back. He was laughing too. I took his foot off my back and stood up and fell sideways onto the crew-cut grass of the green. He fell on top of me and I was feeling passionate so I pulled him close to me and kissed him hard on the cheek. He resisted me, so I stood up and finished digging the hole.

We jumped into it and lay down because it was midnight

and we were tired. I curled up into a tight ball and Paul curled around my back in a loose arc. "I like how the dirt feels, Paul," he said to me. "Thank you for digging the hole."

"Thanks for the wonderful idea, Paul," I said. "Is there anything else?"

"What do you mean?"

"Do we have to do anything else on your idea?"

"No. We just fall asleep and wait for some grown-up to come along and get angry at us."

I closed my eyes and immediately began the descent. I heard Paul say, "Can I hold your hand?"

"Sure." I was lying on my right side, and I reached across my own chest and gave Paul my right hand.

"I like to hold your hand," he said. "When I touch you I tingle with how alive you are." I continued to let myself down into sleep as I felt Paul settling into place behind me. Half asleep, I felt him creeping over the surface of my back, whispery light, a faint tickle on my skin. At this moment, I have a palpable image of him as a long animated skeleton with soft white bones and powers of speech, the shadow of my inner life, clinging to the warmth of my flesh.

THE GROWN-UP whose anger we were waiting for was Tommy, our unlucky uncle. He was a mean, delicate, pretty, fine-featured blond man who repaired televisions and other appliances for a living. He was mean because he was pretty. Prettiness was a terrible burden to him because its mute prophecy—wealth—had gone unfulfilled. Prettiness ruined Tommy for a life of subsistence. It was an outrage to have to live modestly, having been born into the aristocracy of looks. If you have a tendency to be self-regarding, and then you're also poor and delicate and gorgeous and a man, it's a hard life. Tommy had little energy for niceness because he had to devote himself to the tragedy of prettiness. The tragedy was that the prettiness kept him enclosed in a stifling little atmosphere of mediocrity not much bigger than his own body that he expected someone taken with his beauty to lift him out of.

If he could only have convinced someone to let him play golf at the country club, for instance. He practiced his driving and putting at the driving and putting range in the next town, and if he could play just one round of eighteen holes, he'd be in. That Tommy thought he was on his way to insinuating himself into a club membership by signing a service contract with the grounds manager of the club to repair its TVs was proof that he carried around with him this bubble of mediocrity that was impenetrable from both sides. This is only my opinion, of course.

We were discovered at six A.M. by the aforementioned grounds manager, Hawthorne, the other grown-up whose anger we were looking forward to. He was a big, robust, crimson man in his early sixties who loved his morning constitutional on the golf course in crisp khaki shorts and saddle-style golf spikes. He came upon this huge hole in the first green. He peered down into it and saw the two skinny weirdo new foster children of the TV repairman sleeping. The wrongdoing, I imagine, was so categorically pure that the outrage it inspired in him must have felt something like delight. He had thin white hair, and his whole head turned dark purple with what seemed to be happiness when he woke us up. He grabbed my arm and yanked me out of the hole. As I came up, I put my lips next to his ear and said, "You can't pull my brother's arm like that. It'll come off in your hand." He thought that was very funny, and Paul came up on his own.

"I feel like I'm dreaming here," Hawthorne said. "Tell me this isn't happening."

"This isn't happening," Paul said.

Hawthorne thought that was even funnier. Without taking his eyes off the shovel he said, "Your uncle's gonna go nuts over this. Your uncle is going to go nuts. I just hope I can get you kids up to the house before he wakes up this morning so I'll have the pleasure of getting him out of bed for this one. I mean, this is inspirational."

Paul said, "I'm sure the golfers will think so." Hawthorne's mirth subsided then. As he walked us down to his station wagon in the clubhouse parking lot and drove us up to Tommy's house he tried to laugh a few more times, but it was a big effort for him. In fact, we were not prepared for just how upset it would make Hawthorne to contemplate the indignation of his bosses, the golfers.

Hawthorne and Tommy had shared an incident. The very first time a TV set had broken at the country club, Tommy showed up to repair it in a black-and-white houndstooth check blazer and white pinpoint oxford dress shirt and pale blue tie with small bright-yellow polka dots. Hawthorne had a fit. He told Tommy to hurry up and fix the TV and get out of there and next time come dressed for the job he was doing. Tommy was bewildered. Not only did Tommy have better golf skills than Hawthorne without being allowed to play golf where Hawthorne was allowed, but Tommy had a better wardrobe and better taste in clothes than Hawthorne, and Hawthorne could wear his nice clothes in places where Tommy couldn't wear his even nicer ones.

We arrived at Tommy's doorstep with the great discomfort of Hawthorne looming above us.

Our Aunt Myra answered the door, a non-churchgoer up and dressed on a Sunday morning at 6:45 A.M. Hawthorne stood between and slightly behind Paul and me, one hand on a shoulder of each child. At ten years old I wanted to think of myself as a person who knew who she was, but now, many years later, when I think of the way I focused my attention on the faces of adults, I know that I needed those faces to find myself in. Myra's was the hardest possible face for this purpose. Before Hawthorne spoke, I saw a look of confusion on her face. Then Hawthorne said, "The children have vandalized the first green." Then the look on Myra's face was gone, replaced by a frozen expression that I had been seeing for a month. It was an expression that said here was another of life's generalized difficulties. To give more of herself to an event like this would have been something too wild for Myra. Where inside a person do all the events go when they go almost unnoticed? To the event graveyard.

"I'll get my husband," she said.

Hawthorne stood silently with Paul and me on the flagstone stoop, none of us yet invited into the house.

After ten minutes, Tommy came to the door. He had not been awake. About him was the smell of stick deodorant fermented for hours in dark armpits. He wore a neatly pressed dark blue paisley satin robe that showed some of his narrow, hairless chest. His pale, gently freckled skin looked even softer at this, a wee hour for him. His fingers were long and delicate and tapered, the finest fingers of any TV repairman in town. His blue eyes were shiny and his facial features looked small and fine and hurt. Tommy always looked hurt. If, in the morning, he poured milk into his cereal and the milk splashed on his clothes, that was a small example of injustice. Hawthorne at his door in the morning with the two brats was a big, vulgar, bodily injustice standing at his door with the two brats. Hawthorne overseeing the TVs down at the club presented a professional and personal challenge for Tommy that was unpleasant but workable. Hawthorne on the border of Tommy's sleep, however, Hawthorne authoritatively touching the children whom Tommy had brought into his own home for the sake of guilt and duty and love of his dead sister and how it would look to the people who would care how it looked—and even for the sake of the children themselves, whom he worried about perpetually on top of his own worries—Hawthorne, in short, in the tender private places sent Tommy into a quiet tizzy. Did he have to bow to Hawthorne on the threshold of his own house? He needed Hawthorne.

Partly because of the manly discomfort Tommy's prettiness caused in him, Hawthorne wanted to get out of there and order someone to fill in that hole, so he gave Tommy the basic information and was ready to leave when Tommy said, "I'll pay you whatever it costs to repair the hole."

"No need."

"I want to."

"Don't."

"I will."

"You will what?"

"Send you money for the damage."

"I'm not gonna tell you how much it is."

"I'll guess."

"It's stupid."

"It's the right thing to do."

"It won't get you anywhere."

"I don't care."

"Gotta run."

"You'll be receiving a check."

"I'll send it back."

"I'll send it back at you."

"Do whatever you want," Hawthorne said, and walked away.

I understood why adults were inclined to hate or at least fear Paul. Paul had an aberrant philosophical cast. He knew things other people didn't know—secrets from the womb, perhaps—and he had a genius for expressing them in unhappy prophecy. "They're not ever going to let you into the club no matter what you do," Paul said to Tommy, and Tommy, who had had no practice at child rearing, grabbed a hunk of Paul's curly hair close to the scalp and used it as a handle with which to rattle Paul's head vigorously for fifteen or eighteen seconds.

WHEN I'M FEELING sad, which is quite often even now that I'm all grown up, I look for ways to console myself for Paul's crippling illness of that summer. Illness, I think, taking my lead from Paul, was the form Paul was meant to inhabit. Appropriately to his condition, he was a boy without hope, and it is the memory of his lack of hope that leads me unfailingly back to the beauty of Paul. He was not happy or charming or pleasing to the eye, and he understood these things about himself, and he was not indifferent to them, but he also did not rail against what he was, the way Tommy did and the way everyone else does whom I've ever met, either right out in the open for all to see or else secretly in some place that may be hidden even from themselves.

Until September of that year I divided my time between the boy who was already little more than a mind in a dark room and the two strangers who were now my parents. More time with Paul than with the others. I felt I had no choice but to stay with him in that dank little space. I did not do enough big, muscular activity to subdue the rude and contemptuous feelings an unhappy girl like me harbored in her breast, but Paul appreciated my sacrifice, and in return he tried to teach me to think with rigor and passion, if not exactly with the joy of intellectual activity.

"I have another conundrum for you," he said, lying supine on his army cot, looking grim on the night after the head rattling.

"Okay."

"Let's say Mom and Dad are still alive."

"Let's say they are."

"No, I mean let's believe they are."

"I can't do that."

"I'm trying to help you think."

"Don't."

"Fine. Just say they are, then."

"Fine."

"And then they're kidnapped by these evil guys and the evil guys call you on the phone and tell you to go to where they're holding Mom and Dad, which is this big abandoned armory out on the edge of town with a quarter-mile running track. You walk into the armory and it's all lit up by these bare bulbs that are hanging down from the ceiling, and from where you stand by the entrance there're four tiny specks in the huge area of concrete inside the running track. Two of the specks are Mom and Dad, tied up and sitting in chairs. The other two specks are the evil guys, standing over Mom and Dad, and one of 'em's pointing a gun at Mom's head and the other one's pointing a gun at Dad's head."

I was sitting on Paul's bed next to his body and I cried a little.

"We have to do this," he said. "It's important."

"Okay."

"Then one of the guys says, 'Listen, girlie, here are some very lightweight running shoes that are just your size,' and he hands you the shoes and he goes, 'You have to put them on and get on that track and run a mile in four minutes or less or we shoot your parents.' So, Paul, the conundrum is, what do you do?"

"I run the mile, what else?"

"You can't."

"Yes."

"No."

"Shut up. Why are you even saying this?"

"Because you have to start thinking of these things. You don't have any parents to help you when life gets confusing."

"I have you."

"I wouldn't count on me."

"I said I'd run the damn mile."

"Even professionals can only do it in like 3:59.99999. How are you gonna do it?"

"Because I have to."

"You couldn't even stop Tommy from breaking my neck, practically."

"Paul, you make me feel so helpless."

"You *are* helpless, Paul."

On the first morning of his convalescence, Paul asked me to travel from my army cot across the rust-colored deep pile carpet to his army cot, sit down beside him, and tickle him. He couldn't have borne the invasive tickling that causes convulsions of laughter. He wanted the kind that is light fingertips rushing along the surface of the person, leaving a wake of little outstanding nubs. I tickled him in this way and we observed the effects of the tickling on Paul's body. We discovered that it was interesting for me to tickle his chest in particular because of the changes in his nipples: they shrank slightly in circumference, and grew darker, and stood out in pointy relief from the rest of his chest. For that summer at least, my own body remained a private space that I could do whatever I wanted with, except for my hands, which, beginning on that morning, I submitted to the behest of Paul and his body. Paul's body became the joint property of me and Paul—a fascinating little domain full of mystery and foreboding.

Myra came into the room that morning at eight o'clock, as she would do every morning that summer, with a bowl of sugared cereal for Paul. She did all the external things that a good mother would do for her own child. She was gentle and meek and almost sweet. Whatever feelings of unmitigated sweetness she had were trapped inside her body. All of the feelings were in there, and they rarely could come out. She entered the room and opened the curtains and, because the room was dark, turned on the bare ceiling light. She put the raised breakfast tray over Paul's abdomen and put her hand on his forehead and asked him how he was feeling. She asked me how I was feeling, too. "Come downstairs and I'll fix you breakfast," she said to me.

I don't remember how I began helping Myra—if that's what you would call what I did—in her garden. I can't imagine that she asked me. She didn't ask people to do things that would benefit her. She didn't ask me to set the table or clean up after meals or wash the dishes or take out the garbage. Tommy told me to do some of those things some of the time, when he remembered. I must have volunteered to help Myra in the garden on that first morning of Paul's illness, seeing an opportunity to be away from Paul, out under the sun, moving around and smelling the earth.

It was also an opportunity to be near Myra. The emotional comfort she had to give voluntarily was, as I said, locked inside her body, but I found, with Myra, that I could get it by taking it. For an hour that first morning I watched her in the garden. Her body was the opposite of Tommy's body. It was big and coarse and earthy. She was an inch taller than he was, and wider, and deeper. She had big round hips and heavy breasts and thick, muscular arms and legs, black dense hair, and a wide nose. She worked in the garden for hours under the sun and her skin didn't burn and her body didn't wear out. It was so clearly Tommy who had not wanted children of his own because even a ten-year-old could see that Myra was made for intense, purposeful sex and birthing. (I say this now, though who but a ten-year-old knows what a ten-year-old can see, except perhaps someone who has just turned eleven?)

After an hour in the garden, it was no longer enough to look at Myra, crouched with her spade. I ran at her and pounced on her back, trying to knock her over. She let out what I thought was a laugh, but might just have been an expulsion of air from the blow. I clung to her with my arms and legs. Was she smiling? Could she?

"Can I help you with your work?" I asked.

"No, thank you."

"Please?"

"All right."

"What should I do?"

"I don't know."

"Come on, just tell me something to do."

"All right. Dig a long trough from here to where those sticks are."

"What's a trough?" (I knew what a trough was.)

"It's a long, shallow hole."

"How shallow should the trough be?"

"Six inches."

"How long should the trough be?"

"To where those sticks are."

I dug the trough for a minute and put the spade down and ran around the house as fast as I could. When I got back I told Myra I would run around the house again and she had to time me.

"How?"

"Does your watch have a second hand?"

"No."

"Then go one one thousand, two one thousand, three one thousand."

"But I'm gardening."

"Please? Please, Aunt Myra?" I bent down next to her and kissed her cheek. She continued to garden. I knelt down next to her on top of a marigold and felt the cool, uneven surface of the marigold petals crumple against the skin of my knee. She didn't tell me to get off the marigold. Maybe she didn't care how her garden turned out. I knelt there crushing her marigold and tasting the sweat from her cheek that clung to my lips when I kissed her. I watched the places where the sweat came from, which I thought were the shallow pockmarks on her skin. I thought of her own big lips touching my cheek once a night before bed; one regimented kiss per twenty-four hours was Myra's shy charm. "Please?"

"Please what?"

"Time me."

"How could I time you? I don't know how to do it." She seemed almost desperate.

"One one thousand, two one thousand, three one thousand."

"One one thousand, two one thousand." She paused for a moment. "Three one thousand." She looked at me questioningly, as if I were teaching her calculus.

"Four one thousand," I said.

"Four one thousand," she said.

"Okay, now you say go and I'm gonna run around the house three times. The whole time I'm running you're going 'something one thousand, something one thousand, something one thousand,' and when I come around the first time you have to be saying the numbers loud so I can hear you, so I can pace myself. When I come around the second time, same thing. When I come around the third time, same, except we both stop."

She had paused in her work, and I could see she was torn between timing me and going back to work.

"I'm gonna start at these sticks here."

"Okay."

"Okay, I'm ready."

"Okay."

I stood facing away from Myra, ready to go. Nothing happened. I turned around and Myra was staring at the ground, not doing anything.

"What are you doing?" I said.

"Waiting for you to start."

"You have to say *go*."

"Oh. All right."

"I'm ready. Say it now."

"All right." I stood there looking at her and she looked at me.

"Right now," I said.

"Go."

I ran as fast as I could and it felt good in my legs. There was the little gray wooden house on my left blurring toward me, toward me. When I came around Myra was gardening again and who knew if somewhere inside of her body she was saying one one thousand? I tore around the house a few more times until I was breathing hard and my chest hurt and I couldn't make my legs go fast anymore. Then I piled into Myra and collapsed on top of her, saying, "What was my time?"

"I don't know. About two minutes?"

"Thanks, Aunt Myra."

She gardened with me on her.

"Do you want to do this again tomorrow?"

"If you like." This is the way I helped her garden each day until noon, when the sun became too hot and there was no more gardening to do.

AT 5:00 P.M. on the day I began helping Myra in the garden, Tommy arrived home and removed his blue service uniform and bathed and put on a white cotton dress shirt and pink

Bermuda shorts and suede athletic shoes with no socks. He could have been living in Darien, Connecticut, in that outfit, with the rolled-up sleeves that fell away gracefully from his thin forearms, and with his narrow, elegantly muscled legs sparsely covered with golden hair. He walked into the kitchen, a room still bright at 5:20 P.M. Myra had mixed up a batch of powdered lemonade, which he preferred to the kind she knew how to make with real lemons and sugar and water. There was such a lovely feeling of coolness about a room Myra had cleaned and arranged, in which Tommy stood wearing his Bermudas and drinking lemonade.

"You want to throw around a baseball?" he said. "Hey! You deaf? Mary. Baseball?"

"Me?"

"No, all the other people named Mary."

"Okay."

I ran and got my glove and joined Tommy in the backyard, which Myra had mown short the way he liked it.

"I'm gonna pitch first for a while. You squat down over there, and when you catch 'em, just toss 'em back lightly. If there's time before it gets dark, you can pitch a few also."

I squatted and Tommy, holding the ball, got himself up into the sequence of preparatory attitudes of the major league pitcher—scuffing at the ground with the toe of one shoe, hands behind him, left side toward me; staring down the opponent, which, since there was no batter, was me; left foot back, arms up over and behind his head, arms coming down as the left foot came forward and up; right arm back, left foot toward me, left foot planting in the grass, left arm pointing at me, body pivoting, right arm releasing the ball in my direction.

He went through some staggering, spinning motions, which I paid attention to instead of watching the ball coming at me. The ball hit me in the forehead.

"You're supposed to catch that. You all right? Yeah, you're okay. Let's try another. Toss it back."

I threw a wild one way over his head that he had to run for. He came back and pitched another viciously hard one at me, which I caught, stinging my hand. I chucked another wild one—even farther away this time—and he ran and got it and really tried to wound me with his next pitch. We went on in that vein for an hour. I didn't care if I got hit by his pitches. The pain distracted me from other concerns.

After an hour, Myra tiptoed into the backyard with her hands behind her back and her head slightly bowed and stood between Tommy and me, just out of the ball's path—she was another one who probably would not have minded if she'd been hit; would not have noticed was more like it, in her case. Though she had come to indicate in some way that we should go inside for dinner, she did not speak.

Tommy said, "Is there something we can help you with, dear?"

"Dinner's ready," she said, as if dinner had come into being without agency.

The game of catch became another of that summer's routines.

When dinner was over I rejoined Paul in the dank little cave that was our private space. In the hour after dinner he liked to keep the electric lights off so he could watch the natural daylight drain from the air and from each object in the room. Paul didn't like to speak during the darkening of the room, so I sat by him in silence, idly tickling the bottoms of his feet. Then, in the darkness, his rigorous mental conditioning of me would begin again:

"Let's say you're on a desert island with one other person . . .

"Let's say you're in a burning house. . . .

"Let's say you're driving a train headed for a busload of schoolchildren. . . .

"Let's say you reach the age of ten and stop being able to think. . . ."

Evening came to its ritual end when Myra entered and said, "Time for bath." I would then turn on the light in the room, and Myra would carry Paul to the bathroom as if he were a damsel in distress and she the brave hero, only in this case the damsel, while being bathed, always got an erection.

So now you know about Paul and Tommy and Myra and me, and the little life we all had together.

AND THEN, READER, there was the morning at the end of August when Paul stood up out of his army cot, announced, "I can walk!" and took a few small, stiff-legged steps toward me, so much like an idea of a skinny, pathetic, invalid boy and so little like an actual boy that I hardly believe anymore that it happened.

Tommy was at work and Myra was out shopping. I led Paul out to the tiny hill by the fence that separated our backyard from our neighbors' backyard, where I had recently made a thrilling discovery.

"Look, Paul," I said.

"I don't see anything."

"Look down."

"What?"

"The bees."

"What bees?"

There was a fearfulness in Paul's voice that I didn't recognize.

"What are you right now?" I asked him.

"What?"

"What are you?"

"I don't know what you're talking about."

"Just, come on, say what you are."

"The sun is hurting my eyes."

I was trying to get at something: Paul's attitude at that moment was so different from the attitude of the Paul I thought I knew that I wondered if he were not offering some more advanced type of Philosophical Conundrum: let's say I cease to think or behave like the Paul you know; am I still Paul?

We stood for a moment and watched a half a dozen bees hovering above a three-inch-wide hole in the ground by the fence where the grass was thin enough that you could see the dry, pale brown dirt beneath it. I went inside the house and came back with one of Tommy's golf clubs. I escorted Paul away from this new hole in the ground in our lives. The network of hair-thin red veins seemed closer than ever to the surface of the skin of his face and his fragile, white little arms and legs. In that way, the inside of my brother was becoming the outside. I returned alone to the hole with the golf club in my hand. I shoved the golf club down inside the hole and pulled it out fast and ran away from the hole to join Paul. I made Paul lie down on his belly in the grass next to me because I thought the bees wouldn't see us that way. The air above the hole filled up with bees. I could see nothing that was behind the place where the bees were—a small place in the universe made up of the simple hatred of self-preservation. I felt as if all the bees were telling my body something. A shudder and a chill ran through my torso and limbs. I grabbed Paul and shoved myself against him and kissed his cheek. He was limp. "Hug me," I said, and he did, at first because I had told him to and then, seemingly, because he needed comforting, though it was I who had caused him to need it.

The air above the hole was thinning out. The decreasing number of bees in the sky above the hole corresponded to the subsiding of the thrill in my torso and limbs. I released Paul but he did not release me. He kissed me softly on the lips and I kissed him back, thinking it might ease the restlessness that replaced the thrill, but my mouth was indifferent to his mouth. I stood up and helped him to his feet.

"You try it now," I said.

"Try what?"

"Making the bees go crazy."

"I don't want to."

"You have to."

"Please?" he asked very weakly, the ritualistic resistance of the hopeless.

I handed him Tommy's golf club and began to escort him by the arm toward the hole. He pulled his arm away from me and walked slowly forward on his own. He looked calm now. He stood above the hole, meditating on the six or seven bees that flew around his ankles. Now there were ten. Now there were fifteen. As if he had many other things on his mind—idly, you might say—he eased the golf club down into the hole and drew it out. He stood there. He turned his head and looked at me. He smiled. I screamed at him to run.

Instead of running, he danced. It was a jazzy dance with whiplike arm moves and crazy, syncopated sidesteps. He danced around the bee hole, in honor of the bee hole. He fell down and seemed to land directly on the golf club. I thought he was shrieking because the end of the golf club had poked him in the belly. I ran to him and took him in my arms and carried him away from the hundred bees in much the same way as Myra, more slowly, had carried him night after night to and from their tender, erotic bath. I laid him down on the ground and felt but did not fully register the sharp jabs on my neck and under my arms.

"They're in my shirt," he said, as someone might complain with casual annoyance, I stubbed my toe.

I took off his shirt and brushed away the dirty yellow-and-black bees that were writhing and the ones that were already dead. He had nipples all over his body now. They protruded farther from the surface of his skin than the original two and were growing larger in circumference.

I knelt above Paul, studying him. He looked at me sweetly. "Paul, I can't breathe so well," he said.

"What should I do, Paul?"

"Just stay here with me for a while."

"Okay."

"This is not so bad."

"It isn't?"

"I'm glad Tommy and Myra aren't here. It's nice to just be alone with you."

"Yeah, it's nice."

"What are you gonna do, later tonight?" he asked, as if asking about the customs of children in a country he would never visit.

"I don't know. Have dinner."

"What else?"

"Play catch with Tommy."

"I think you should mate with Myra," he said. "It would make her feel good to have a baby to take care of."

Some of the pink bumps on Paul were connecting up with one another, making long, thick, pink fingers along the surface of his belly. He said, "I'm glad it was you, Paul."

"You're glad what was me?"

"You know."

This was his final puzzle, not a hard one. Then—at least this is the way I remember it—my brother became an idea.

1

The Horror of Grade School

PLEASE INDULGE ME here, reader, as I ease out of the "prologue" and into "chapter one" of "my" "life"; take a moment and try to think of everything that happened to you every day for a week of your life starting in, say, September of the year you were ten years old. Did you try it? It's really really difficult, right? In my case it's especially hard since around that time my mind, unbeknownst to me, began its own program of forgetting. My mind's reason for forgetting was, I assume, to banish grief from its domain, and in this it was only partially successful. Some of the grief remained, while certain other virtues of mental and emotional life fled; kindness was one, memory of daily events was another.

So what your humble memoirist is doing now, for your reading pleasure, is she's opening the gate of her mind, flinging it open to memory, to kindness, to grief. Well, okay, she's nudging the gate open. She's leaving the gate ajar with the security chain still attached. Let's not get carried away here—a memoirist needs her amnesia, her cruelty, her euphoria.

Here's something I wish I could remember that I can't: my parents, the original ones. After Paul died, I began to forget them. All that lingered were certain songs my father had often sung to me, but I am uncertain even about those. To this day, when I sing the songs, I know that some of the words are wrong, but I don't know which ones. "Love, oh love, oh careful love," I sang, the autumn after I killed my brother. (Which word is wrong there?)

SCHOOL BEGAN AGAIN that fall. I stopped working in the garden with Myra, and I stopped playing catch with Tommy, and I did not ever do those things with them again. I became preoccupied with people my own age, and I developed my ongoing involvement with myself. I had some difficulties with the other children in school, and without parents or a brother I sometimes felt desperate, so I took refuge in the sensations of my deluxe body. After school, I ran around and around and around the house, with no interest anymore in being timed but only in exhaustion. At night in bed, I softly tickled my own arms and legs and chest. I lay on my back and hummed with my mouth open and lightly punched my breastbone in varying rhythmic patterns. During the day, when other children were watching, I merely thought of doing these things. As I reveled in the pleasures of my own robust health, so Tommy and Myra became more fragile, it seemed. This may be what happens to people whose secret wish comes true, or halfway true.

I went to a small rectangular brick school that housed grades K through six on a wooded hillside. If Tommy was an overly elegant dresser, then Myra was a simple, tidy dresser with a decent sense of the rightness of clothes—at least of the clothes she dressed her adoptive daughter in—and therefore it was probably not the pale flower-print dress that I wore on the first day of school that caused the other kids to stare at me. I like to think it was the grief, which must have migrated from my mind to the surface of my skin. That would explain why I got punched a lot and seemingly at random: people testing the properties of the grieving skin.

In particular there was a group of boys who liked to hit me. There was a big, dirty-blond, smart-mouthed kid named Harry who was the leader of the boys. Hourly, he sent his emissaries to punch my arms. Once a day, he himself wandered over and performed some variation on the arm punch to demonstrate the kind of innovative thinking that made him worthy of leadership. Smiling, he approached the table where I sat with my head down as usual—like the rest of the boys he mistook my unwillingness to engage as a sign of submission rather than disinterest. He punched me in the chest or brought the side of his fist down on top of my thigh, walked back to his friends, and exchanged nods of affirmation with them, whereupon they proceeded to microevaluate the transaction, in preparation for the kinds of work that boys do when they grow up. As a form of social intercourse, this was tedious and stung for about a minute. As a bodily sensation to savor in private later on, it had its uses and pleasures.

We had what was called at that time an open classroom, which meant that no one had to do any work. Bulletin boards hung from the wall at the front of the room; stapled to each bulletin board was a piece of paper with a list of the names of all the children in the class. One bulletin board was labeled

MATH and one was labeled LANGUAGE and one was labeled SO-
CIAL STUDIES, et cetera. At the end of each day we had to write
on each bulletin board a several-word description of the work
we had accomplished in the area of discipline of the given bulletin board. So it is actually a slight exaggeration to say that nobody had to do work. Four people had to do work and write
about what they had done so that the rest of the class would
know what to write when they wrote about the work they
hadn't done. Sadly, the very children who did do the work
lacked the imagination to write down any more or less than
what they had done; that too carries over into adult working
life.

At first I myself did not document the work I had not done,
and so the space next to my name was blank day after day, not
because I felt myself to be outside the system of small rewards
and punishments for which the bulletin boards served as a
clearinghouse, nor because I was immune to the keen feelings
that attended success and failure at school. I just didn't
wanna. I didn't wanna do any work, I didn't wanna say I'd done
any work, I didn't wanna talk to anyone at school. I wanted to
go home and run around and around and around the house
and eat dinner and sit in my room tickling my arms and tickling them until all the arm skin nerves were worn out and
delirious and subdued.

Because I was doing no work, Mrs. Building, my teacher,
began actively to pity me. She was small and thin and sweet
and naïve, with medium-successful authority over her students. Twice a day she took me by the hand, led me to her
desk, and sat me down in a low hard wooden chair next to her
high cushioned metal chair and devoted twenty solid minutes
to trying to soothe me and bring me out. The first tactic I tried,

to avoid the horror of the pity of my teacher, was viciousness. Harry, the leader of the boys, came over one day with all his big cream-colored flesh. His avant-garde statement of the day was to punch me lightly in the throat. I punched him hard in the nose. He looked at me stunned. I punched him hard in the nose again and it bled. Then I punched him hard in the nose again. Then I did it again. Then I stepped on his foot and he fell down. I got on top of him and punched him and scratched him and spit on him. Mrs. Building pulled me off and hugged me and said, "You poor thing." That was not at all the result I was looking for. However, there was another result that was quite pleasing: with one easy and reasonably enjoyable act of violence I had ruined Harry's social standing among the boys.

Building continued to pity me each day from 11:00 to 11:20 A.M. and again from 2:00 to 2:20 P.M. I was at a loss. Dierdre noticed. She was to the girls what Harry had been to the boys until I beat him up: mean and influential. Now, there may be some grounding in reality for the kinds of statements people make about girls at that age—that they are subtler social beings than boys are—because instead of hitting me, Dierdre befriended me. She came over to my table after one of my conferences with Building and sat down sweetly in the chair next to mine, our first social contact. She had nice flaxen conspiratorial pigtails and a concerned frown as she hunched toward me in the chair: her elbows were resting on the innermost part of her lap, her left hand held her right hand on her knee, her toes were half facing each other, half facing me. "I know what you can do about Jane Building," she said.

"What?"

"You hate the conferences, right?"

"How did you know?"

"Listen, here's what you do: be average. Do work. Get along with others. That's it. Then she won't bother you."

I thought maybe she was giving good advice. After all, she herself had the bases covered: she was the smartest girl and the most popular girl and the meanest girl *and* she was not the teacher's pet.

"Do I really *do* the work?" I said.

"No. What are you, stupid?"

So, as camouflage, I began doing what everyone else did. At the end of the day I approached the bulletin boards and wrote *fractions* and *spelling list number 7* and *Treaty of Brest-Litovsk.* Treaty of Brest-Litovsk, by the way, was a very popular one to write, especially among the boys. They were fascinated by the ramifications of this treaty. At any hour of the school day you could hear a couple of boys discussing Brest-Litovsk, finding nuances of significance that had eluded all other historians for most of the century.

Mrs. Building called Myra to talk about me, which was like calling a child about another child. They arranged a parent-teacher conference. When Myra told Tommy about the conference he got very excited and bought a cape. He loved to meet officials like teachers. Anything could happen in the presence of an official. He would be recognized for his good qualities or be able to change jobs. Thus the cape for the conference with Jane Building, who was skinny and sweet and twenty-six years old and three months pregnant. The cape was made of black wool on the outside and red satin on the inside. He wore it with a black turtleneck and black trousers with suspenders and black low-cut suede zip-up boots. He held his chin up when he wore the cape. His eyes were close together and blue, and his skin was soft like the freckled skin of a

French film actress. Myra wore a brown corduroy jumper with a belt at the waist and a white button-down shirt with a small faded bluebell pattern. The conference took place one Friday afternoon in the classroom after school. I waited in the hallway and peered through the glass panel in the door. Tommy had the hopeful, hurt look on his face that always anticipated the failure of an event. Myra's eyes began dripping tears shortly after she sat down by Building's desk, and continued to drip for the whole conference, as if the entire contents of her body were going to leak out onto the floor.

Building's twenty-minute sessions with me did not cease. The main outcome of the parent-teacher conference was the cape.

I JOINED DIERDRE'S group of friends in the specific way that the person who will be sacrificed joins the group. I became especially close with Dierdre and two other nasty little girls, Melissa and Toni. They liked me a lot. People relish the person they are going to inflict pain on more than they relish each other. One afternoon I found myself in the bathroom with these three: the girls' bathroom, to be exact. Dierdre and I went into stalls to pee and the other two went to stand in front of the mirror above the row of three sinks. They didn't yet know what to do in front of the mirror except stand there and talk. Dierdre, in the stall next to mine, saw that my feet were facing the back of the stall and she peered over the top of the partition separating our stalls. I had pulled my dress up and almost off. My arms were still in the armholes but I had taken my head out of the head hole, and the bulk of the dress was bunched up behind my neck. My underwear was around my knees. I stood over the toilet and peed into it.

"How the hell do you do that?" Dierdre said.

I said, "What, you don't pee?"

"Not like that!"

"Why, how do *you* do it?"

"Sitting down. Hey, you two!" she called to the ones by the mirror. They came over and stood in front of the stalls. "Open the door," Dierdre said to me. I opened it. The urine was still flowing out of me. I had eaten a beet salad from Myra's garden for lunch and it was making the water in the toilet bowl red, which added another layer of meaning and/or incomprehension for the girls. "Look at her," Dierdre said. "Is that amazing?"

"How are you doing that?" Melissa said.

"Give us a demonstration of how you do that," Dierdre said from above me, her arms dangling into my stall.

"Why should I?"

"Because."

The urine subsided and I used a piece of toilet paper to clean myself.

"Okay, so that's something. You wipe yourself," Dierdre said. "What else do you do? How do you aim it, basically?"

"You take it between your hands like this," I said, exasperated, turning around so she and the other girls could really see.

"Take *what* between your hands?"

"The genitals."

"The genitals!"

"You know, the little area you pee out of."

"Little area, that's what you call it?"

"Why, what do you call it?"

"I call *that* a penis."

"This isn't a penis. Haven't you ever seen a penis before?"

"I'm looking at one right now."

"I can't believe Mary has a penis!" Toni, giddy with horror, said.

"Mary has a penis," the others said.

"What's going on in here?" That was Mrs. Building. She had come in and was staring at my crotch. "Oh, my word," she said. "Girls, all of you get back to class. You too, Mary. What are you doing in here showing these girls *that* for?"

Building stood by the bathroom door and shooed us back to class. I knew this to be the end of her reign of pity. "Thank you," I whispered to Dierdre in the hallway on the way back to the classroom, and she looked dismayed.

After school Dierdre and the two others cornered me alone between the Dumpsters behind the school. The two girls sneered and Dierdre said, "You're not allowed in the girls' room anym．．．."

"Why?"

"We don't want you in there."

"What if I go in anyway?"

"You know how Harry and the other boys used to punch you? Well, Melissa and Toni will come up to you in the girls' room and hold your arms and I'll smash your face into the sink over and over till it's a bloody mess."

I considered that. "So where do I go if I have to pee or something?"

"The boys' room."

Next morning I went to the boys' room and was peeing in a urinal when a kid named Mittler came over to me. He often had a thin coat of dried saliva on his chin and was the soul of politeness, having punched me only half a dozen times in all. He had been second-in-command of the boys until I beat up

Harry. Now he was their leader. Mittler possessed many qualities of the philosopher-king. He ruled with an extraordinarily soft touch and had brought the boys into an era of enlightenment and peace. He waited until I finished peeing before he addressed me.

"So you're using the boys' room now," he said.

"You got a problem with that?"

"Nope. How come the girls won't let you use theirs anymore?"

"How do you know they won't?"

"Dierdre told me. She asked me if I'd let you use the boys' room."

"Gosh, I guess she was doing me a really big favor."

"I told her you could use it."

"Gosh."

"Dierdre also said you showed her your Litovsk." Mittler made a gesture with his hand as if he were tipping his hat, turned, and walked out of the boys' room. No one had ever been so polite to me before. That really got me.

THE NIGHT AFTER the parent-teacher conference, Tommy wore the cape to dinner in our kitchen. Beneath the cape he wore a dark blue blazer and slacks and a white dress shirt and red tie. He strode into the kitchen clutching the edges of the cape. He held his chin high. He looked down at Myra and me, waiting for us to sit that he might sit. In the autumn, the kitchen was spacious and neat and bright and cool. In his dark outfit Tommy stood out in relief from the room. While waiting for us to sit down, he manipulated the cape meaningfully about his body. He could be quite articulate by means of the cape and the dark outfit and red tie. The red tie in particular was a solid, stable, vertical red line in the visual center of his body around which gathered small fragments of the red underside of the cape in quick, elliptical flashing movements. I thought the redness of the tie and of the inside of the cape stood for the red insides of Tommy's body. Myra created a quietly tragic setting for the cape by continuing to leak tears. In relation to Tommy's financial and social standing, the cape in the kitchen functioned in much the same way that the paintings of animals in caves are said to have done in relation to the animals themselves, once upon a time. The cape, I mean, would magically draw the aristocratic life to itself. The cape was Tommy's primitive get-aristocratic scheme, surprisingly effective as you will soon discover.

HOW I TRIED to have sex with Mittler on the last day of school is something I don't want to leave out of this account, God knows. (In fact, every single event in my life that I can think of seems to have a purpose, each event somehow causes the event that follows it. Isn't that amazing?)

Had I been older, I would have known to give the name *longing* to the feeling I had been harboring for Mittler since the day he had faux-tipped his hat to me in the boys' bathroom; but, as I was eleven, I didn't call it *longing,* I called it *Mittler. Mittler* also became the name of an enduring confusion in my life.

A small enclosure had been created at the back of our classroom by a cork partition. I stood just outside the partitioned area playing with clay. Mittler was inside the partitioned area extemporizing thoughtfully to some of the other boys. "It's spring and the weather is warm," Mittler said. "Everybody feels wild on the last day of the year," he said. I was not so much playing with a hunk of clay on the Formica table as I was having a tactile experience of Mittler in the clay. Touching his words with my hands. "Everybody feels desperate on the last day of the year. Everybody feels hopeful. This is a good time for a man to get in touch with his dick."

I feel lucky that I've met a lot of people in my life, beginning with Paul, who knew how to expound. Some have used the Socratic method and some have pontificated and some have quietly generalized or instructed, and some have let an aphorism fall so quickly from their lips that I have had to be waiting to catch it.

"You take all that energy of the last day," Mittler went on, invisible to me. "You take it all inside you and you bring it quietly to somewhere private. It has to be quiet, because when you unzip your zipper it's like the roar of a lion. And: you take out your dick. And: you focus all the energy *to* your dick. And listen," he whispered. "Then, you hold your dick. You're holding your dick. Then, your dick is, like, everything."

Jane Building was eight and twenty-nine-thirtieths months pregnant, as we liked to say. For the last hour of school of the year, she gathered us around her to read the finale of *A Wrinkle in Time*. I understood Mittler well enough to know that he would choose this moment, when everyone else was in the thrall of the end of the story and of Building's soft, crackling voice and her full-term pregnancy, to put his philosophy into practice. So I snuck out before the reading began and secured myself behind the door of the stall closest to the urinals in the boys' room, standing, of course, on the toilet seat so as not to be detected by careful Mittler.

With its tiles and high ceiling, the bathroom made a resonant sonic environment. I passed a happy half an hour listening to the echo of the silence, and then it happened: with an explosion of sound, Mittler kicked open the door of the boys' room whistling the mouthwash theme song, which is the song of the heroic bottle of mouthwash swinging through the wild jungles of Africa from vine to vine.

I considered it a pity that the stalls stood opposite the urinals: as I peered over the top of the stall door I was directly behind and slightly above Mittler, and once he took the basic urinating stance I could not see exactly what he was up to in front of his body where the action was taking place. A long moment of utter stillness followed and, from where I hung, an even longer one of only small movements of his shoulders and elbows. His head had rolled forward. Two peninsulas of dark down grew on the back of his neck, softest hair on his body. I looked at his amorphous brown pants and green short-sleeve shirt that seemed never to have been made but always worn—the standard outfit of the eleven-year-old sage. Then came that sigh. I wish I had had a tape recorder handy every time in my life that I heard a boy sigh at the outset of a urination. What a lovely sound. So much satisfaction. Girls sigh far less often before they pee, and not with the same devotion, I think. If only I had such a recording of boys' sighs. I would lie on a pillow in the sunlight of the late afternoon, sometimes listening to Chopin, sometimes to Schubert, and sometimes to the sighs, seriatim, of all the boys about to pee.

By the time spring arrived, I had switched over from dresses to pants on a daily basis. On that fateful afternoon, I waited in my pants until the sound of liquid entering liquid subsided before opening the door of the stall and thrusting Mittler against the wall next to the urinal. I accidentally knocked his chin

against the wall and he started crying and getting an erection.
"Sorry, Mittler, sorry, Mittler," I said, without letting him up.

"What are you gonna do?"

"Pull your pants down."

"Then what?"

"Pull my pants down."

"Then what?"

"Have sex with you."

"I don't want to."

"Too bad."

"I don't love you, and if you have sex with me I'll never love
you."

Ah, Mittler. Mittler, how could you have said such a thing?
Even now it burns in the telling. If you could kill a person by
having sex with him, that's what I would have done to Mittler
then. I got his pants down and, with some effort, mine, when
the two girls who were the emissaries of Dierdre ran into the
bathroom and told us Mrs. Building's water had broken.

"So?" I said. "Get out of here."

"There's a big puddle on the floor and she's having her baby."

I released Mittler. He withdrew a sharp knife from his
pocket and made a gift of it to me blade-down in the palm of
my hand. He left the bathroom with the girls. Jane Building
and her baby: big deal; this would not be the first time in history that a great passion was thwarted by uninteresting news.

2 *I Am Commodified*

THE SUMMER OF that year I will give in summary: though Mittler was wholly absent from the physical dimension of my life, I did not engage in a single activity that was not at least partly a devotion to or distraction from Mittler, including my twice-weekly reopening with the knife of the cut in my palm, or my first ovulation, or my body's production of a pair of small breasts. So much for that summer.

In the fall, our new teacher was September "Skip" Hartman, whom I liked because she so obviously was making a lifelong effort to cultivate the raw material of herself through things like posture. She stood up in front of the class with her lovely spine and her blond hair saying, " 'Be silent and take defeat' " and " 'I knew a woman lovely in her bones' " and " 'In sooth I know not why I am so sad' " and " 'In the old age black was not counted fair' " and " 'Time will say nothing but I told you so.' "

The first time Skip Hartman spoke with me in private she said the word *sensation*. Ms. Hartman was not an exclusive proponent of the open classroom. With her it was sometimes open, sometimes closed, sometimes halfway open or closed. One week the class resembled an old turn-of-the-century schoolroom with desks in rows; the next it resembled Gertrude Stein's salon with chairs in loose circles and, on the walls, abstract line drawings imported from the kindergarten, where the five-year-olds were busy producing them ("It's good not to lose touch with what the younger generation is doing," Skip Hartman said). All of which is to say that early in the semester, during the first grid era of the classroom, she came down along the column of desks and chairs I was sitting at the end of, with her hair and her posture and her loose silk chemise. Her dark-blond hair when she was walking toward me was a machine like a music box with diverse moving parts that operated smoothly in concert with one another. She stopped by my desk and asked to speak with me about the report I was then preparing to write on Samuel de Champlain. She pulled a tiny children's chair next to mine and sat in it with her soft beige skin under the dark chemise. I elaborated on my plan to build a canoe or hut from paper and twigs and glue. Then, in the middle of a sentence, she told me *sensation* and, to illustrate, touched her own bare forearm below the chemise's rolled-up sleeve.

Some words (like *sensation*) she spoke, and some words (like *chemise*) she gathered around her, in the way that I imagine Saint Francis of Assisi gathered starlings. Her lips were thin and gave the words that passed across their threshold distinct shapes in the air; she imbued them with independent lives of their own. I wanted to use words that she had used, or words that accurately described her, the former because I was touching something that she had touched, the latter because I was touching something that was touching her. *New England* was another thing she told me, on more than one occasion. I liked her shoes.

Skip Hartman taught by implied confession. She was always in the process of revealing her own close relation to the knowledge she imparted: "'Whose woods these are I think I know.'"

In the encyclopedia, I looked at the photograph of the mud hut of Samuel de Champlain—or Samuel D. Champlain, as I liked to call him—and built a quick version of it in my bedroom and carried it to school on one of Myra's food trays. This was the first schoolwork I had ever done, and I think Skip Hartman recognized the birth of an interest. Whereas Jane Building had conducted all her meetings in the shadow of the great mansion of her adult desk at the front of the room, Skip Hartman invited herself into the dwellings of the hoi polloi. At our second private meeting—where were all the other children? at lunch—we were alone at the back of the classroom amid the furniture of children. She said to me, "I'm *very* excited about your hut."

Having now the organized movements of Skip Hartman's hair as she walked toward me on low heels, I stopped carrying Mittler's knife, which ceased to have the voodoo power to cut me. I didn't stop loving Mittler, but this adult had enchanted me more than it was in the power of a child to do. So I would say that the intense bodily feeling I was in the habit of calling *Mittler* was crowded aside in the fall of my twelfth year by a new sensation named *Skip Hartman.*

Many of the same children populated Skip's class as had populated Building's. A new disaffection settled upon them.

Perhaps this was a result of the previous spring's humbling spectacle of childbirth. Or perhaps the new teacher—voted Teacher of the Year for the two previous years—had a kind of charisma that did not invigorate her students so much as it made them experience their own inadequacy more keenly. Mittler and Dierdre found some consolation in smoking filtered cigarettes together by the smelly Dumpsters on the dark north side of the brick school building, but even that they did languidly, not in grandiose imitation of a wise and world-weary adult but out of heartfelt torpor and the inability to locate the interest in their own lives.

One day in October, Dierdre dragged Mittler over to see me on the playground just as school was letting out and said, "We think you should come and smoke a cigarette with us." The attitudes of cleverness and excitement she had used the previous year to woo me and then to cast me out had vanished. Her freckled eyelids were heavy now. Her thinness, once a sign of energy, had become anemic. Mittler stood by, doubtful, looking away. "She won't smoke," he said. "She loves that body of hers too much."

"I'll smoke," I said, "but not if Mittler comes along."

"Mittler, get lost," Dierdre said. Cruelty without pleasure, reduced to its essence of need.

Mittler shrugged and left.

"We can go to my house," she said.

The school was on the side of a long hill. Behind it there were a few dozen acres of woods sloping sharply upward. Dierdre slipped her little arm into mine and leaned into me as we walked up the path through the woods.

"Why are you inviting me to your house?" I said.

"Feel like it. How did your brother die?"

"I killed him."

"That's what I figured. Would you kill someone else?"

"Shut up."

We reached a metal fence that bordered someone's back-yard, where there was a small swimming pool resting on top of the ground. I crawled through a little hole at the bottom of the fence and Dierdre came through after me. Her purple flow-ered dress got caught at the hip on a sharp piece of the fence. "Ow! It stuck in me, and now it's on my dress. Get it off! Don't rip my dress!"

I grabbed her elbows and jerked her through the hole in the fence, which tore a hole about a foot long in the side of her dress.

"You made me scrape my knees and you tore my dress!"

"Too bad," I said.

She was about to continue berating me but stopped. She nodded thoughtfully. "Too bad," she agreed softly, learning, it seemed, something she had wanted to learn. I suppose I have had a kind of luck in sharing my misery with others and re-ceiving their gratitude in return.

She took me directly to her parents' bedroom and showed me the illustrated sex books. "I figured you'd want to see these. Do you want to smoke a cigarette now?"

"Could I borrow these books?"

"No."

"How about just one?"

"No."

"I'll give it back tomorrow."

"No."

"Why?"

"My parents will know."

"Why, they're gonna have sex tonight?"

"I don't know, they could."

"Don't they know how to do it already?"

"Duh. They had me, didn't they?"

"What are the chances of them doing it tonight?"

"Forget I even showed you the books. Put that book down."

"You can't take back showing someone something."

"I knew you would be into these books. I don't even get what the big deal is."

"All right, listen: you go and smoke a pack of cigarettes and I'll stay here and just read this one book and I won't even take it out of the room, I'll just read it in here."

Dierdre left. I became a scholar of that one book, which surprised me here and there and confirmed some of what I had recently been suspecting was the case. Still, it was quite narrow in scope and prepared me only in the most rudimentary way for the astonishing thing that was about to happen to me.

I came out into Dierdre's backyard as the sun was setting and she looked sick from smoking a pack of cigarettes. "Do you want to try some of the stuff in that book?" I asked.

"With you? *Eeew.* We can touch tongues if you want."

We touched tongues for a second and Dierdre vomited in the dark grass of her backyard. I went home.

THERE ARE CERTAIN objects meant to be looked upon by certain eyes and vice versa. Such was the case with my Uncle Tommy's cape and the eyes of Skip Hartman. Things Tommy didn't quite know about himself were absorbed and understood by Skip Hartman, who was, it should be said now, independently wealthy. As for Tommy, when he entered Skip Hartman's classroom one Thursday evening in mid-autumn for the first parent-teacher conference and witnessed the erect posture, the short, straight, segmented blond hair, the crisp, pale-blue linen sleeveless dress, the black silk scarf, and the black suede lace-up boots with the Louis Quatorze heels, he gasped. "I hope you don't mind my saying that's a delightful dress."

"And I hope you don't mind if I tell you something you are no doubt already aware of: namely, how precious is your niece."

There was everything that needed to be said. The rest of the conference was a mere formality, ending with Skip Hartman's grateful acceptance of Tommy's invitation to dinner the following night. On the way home in the car Tommy spoke passionately about the importance of a good education. Myra was at the conference too, in her way.

AN HOUR BEFORE the arrival of Skip Hartman at our house for dinner, I entered the kitchen to find Myra's eyes, which had been dry for several months, leaking again. I have not ever come to a good understanding of the folkways of the kitchen, but I liked to observe Myra doing somber, orderly things to food in vessels with tools and heat. When she moved, I followed her. When she stood at the counter surrounded by the bright light of the kitchen, bashing something soft with a wooden hammer, I stood behind her.

"Why are you crying?"

"I'm not crying."

"What are those tears?"

"What tears?"

"The ones coming out of your eyes."

"I guess allergies."

"You don't feel sad inside right now?"

"No."

"What do you feel inside?"

"I'm trying to concentrate on making dinner for you and Uncle Tommy and Miss Hartman."

"Are you making a special dinner?"

"Just trying to make something everyone will like."

"What are you making?"

"Veal."

"Do you like Miss Hartman?"

"Yes. Uncle Tommy likes her very much."

"Thanks for making such a great dinner for Miss Hartman."

"Trying to make something people like."

I was a skinny girl and short for an eleven-year-old. Myra was tall and big. I leaned in over her broad behind and hugged her ribs. Her large breasts rested lightly on my skinny arms. I pressed my belly and my little chest against the great contour of her behind. She continued bashing as if nothing had changed.

"Aunt Myra?"

"Yes."

"You're so beautiful."

She missed with the hammer and broke something delicate that fell on the floor in pieces. I felt a tremor shuttle through her body and heard a noise come from her. I let go of her and tried to get around to the front of her to see what was happening on her face, but she ducked down and away from me to pick up the shards of ceramic off the floor. "I think you ought to get out of here with your bare feet," she said.

"I want to see what everyone is going to wear for Miss Hartman tonight," Tommy said twenty minutes before she arrived.

"I will stand by the back door in the kitchen, since that's where she'll come into the house and see you first. I'll stand right here and you two come in wearing your outfits and I'll tell you if they're working or not."

Everyone became excited for this fun family activity. Our first outfits were all wrong. "Elegance, elegance, supreme elegance for the meal."

We returned in a pair of frilly pastel outfits that made us look like people who owned one good costume and saved it for Easter, though I didn't believe in God and if Myra believed in anything in particular, it's doubtful that she knew it. Tommy stared at the outfits for a long time with his close-set eyes and the hurt look that was really a quality of the skin. "This will be fine. I think we could do better but we're out of time. Why are these important decisions always rushed? Myra, why are these important decisions always rushed?"

"I'm sorry," Myra said.

In a stage whisper, I said to Myra, "Call him 'dear.' He wants you to say 'I'm sorry, dear.' "

Tommy said, "Ah, Christ, are you just gonna make weird remarks when the teacher gets here? Is that what I have to look forward to—you throwing off the whole dinner conversation?"

"If I just said normal stuff, I don't think Miss Hartman would be coming to dinner."

"Hell, Christ, what do I know, right, Myra?" Tommy said, looking at me. "I'm just the guy who bought the house where the whole dinner is going to be. What does that make me? Just some idiot with a tiny house in the suburbs."

Skip Hartman's long legs were sheathed in black leather when she stalked into the kitchen. She carried a lily of the val-

ley and wore hand-stitched cowboy boots and an oversized
white cotton chemise that hung loose over the pants.

After swallowing a first small mouthful of prosciutto at the
family dinner table in the kitchen, Skip Hartman said to
Tommy, "I am making the supposition that you are some sort of
public-interest lawyer."

"Nope." Tommy beamed. She had instinctively picked the
best lie. "I would have been a lawyer but I did poorly on the
LSAT. I would have done well if it weren't for the time limit. I
think there are plenty of jobs in the field of the law where you
don't have to think fast. Oh, I can think all right, but I need
time. I wouldn't make a good trial lawyer—I know that about
myself and I accept that limitation about myself—but there
are plenty of jobs within the field of the law I could have done,
if it weren't for the damn time limit on the LSAT."

"It is perfectly all right—I daresay advantageous—to think
slowly, if one thinks thoroughly. Many people who think
quickly think sloppily," Skip Hartman said, indicting by impli-
cation anyone whom Tommy might have envied.

For the sake of the rapport that had to develop between
Uncle Tommy and Skip Hartman, I refrained from making
what Tommy would have called weird remarks at the table. I
tried to interject funny, niecely things into the mutually respectful dialogue, just as Myra provided the kind of wifely silence that deepens the harmony between the husband and,
shall we say, the husband's prospective business partner.

After two glasses of brandy in the living room (did he get
these moves out of a book?) Tommy, talking more and more
like Skip as the evening wore on, said, "Miss Hartman, I'm
glad my niece is in such capable hands as yours. Mary, would

you like to show Miss Hartman your bedroom, where you do all your schoolwork?"

Skip Hartman and I strolled to the threshold of my room. "Well, my child," she said, looking dizzy and frightened.

There was only one thing I wanted to show her in that dark little room with the false wood paneling and the cheap orange carpet. I took her hand and led her to the empty army cot by the window and stood with her before it, saying nothing.

"This is where your twin brother slept," she said.

I nodded.

" 'Doesn't everything die at last, and too soon?' " she said to herself and me. And to me: "You miss him terribly."

I nodded, and the tears started leaking, and then in the presence of Skip Hartman I let my body go. I felt jolts of electricity pulsing through me and when Skip Hartman took me in her arms I could not imagine a more intense pleasure than sobbing and being held by Skip Hartman. She was a head taller than I, and presumably knew what she was doing while I did not, and yet what we were doing did not feel like an adult hugging a child. No doubt the treachery of retrospect comes into play here, but those two people in that room seem to me now like two women hugging, each with something to give the other for comfort.

I stopped crying, and some space opened up between the fronts of our bodies, which had been pressed together. Skip Hartman lightly touched the sides of my body underneath my arms. She put one hand on my face, in my hair. "You are such a beautiful child," she said, and kissed me on the mouth.

"Did you two have a nice time in there?" Tommy said, back in the kitchen, showing Skip to the door.

"Splendid," she replied.

"It got cold outside, and you in your cotton blouse. Take this." Tommy removed the cape from his shoulders and held it out, gorgeous black wool with the crimson inside.

"Mr. White, I must admit that I have been admiring your cape all evening, and I must also say that I find your generosity breathtaking," she said, leaning against the wall in the tiny foyer for support, dizzy again, overwhelmed by the luck, if you could call it that, of having discovered such a family, if you could call it that, "but I have also observed how very important your cape is to you and I do not wish to be the cause of a separation between you and your cape."

"You can give it back when you come to dinner a week from tonight," Tommy said.

"That I do wish for, and that I can accept," Skip said, and grinned. "That I wholeheartedly accept."

On the night that followed, Tommy asked me to play catch with him. I said no. "Please please please please please?" he said. We gave it a shot, but I kept forgetting to catch the ball or throw it, and that was because I was thinking of a song. It was called "You Do Something Something Something" and was one of the show tunes my father used to sing, incorrectly I suspect, when he was alive:

> Let me live 'neath your skin,
> I will not leave you if you lock me in.

"HOW DO YOU FEEL about mutual funds?" Skip Hartman said to Uncle Tommy at dinner number two.

"I'm not sure."

"What's your gut instinct, yes or no?"

"No?" The blood roiled up beneath his pale freckles.

"Me too!" Skip exclaimed, the pleasure of *this* mutuality shooting up through her straight spine into her neck and head. "I feel I can talk to you about my financial instruments," she said.

"I'm not sure I could add much to the conversation, embarrassed to say," Tommy said.

"No, no, that's quite all right. I feel I can talk to you nonetheless and you will listen. I'll show you my portfolio of investments and you either say nothing or you say anything that occurs to you."

I have never in my life seen someone understand someone else as uncannily as Skip understood Tommy. It was now Tommy who looked dizzy. Myra's face was blank and indecipherable as usual, and Skip had the good sense not to try to draw her into the conversation more than perfunctorily. I can't even tell you how hard it is to remember Myra. For all I know she spoke all the time, and I have simply forgotten everything she said.

In my room, Skip Hartman sat on Paul's bed and held me in her smooth arms as if I were a baby. I liked when she walked toward me and I liked when she held me in her arms. Then I held her in my arms and played with her hair. I rubbed it and tried to mess it up. She thought that was funny. We went over to the little mirror above the dresser and watched ourselves put Skip's hair in different positions. She made faces at me. She asked to feel the muscles of my upper arms. "Oh, my, but you are a strong little girl," she said. She felt the muscles of my calves and said, "Oh, my, but you *are* a strong little girl." She felt the muscles of my thighs and said, "You are *such* a strong little girl." This seems like a good time to say, if I have not said it already, that I both did and did not know what I was doing at age eleven, just as now I do and do not remember what really happened, because I think that after Skip Hartman said, "You are *such* a strong little girl," I climbed on top of her on the rug and affectionately gave her my virginity.

"Should I still call you Miss Hartman?" I asked.

"Call me whatever you would like to call me."

"I like Miss Hartman."

"Miss Hartman likes you. And what shall she call you?"

"She shall call me Paul."

"All right, Paul."

"She shall call me Paul only sometimes."

"All right, Paul Only Sometimes."

YOU MAY WONDER what it was like to continue to be a student in the sixth-grade class taught by the first person I had ever made love to. The answer is that I wanted to see her as often as possible, and that seeing her and speaking with her at school, yet knowing that we could not speak as we spoke in private, caused in me an excitement that slipped easily into discomfort and confusion. The confusion came about when I tried to understand what the words we said to each other in that public space really meant, because they did not seem to mean the most obvious thing that was conveyed in them. "Mary," she happened to call out one day in the classroom, causing a small commotion just below my chest, "would you please demonstrate for the class the proper way to add fractions, using the case of one half plus one half as a straightforward-enough illustration?"

"Yes Miss Hartman."

I went to the blackboard. The air near my head was buzzing. I looked around and tried to see my classmates, which I did, but I had a hard time composing them in my mind; I saw individual elements of them, and of objects in the class—some-one's neck, a plastic hairpin, the bottom of a chair leg. I drew the two figures on the board and made some manipulations of them using a logic that was perfectly clear to me in the state of mind I was in. I then turned to my teacher and said, "Miss Hartman, I believe that one half plus one half equals two."

"All right," she said, and approached me. She took the chalk from my hand and, in doing so, touched two of my fingers with one of hers. She redrew the equation on the board and arrived at the correct answer, which was apparently one, and explained how she had done it.

"I still believe it's two," I said, standing next to her.

She looked frightened, as she had in the foyer of our house. "Mary," she said, controlling a quaver in her voice that was audible to those who knew to listen for one, "perhaps you are confusing arithmetic with religion or poetry. Religion and poetry are matters of belief. Arithmetic is, unfortunately, not. In poetry in particular, one half plus one half may sometimes equal two. In arithmetic it cannot and will not."

I returned to my seat. Nobody knew about the quaver except Skip Hartman and me, and possibly Mittler, the disaffected prodigy; I thought I could sense this in the way he stared out the window, whistling to himself very softly.

TO DINNER THE following Friday, Skip Hartman brought pairs of shoes. For Tommy she brought two-tone brown leather wing tips. He squealed with delight. He put them on during the gaz-pacho and paraded them around the kitchen. He left the kitchen and shouted from the hallway, "Watch when I enter the kitchen. The shoes will be coming in first. I want to know everyone's reaction."

He reentered the kitchen with elongated steps. We all applauded, even Myra. Then Skip held out Myra's shoes to her across the table. They were wisely moderate black flats.

"Please, you mustn't give these to me."

"But I must." She continued to extend the shoes over the table.

"It's so kind, but I couldn't wear them."

"Try them on. If you can't wear them I'll get you a size you can wear."

"It's not that."

"Oh, you're being demure!"

Myra looked down abruptly at her plate of linguine with fennel and sausage. If only Skip had understood Myra one hundredth as well as she understood Tommy (arithmetic being, here, a matter of belief). She didn't realize she was causing Myra pain, as anyone did who described or noticed her. I whispered in my teacher's ear, "Take back the shoes and she'll feel better, but do it quietly."

"You know perhaps I'll see if there's a different color that would be more suitable at some future date as yet to be determined at which point everything may not be so . . ." She rounded out the sentence by pulling the shoes back over to her side of the table and slipping them into her oversized purse. Even if one did not understand Myra, one wished to do something for her. Just as Skip Hartman was rescuing me from my orphanhood swashbuckler style in her leather pants, so I wished that someone would find a way to rescue Myra from wherever it was that she was stranded—inside her body, was how I chose to locate it. But some people never get found, never get rescued.

To this third dinner at Tommy's house, Skip Hartman had

also brought a toothbrush and deodorant and fresh underwear and a sweatshirt and jeans. When we were alone in my room after dinner she said, "And would you like me to call you Paul this evening?"

"I would like you to call me 'teacher.'"

"Oh, really." She took a step back away from me and folded her arms and frowned.

"Yes, really. And you have to go sit in that little chair over there, and if you want to speak you have to raise your hand."

She looked at me, not sure what to do. "And what will you call me?" she said.

"I shall call you Skippy. Skippy, sit down now, please."

She sat down. She raised her hand.

"Yes, Skippy?" I said, prancing back and forth in front of her.

"How much is one half plus one half, teacher?" she asked.

"One half plus one half plus religion plus poetry plus arithmetic plus Skippy plus teacher plus you plus me plus you plus Skippy plus Skippy plus Skippy. Skippy?"

"Yes, teacher."

"Now I have a question for you, Skippy."

"Okay."

"Here's what I want you to do. I'll stand on the bed and you hop around the room in circles like a giant kangaroo."

"I don't think I want to do that."

"Excuse me, Skippy?"

"I will not do that."

"I will not do that *what*?"

"Mary, please."

"Skip-py!" I commanded, leaping onto the bed with both feet.

"What?"

"Do it. Now!"

Skip Hartman stared up at me. I stared back down at her. Slowly, she stood up. She took one cautious hop.

"Good girl, Skippy," I said very gently. "Try it again."

She removed her pumps and took a few more hops.

"*Very* good, Skippy. Oh, Skippy, I'm so proud of you."

She hop-hop-hopped around the room. Her head, which she usually held vertically in place atop her spine, bounced from side to side on her shoulders, which I found perfectly charming.

"Now I will ride you."

Skip Hartman hopped over to me and turned her back and bent down. I jumped onto her back and grasped her kangaroo flanks tightly between my legs. She hopped around the room while I messed up her hair with my hands. "Now make kangaroo noises!" I said.

"Arf!" she said. "Arf! Arf!" We both were laughing now and we collapsed onto Paul's bed and laughed for a while. Her face was bright red. "Oh, my darling teacher," she said.

"Yes, my darling Skippy?"

"Come put your ear close to my lips. I must whisper something." I did as she said. She whispered, "I am discovering aspects of myself that I had not an inkling existed, thanks to you, my teacher."

"My little Skippy is soooo cute," I whispered back, and patted my excellent pupil on that fantastic machine, her head.

ON THE DAY before the first day of summer, a big door at school slammed on my fingers and September "Skip" Hartman lost her place in the world. She happened to see my fingers resting lightly on the door frame as the door approached them. She happened also to be the person who had pushed the door with mild vigor, not knowing my fingers were there at the time she had pushed it, a big oaken door easy on its hinges. "I saw your hand and I looked very quickly up at your innocent face," she said to me the following evening, when we were reunited in my bedroom and she was helping me to pack my things. "Your face was turned the other way. You did not see the door coming." She perched on Paul's bed, controlling the skeletal muscles and tear ducts of her erect body but unable to keep her voice from rising and rising. "Mary, all in a moment I felt myself about to shriek, was seized with fear, and then did a terrible thing: I did not shriek. I did not warn you, my dear child, of the pain I was about to cause you," she said, as Tommy sauntered into the little bedroom to supervise the packing.

The pain was surprising and intense, and you might say that the shriek Skip Hartman did not utter came out of me. She had been leading our entire class through the hallways of the school to the gym. After the door slammed, she put my hand that was not hurt inside of her hand and commanded the other children to remain still while she took me to the nurse's office. Once we had rounded the corner she stopped a moment and could not prevent herself from bringing my injured hand to her lips and whispering into it, "Oh, my precious precious."

"I hate you people," Mittler said. He had rounded the corner behind us. "I knew you couldn't wait to kiss her hand, I knew it! I'm telling everybody about you two. I'm telling the principal, I'm telling all the kids, I'm telling *everybody*! Mary, I want my knife back right now!"

"I threw your stupid knife away!" I roared back at him. "Miss Hartman sleeps in my room once a week!" I roared, and turned to my lover and threw my arms around her neck.

"All right, dear, we'll go to the nurse's office now," she said and removed my arms from around her neck. "Mittler, I understand your agitation. Please join the rest of the class and I'll speak with you later."

The rest of the class, however, had joined Mittler, and most of them had heard what he'd said, and what I'd said, and seen a few things they didn't quite know how to see, and now they stood there, some of them staggering like people newly blind, as if they had used up all their eyesight looking at the strange pair of us. Skip Hartman took me by the elbow and led me to succor.

IN LIGHT OF September Hartman's six years of devoted and intelligent service, and to avoid a scandal, the school administrators canned her quietly and did not make public the wrongdoing of the Teacher of the Year, nor did they press charges. The central outcome of the door slamming was the transfer of guardianship of me from Thomas and Myra White to September Hartman. In exchange for the transfer, the Whites received from Ms. Hartman a lump sum of $100,000, and would also receive weekly payments of $500 for the duration of such time as she remained my legal guardian.

On the day that Skip and I moved to Manhattan, the weather was hot enough for Skip to put the top down on her little black Porsche when she came to pick me up. Just the same, Tommy wore the woolen cape in his driveway to send us off. Myra did not appear to be on the verge of voluntarily kissing me good-bye, so I leapt on her in the driveway and knocked her down, accidentally breaking her elbow. I didn't care about her elbow. At the time, caring did not strike me as a useful activity. Little did I know that all the caring I didn't do then was being stored up inside me and that I would eventually become a young lady full of care.

Tommy did not kiss me good-bye, but he made a definitive flourish with his cape, bowing deeply before me and the Porsche, such that I saw the individual drops of sweat lined up along the border of his pale forehead and his delicate blond hair. He whispered, "I'm sorry if I have failed you." As Skip and I climbed into her car, Tommy went to where Myra was lying in the driveway to attend to her elbow, which had already swollen up in much the same way that Paul's face and torso did after the bees stung him and just before he died. New York City, here we come!

More Wrong Songs

SOONER OR LATER everyone finds a way to be mistreated. Some find it more easily than others: Skippy and I, for example. But sometimes mistreatment is better than no treatment at all.

In the early days of living in her house in New York City, Skip and I lay on top of the white duvet on her king-size bed facing the French windows that opened out onto one of the pristine streets near Fifth Avenue on Manhattan's Upper East Side. My favorite time to lie on the bed with her there was early in the morning. At that time we heard four or five or six kinds of birdsong, and Skip was someone who could attach a great many bird names to the songs in the world that belonged to them.

At other times of day I did not like to lie on the bed. Late morning, for example, or early afternoon, or late afternoon, or anytime in the evening before ten-thirty. But Skip Hartman wanted me on the bed with her, and I thought the arrangement was that either I stayed on the bed or I got kicked out of her house. If she kicked me out of her house, I thought, she would also stop paying Tommy the weekly stipend, and then he would not take me back into *his* house. At the age of twelve, I was not ready to live on the street without knowing a soul who would help me, so I stayed next to her on the bed, usually naked, eating or listening to her pronounce the litanies she had taken pains to learn and loved to say, such as the names of all the popes or all the kings of England, or the countries of South America, or the lakes of northern Finland, or the provisions of the Bill of Rights, or, as my father used to sing, "'I'll quote the facts historical, now please don't get hysterical.'"

One afternoon when I was feeling especially perspicacious and Skip especially vulnerable, she revealed to me in a vocal tremor and tic of the mouth that it was I who allowed her to keep me in her house, not she who allowed me to stay there. I may desperately have needed the enclosure of her house, but she needed the enclosure of the slim radius of air around my body. She could not bear to be away from me. Or so I became convinced that she imagined.

I got out of bed and got dressed and walked out the front door and onto the sidewalk. She followed me. "Where are you going?"

"Need some air."

"Tell me."

"Tell you what?"

"Tell me when you are going to do something like go out for air. I cannot abide a system of communication wherein you do not consult me before leaving the house. We need to, I think we ought to, we need to—" Skip stood at the top of the short flight of stone steps between our house and the street, while I stood at the bottom of it. Her face was flushed and even her hair was beginning to show signs of disorder.

"Okay, okay, okay, so don't have a fucking fit," I said. I saw that the word *fucking* startled her, coming from me. "Don't have a cow," I added. "Don't have a pig. Don't have a goat. Don't have a canary," I said, to make her laugh and bring her back to an area of comfort: lists of names of things—animals, in this case, that a woman would not ordinarily give birth to.

"Mary, would you like to go out to a restaurant?"

"I want to *do* something."

"Such as?"

"Do you have a stopwatch?"

"I have a wristwatch with a stopwatch function."

"Go get it."

Startled again.

"Please."

She stood still for a moment, thinking perhaps that when she returned with the watch I would be gone. She went inside and came back, breathing hard. "Now what?" she said.

"Now I run around the block and you time me."

"Where are you going to run?"

"I said around the block."

"Which block?"

"Duh. The block that we're on."

"Do you mean that you'll run to Fifth Avenue, take a right and go north for one block, take another right and go east to Madison, take another right and go south for one block, another right and return here?"

"Yeah, okay."

"Go!"

It was five P.M. on a Thursday in early summer. The sidewalk along Fifth Avenue was crowded with wealthy adult pedestrians and tourists. I liked weaving among them, defining my speed by their slowness, my youth by the rigid expressions of fear and annoyance on their faces. As I reached the farthest point in my journey, I began to miss Skip Hartman. My heart beat wildly inside my chest; I missed the pressure of her hand on the skin that surrounded my heart. I tried to picture her face and could not. I sped up. As I rounded the corner onto our block I saw her lips moving. "Forty-nine," she was saying, "fifty, fifty-one—"

I ran to her and threw my arms around her, being careful not to knock her to the sidewalk, as I had done to Myra. (Fancy that, reader: Mary learned from a mistake. She's growing up so fast!) "Fifty-one point three two seconds," she said.

Varying the route, we enacted this little game many times that summer and over the next several years. We called the game Going Away and Coming Back. It was one of the ways we loved each other.

"YOU MUST LEARN to lie still," Skip Hartman tried to explain to me, on her bed one morning after the end of my brief period of compliance.

"Why must I?"

"Just as it is important to cultivate useful activity, so it is important to treasure idleness. One might even consider idleness a skill."

"You're full of shit."

Startled yet again. (To startle and be startled: this was another of the ways we loved each other.)

"Why's everything have to be *useful* and *cultivated* and *treasured*?"

"Because life is short."

"I don't care."

"Don't say that."

"Why, because not caring isn't *useful*?"

"No, because it hurts me."

Across the hall from the bedroom where we slept on the second floor of the Hartman apartment was another, slightly smaller bedroom. Most of the available wall space in this room had been covered with bookshelves. The books, which nearly filled the shelves, were arranged both alphabetically and by category. I had not seen such a room as this before in a private home. By the window there was a small antique rosewood desk and matching chair. Next to the desk there was a four-story wooden filing cabinet, and on the wall beside the cabinet hung a large glass-framed print depicting a small unhappy child flying a red kite in a scarred purple sky.

Just after the beginning of the unending period of my non-compliance, there followed the period of Skip Hartman's weeping. She sat at the desk in this room and looked at one particular page of a certain book and wept for most of the day. I didn't want to go into the room where she was weeping, so I sat on the wooden floor in the hallway just outside the open door. There I tried to re-create my dead brother, Paul, inside myself in the form of a Philosophical Conundrum. The conundrum was not supposed to replicate exactly the situation of the weeping; it was meant as an idealized conundrum *about weeping*. Let us say, the conundrum began—for all conundrums must begin with this supplication—let us say that you are in a room. And let us say that there is a room adjacent to the room you are in and that someone is weeping in this second room. There is no door to the room in which the person is weeping, and there is no door to the room you are in. Nor are there windows to these rooms. Each of you, then, is sealed in a room with no way in or out. The walls of this conundrum, then, are the walls of the two rooms, which are the walls of the world, for the purposes of the conundrum. It is your task to stop the person in the adjacent room from weeping. Why is it your task? It is your task because it is your task. And it is your task because you cannot sleep with the ceaseless weeping. The weeping distracts you from everything in your life that is not the weeping. You have already tried calling to the person. First you called softly and tenderly. You said, "Oh, my child, I am right here beside you, and though you cannot see me or touch me, I will always be here beside you." But that only made the weeping more abject, more disconsolate. You have also tried calling loudly and angrily: "Will you shut up already! I am your neighbor, and your sorrow is not my sorrow!" That, too, intensified the weeping. At this point in the conundrum, reader, I noticed a difference between this conundrum and the ones Paul used to instruct me in. In Paul's, there was generally a choice to be made among two or more distinct courses of action, and it was implied that only one of these courses of action was correct. Whereas the conundrum I had invented to instruct myself presented a situation unresponsive to anything I might do to attempt to change it. Either it was a conundrum without a solution or the solution consisted of a mental adjustment to a situation I was powerless to affect. I believe this was the point in my life at which I abandoned conundrums altogether. In this way, the memory of Paul's life loosened its grip on my mind.

For a few days, I sat outside the door to the room of the weeping woman playing the game of jacks that I had brought with me from the suburbs in a red cloth bag.

Then I went into the room.

"Hi," I said.

"Hi."

Skip Hartman sat in her chair. She was not actively crying now. She was in that red-eyed resting place between crying and more crying. She was looking down at a picture in a book about northern Renaissance painting. I pulled a book down from one of the shelves and opened it and touched the pages and tried without success to figure out what the book was about. I put it back and pulled down another book and touched its insides and put it back. I did this to maybe two thirds of the books in that room. Then I left the room and went out of the house. Skip Hartman did not follow me this time. I imagined she was still in that chair looking down at that page of that book. I went into Central Park and wandered down to Bethesda Fountain and watched two squirrels alternately frol-icking and standing still. I came back to the house and made a sandwich and ate it and went to sleep. When I woke up I went to the book room again. She was looking down at the book, crying.

"Hi," I said.

"Hi."

I wanted to do something nice for her but I didn't know how, so instead I pulled down the books again, all of them, and I did not replace each book before pulling down the next. In the middle of the floor, I made a huge unruly pile of every single book in that room except the one that Skip was staring down into. Then I put the books back on the shelves in no particular order, as if I had not already left my smudge of randomness on Skip Hartman's life.

"OOH, THIS IS fantastic," Tommy cooed in the entrance foyer. He was looking at a tall, ancient, rectangular mirror with a mahogany frame, to which a pair of coat hooks was attached on either side of the reflecting glass. His pale red silk shirt, his lavender cravat, and his delicate, smoothed-out-baklava skin looked patrician in the tarnished surface of the old mirror. Myra was still wearing the hard rough white-plaster shell that the doctor had put on her forearm the day I felled her on her driveway. She was dressed in a brown cloth in which fragile produce might have been wrapped to be shipped overseas.

Tommy gazed at that mild narcotic, the image of his own face in the mirror. "Oh," he said. Myra looked at an area of the white wall in the foyer that had no mirror or window or painting.

"Would you like to see the rest of the house?" Skip asked.

It was the end of August and the ostensible purpose of this, the first visit from my aunt and uncle, was to discuss plans for my education, but nobody seemed to want to do that, except possibly Myra, but then one has to invent virtually all intentions and attributes of Myra.

Tommy checked his collar and cuffs in the mirror. He was not quite ready to leave the mirror. He stepped away from the mirror and rushed back to it. "I forgot the cape!"

"As lovely as your cape is, Thomas," Skip said, "it seems to me more of a winter cape. Perhaps an autumn cape is in order."

Now Tommy could safely turn away from the mirror, having found another place that reflected him—Skip Hartman—and the tour of the house could begin.

"I want books," he said, when we reached the book room. Skip had not returned the books to their previous arrangement but, by using a mnemonic technique she had learned from the Roman orator Cicero, she had asserted the ordering principle of her own mind on the chaos of book placement.

"Perhaps I could lend you some," she said. "What sort of books would you like to read?"

"I don't necessarily want to read them, at least not right away. I just want to have them around. I don't want you to lend them to me. I'll go out and get some. I'll build a nice bookshelf in maybe Paul and Mary's room so it can be the room where the books are, the way you have this room. Do you know where I could get some books like this?"

"In a bookstore, I imagine."

"I don't want the kind of books they have in bookstores. I want this kind. Old books that are about things most people don't know about. I want to read but I'm easily distracted. I want to know things. I think I could work up to reading books by first owning them."

Skip Hartman stood tall in the center of the book room while the rest of us stood around her. She cocked her head to the side to consider Tommy, which gave me the opportunity to consider her long, curved, graceful neck. "I own many more books," she said. "Some of them I keep in the basement. Some are quite rare."

"*Rare*—the word alone gives me a feeling," he said.

"Rare and juicy," I said.

"Succulent," Skip added.

"*Succulent* doesn't give me the feeling," Tommy said.

"Why don't I box up a couple gross of books and have them carted up to you," Skip said, with the faintest Brooklyn inflection waxing and waning in the course of that sentence.

Tommy was too intoxicated with the aura of the rare books in the room to notice the irreverence. In the chair on which Skip had wept for a month, Myra sat looking at the floor, while the fingertips of her left hand grazed the cast on her right arm.

"Further, let me simply hand over some cash to you," Skip said. "Here." She removed several hundred-dollar bills from her wallet and handed them to Tommy.

"Thanks."

"Look under 'Books, rare' in the Yellow Pages and you'll find many more books that I'm sure you'll read with relish."

"And mustard," I said.

"And not only that," she said. "We must now hurry you off to my tailor, who will make you an exquisite autumn-weight cape."

"Maybe after we eat," Tommy said.

"Oh, no! You must visit the delightful hot-dog cart on the way to my tailor on Fifth Avenue. That is where you will have your lunch. Visiting the island of Manhattan without eating a hot dog from a cart would be the equivalent of visiting Paris without climbing the Eiffel Tower."

"Or teaching sixth grade without having sex with one of your students," I said.

"Just so," Skip said.

"Hey, come on!" Tommy said.

Skip hustled Tommy down the stairs and out the door. She stood in the foyer and said, "How often do you suppose we must have this uncle of yours to the house? I don't enjoy his company."

We noticed then that we had not sent Myra out of the house with Tommy. She stood on the stairs above the foyer and had heard what Skip said to me. For an instant, she looked at Skip with what appeared to be hatred, and then the hatred—if that was its name—was swallowed back into the affective abyss of her body.

AT NOON ON Labor Day of that year—the day before what would have been the first day of school in some normative version of my life—I answered the doorbell and saw before me slightly older, wickeder versions of Dierdre and Harry, my elementary school classmates, who had somehow obtained my address. Had my twelve-year-old body not felt so woozy and sated after a morning of love with my thirty-seven-year-old guardian, I would have been shocked to see those two. They were no longer the disgraced elder statesmen of the schoolroom. They did not look wounded and chastened so much as dirty and arrogant and theatrical. Dierdre had dyed her hair black against her pale skin and freckles. She wore black mascara and lip liner. Harry had grown taller than Skip Hartman, and massive. Random light hairs grew from his jaw. He wore a scuffed black leather jacket. He looked down at me with an expression of amusement that suggested he had come as far from wanting to tussle with me as a rhinoceros would be from wanting to tussle with a penguin.

"How's the sex going?" Dierdre said.

"It's about the only thing that's going good," I said.

"Why? What's wrong?"

I heard Skip on the stairs behind me. I turned to look at her. She was wearing a white terry bathrobe and her hair was darkened by water and smoothed down on her skull in combed stripes. The skin on her face glowed as if lit from within. This was the classic postcoital Hartman look. Dierdre and Harry stared at her. "Here comes the pervert," Dierdre said, meaning to be funny, but no one laughed. "Sorry," she said. "Can Mary come to the park with us?"

"Mary may do what she likes. I am not the keeper of Mary." Skip did not descend the few final steps to greet the two children, one of whom had been her student.

"I thought you were her guardian," Dierdre said.

"Legally, yes, but it is perhaps best to behave as if we are equals in all things, even while we are not equals in all things: in age or in experience or knowledge, for example."

"Or money," I said.

"I thought it was understood that you own everything I own."

"But you own me."

"Perhaps," Skip said, "this particular can contains worms enough for only two people, in which case it would be impolite of us to open it in front of your little friends. Why don't you all run along to the park, and we'll discuss this in the evening after they've returned to the suburbs."

"But I want them to stay for dinner. Can they?"

"Here again, a decision is being thrust upon me that is not mine alone to make."

We entered Central Park at Seventy-second Street and walked over a small grassy hill shaded by large trees and down to a concrete area next to the Sheep Meadow where people

were roller-skating to dance music in a tight ellipse. We stood
in a crowd, presumably to watch the skaters. But I was distracted by the pronounced sensation that much of the crowd
was watching *me*. I felt the hair sticking to my neck and I felt
the crowd looking at my arms and my neck and the black
clumps of sweaty hair sticking to my pale, unblemished neck.
Have you ever wondered, sexual reader, if people are looking at
you funny when you're out in public just after having had sex?

"Watch what Harry can do," Dierdre said.

We followed Harry to the low chain-link fence that served
as the border of the Sheep Meadow. A skinny black boy of
Harry's height nodded at Harry. Harry approached him and
nodded back and the boy shook hands with him and described
several arcs in the air with his hands and arms while saying
something to Harry. He handed Harry a small green object,
which Harry brought to his face and smelled. Harry reached
into his pocket and gave some money to the boy, who jerked
his head around in all directions and walked away quickly.

"Scored us some dope," Harry said.

Dierdre said, "I got high just watching you," which seemed
false. She turned to me and said, "You want to get high, Little
Mary Sunshine?"

"By what? Taking marijuana? Is that what you just bought?"

"Yeah," Harry said. "We could go back to Miss Hartman's
house with the air conditioner and 'take' some marijuana."

Skip was not home when we returned. We sat in the kitchen
and Harry rolled some of the marijuana into a little cigarette.
We smoked it and my heart raced and my two friends looked
like insects to me and I burst into tears. They were very gentle
and stopped looking like insects, but I could not stop wheez-
ing and shaking. They fed me bowls of sugared cereal and I

shook until I was exhausted. They poured a quart of oil into a pot and turned the electric stove on high and put the pot on the stove with the intention of deep-frying some strips of potato. But they forgot to cut the potatoes and, in fact, forgot that the pot of oil was on the stove. Starting with a small explosion, an oil fire consumed the wiring of the oven and stove and burnt the wooden cabinets above them.

By the time Skip returned from wherever she was, Harry had found the carbon-dioxide fire extinguisher and put out the fire. When Harry explained how upset I'd become after smoking the pot, and how the fire had started, Skip was gracious. She thanked them for taking care of me. Harry and Dierdre left because they had the first day of school to rest up for.

The walls of the kitchen were smeared black with smoke residue. The smell of burnt wood and plastic mingled in the air. I cannot remember what my reaction to the fire was. I was stunned, I imagine, and drugged. I sat in a kitchen chair and Skip Hartman stood behind me stroking my cheek. "How come you're not mad?" I asked.

"I am grateful to your friends," she said. "They tried to feed you with warm food. It seems this fellow Harry had the presence of mind to extinguish the fire shortly after it began. I am thankful that you are unharmed, that you are here next to me."

Skip Hartman left off stroking my cheek and strolled around the kitchen table slowly and carefully several times. She looked as if she were balancing a stack of books on her head. I liked the way her quiet thighs came down out of her pelvis; the way her hands swung forward wrist first as she walked; the way, at the very front of the pendulum swing of her arms, her fingers flicked forward slightly. She had a monumental style of walking. Watching her walk was like watching the stars fix themselves slowly, over the millennia, into the shape of a woman walking.

"Well, I suppose it's time for bed now," she said, and headed toward the threshold of the kitchen, and stumbled on it, and was jolted, and kept walking away.

"But it's only six-thirty."

She turned and came back to the doorway. "Oh, well, then, I'll fix us some dinner. I'll prepare those flounder fillets I bought at the farmers' market."

"Skippy?"

"Yes?"

"You can't prepare anything because the stove got all burnt to a crisp."

"It did?"

"In the fire."

"Yes, the fire." Skip's pink face was dazed. "I hope you had fun with your friends. I so want you to be happy."

"Skippy-doo?"

"Yes?"

"I love you."

"Come to me," she said. I did.

4 *I Am Stuck*

ON THE MORNING of what would have been the first day of school, Skip Hartman and I attempted to begin my home schooling. I had a stomachache.

We sat in her book room, I in my Snoopy pajamas and she in one of her silk and linen teaching outfits, which she called "a bulwark against the boundarylessness of this household." She tried to give me a lesson in English literature.

"Let us begin at the beginning of the world," she said.

"With swirling hot gases?" I asked.

"With Shakespeare," she said.

"Oh, yeah, I remember him from when I was in school."

"And I suppose that you wish you were in school now?"

"I suppose that I wish I were in heaven."

"'Th' expense of spirit in a waste of shame,'" Skip Hartman

said, "'Is lust in action, and till action, lust / Is perjur'd, mur-
d'rous, bloody, full of blame, / Savage, extreme, rude, cruel,
not to trust.'

"What do you think of the opening lines of this poem,
Mary?"

"I think I have a stomachache. Could I go to the park?"

"I'd prefer if you didn't."

"I'd prefer if I did."

We were sitting next to each other on chairs in the book
room, the oaken floor spreading out all around us. *The River-
side Shakespeare,* volume 2, opened to pages 1772 and 1773,
lay in her lap. She stared at me. She reached out and brushed
a lock of black hair away from my eyes. It fell in front of my
eyes when she let go of it. She brushed it away again and it fell
back again, and she brushed it away and it fell back. "Ach," she
said, which seemed to be a comment on the uselessness of, for
example, trying to brush my hair away from my eyes.

"Go," she said.

"I need money."

"What for?"

"Hot dog."

"You have a stomachache."

"What if it goes away?"

She gave me a dollar.

"That's it?"

"How much do you want?"

"Fifteen."

"What for?"

"Harry says you can't leave the house with less than fifteen,
just like you can't leave the house without ID because if some-

one runs you over and kills you the police won't know who you are."

"Here's ten."

"So anyway, is this that discussion we were going to have where I own everything that you own?"

"Here's another twenty." She walked out of the room.

The weather was cloudy and hot and damp. I went to the same place that Dierdre and Harry and I had gone to the day before. I stopped at the long, thin area of concrete where the people had skated. Today there were only three skaters and no music, except the high, thin, rhythmic noise that came from the tiny speakers they all had inserted in their ears. These people were committed athletic skaters and serious loners, skating around and around privately behind their sunglasses on an overcast Tuesday afternoon near the end of summer.

The tall, skinny black boy who had sold pot to Harry the day before was pressing the top of the low fence around the Sheep Meadow with his elongated forearms. He gazed out at the vast, sparsely populated lawn. "Hey," I said.

His body stiffened. He pretended not to have heard me. "Excuse me," I said, nudging his arm, "do you have pot?"

"Do I have what?"

"Pot. Marijuana."

He stood and turned to me. "What do I look like to you?"

"Like the guy who sold my friend marijuana yesterday."

"I see. You saw a black man sell marijuana to your friend here yesterday, and because I am black and standing here, you think it must have been I."

His white dress shirt was neatly pressed and so were his khaki pants. His brown loafers with gold buckles had just been shined. He didn't look like a marijuana dealer, but then again I had led a sheltered life in the suburbs, reader, and didn't know what a marijuana dealer was supposed to look like.

"I think I know what I saw," I said.

"I think I know what I am," he said, with his hands on his hips.

"Come on, just sell me some pot."

"Listen, would you please get away from me before I call the police?"

"What's that perfume you're wearing?"

His body relaxed into maybe one tenth of a faint, as if what I had just said were so exasperating it could have knocked a person unconscious. "It is not perfume. It is a men's cologne. It is Safari for Men."

"Well, it stinks."

"I cannot sell marijuana to a small child."

"I'm not a small child, I'm a small adult. My growth has been stunted by smoking marijuana."

"Trust me, you're a little girl and you don't know anything."

"I know a lot more about life than you'll ever know."

He made a *tsk*-ing noise with his tongue and teeth and made a little rounded gesture in the air with his long, supple hands that seemed to be a comment on the elaborate wrongness of what I had just said.

"I do," I said.

"Such as?"

"Lust."

"And what do you know about lust?"

"Savage extreme rude cruel."

"So the little girl has read Shakespeare. Big deal."

"So sell me some pot."

He rolled his eyes back in his head. "I can't believe I'm doing this. This is really stupid." He reached into his pocket and removed a small plastic bag. "That'll be twenty dollars, please."

"I have to smell it first."

"Yes, of course. I'm sure that William Shakespeare always smelled it before he bought it." He handed me the bag.

"Well, I have to stand away from you to smell it because of your 'Safari for Men' cologne."

"Fine."

I took several steps away from him and, for no reason that I can think of, turned around and sprinted toward the edge of the park at Fifth Avenue. I looked over my shoulder for long enough to see this boy try to organize his two very long, thin legs into a running motion. He was having trouble getting started, like a young colt. I eased off to a quick jog, which was a mistake, because once his legs got the basic concept of running they did quite well with it and he almost caught me. During a whole summer of running, I had developed a burst-of-speed technique, which I deployed just as he was about to catch me. None of the skaters, nor any of the young mothers pushing strollers, nor any of the drunks, nor the old people feeding pigeons seemed to care that a tall black boy was chasing a short white girl through the park. By the time I reached Fifth Avenue I had maybe ten paces on him. I hailed a cab and climbed inside.

"The toy store," I said to the cabdriver, who moved out into traffic and also didn't seem to care that there was a boy chasing his car. I stared at him out the back window of the cab and wished he didn't look so despondent.

"Which toy store?" the driver said.

"That huge one on Fifty-eighth Street with all the nice toys."

"F.A.O. Schwarz," he said.

"Yeah, F.A.O. Schwarz," I said. "I have thirty-one dollars and I'm going to buy my teacher a nice present."

BACK IN SKIP Hartman's room, I sort of missed the boy from whom I had stolen the marijuana that I was now smoking. I saw delicacy and hopefulness in his face, and a puzzlement that I understood all too well: why am I this when what I wish to be is that?

I don't know how long Skip Hartman had been standing in the doorway watching me meditate and take puffs of pot. She stood in the doorway and I sat on the bed and we observed each other for a while. One of the pleasures of living with Skip Hartman was having the opportunity to watch the quick changes in the color and texture and arrangement of her face. Every gradation of feeling could be seen there. While some people's emotions originate in their hearts, Skip's originated on her face.

"What is it like to smoke pot?" Skip asked me.

"You've never done it?"

"No."

"Kind of interesting. Come here and sit with me and try some."

"No, thank you."

"Why?"

"I do not need to learn another way to lose control of my life."

"How about doing it because you want to keep me company while I do it?"

"I think there is already enough of that kind of sacrifice in this relationship as it is."

"No there isn't."

Skip Hartman held her hand up as if to say *stop*. I had seen her use this gesture in the classroom to signal *please be quiet*. I wondered if the gesture now was meant to signal *please be quiet* about all the topics we never discussed: for example, where she went and what she did without me beyond the confines of the house.

"What do you do when you leave the house?" I said.

She looked at me.

"Do you have friends? Who are your friends?"

"Would you like to meet some of them?"

"Yes."

WHAT I KNEW about Joe Samuels and Ruella Forecourt in advance of their arrival at Skip Hartman's house for dinner was that they, like Skip Hartman, were rich. I knew it by what few details Skip told me about them—that Ruella was a retired fashion model–slash–performance artist and that Joe owned a photography studio—but more than that, I knew it because I knew it. As a twelve-year-old, I already sensed that rich people tended not to invite guests over to the house who had personal financial arrangements other than richness. If someone is poor and comes for a social visit to the house of someone who is rich, the question tends to hang in the air: "Could I have some of your money?" This question does not actually get voiced by anyone with more than a casual understanding of reality, but in the case of Tommy White, for example, it gets voiced and, what's more, it gets granted. You *might* want to take the Tommy tack and focus single-mindedly on the goal of fabulous wealth for its own sake, but as you probably know, there is very little fabulous wealth to go around, and if you do devote your life to attaining it you might really be screwing yourself out of a lot of other pleasures, thus having, at your life's end, a fabulous regret beyond anything that I could describe or that you could imagine, cherished middle- or maybe even working-class reader.

When Joe Samuels and Ruella Forecourt arrived for dinner, Skip climbed the stairs and retrieved me from the bedroom, where I had been engaged all afternoon in drawing women and cars with colored Magic Markers on the surface of the eggshell-white wall between the two French windows. When I came down the stairs in my favorite pink ballerina outfit of that period, I saw the statuesque Ruella Forecourt. She was blond and muscular and wearing a long black dress that embraced her body so tightly it was almost inside her skin. "Oh, look!" she cried in her Swiss-German accent, "the little dancing child is lovely!"

"Kid's cute," Joe said. He was bald and gray and a little shorter and heavier than Skip. He did not have good posture. He held his head forward and down, which I think he did so he would get there a little sooner. He wore a shlumpy gray suit that was probably once very expensive, which he appeared not to care about at all. I thought I recognized him from somewhere.

"I would prefer if you both would address me directly rather than talking about me as if I were not in the room," I said, wanting to make a good impression.

"Kid's smart," Joe said.

"Kid wants man to talk directly to her or get out of her house," I said.

"Oh, sorry, sorry, sorry, kid, I don't have much—what?— grace or aplomb with children."

"Get some," I said.

"I *like* you, dear girl," Ruella said, leaning down almost on her hands and knees as if talking to a baby or a dog. "You are small but with a fully formed personality. Tell me, have you read Nietzsche?"

"What's Nietzsche?"

"September, do you mean to say that you have not offered the child Nietzsche to read?"

"Short of shoving Nietzsche down the child's throat, I don't think any offer of Nietzsche would be accepted by the child, isn't that right, dear child?"

"Ah, but Nietzsche himself said, 'One has regarded life carelessly if one has failed to see the hand that kills with leniency,'" Ruella said.

Skip said, "He also said, 'The good teacher takes things seriously—even himself—only in relation to his pupils.' Shall we eat dinner?"

In the manner of Skip Hartman at her finest, Skip Hartman had seized the adversity of the summer's little oil fire in the kitchen to make some advantageous modifications to her cooking setup. Cooking—like reading, or memorizing poems, or teaching, or loving—was one of the ways she made a meaningful connection with the world. In the delicious taste of the tajine of lamb that she prepared for us that evening, I was given access to yet another expressive venue for the passion of this remarkable woman, who also expressed her passion in posture, in the syntactically baroque sentences that marked her conversational style—in the way she made a bed or sat in a chair, for that matter. There was so much for me to admire in Skip Hartman that the admiration I had to give could not possibly have been adequate, so I often neglected to admire her at all.

"So, kid," Joe Samuels said to me, his head ranging out over the salad bowl, "how you adapting to your situation here?"

"Okay, I guess. I'm kind of bored."

"'Boredom—the desire for desires.' Leo Tolstoy, *Anna Karenina*," Ruella Forecourt said.

"We are attempting to discover Mary's interests and cultivate them," Skip said.

"We're not sure I have any interests. We're hoping I have some," I said.

"Certainly her irreverent wit is not in need of cultivation," Skip said.

"You would love the studio, my child," Ruella said. "You would adore the studio. Joseph, wouldn't the child adore the studio?"

"She might adore it," he said.

"What kind of stuff do you do there?" I said.

"Oh, we photograph people in gorgeous clothing. It is at once deeply rewarding and repulsive to me, for you see I am a feminist and a socialist with Nietzschean leanings. ' "Sympathy for all"—would be harshness and tyranny for thee, my good neighbor.' "

Joe said, "See, what happened was, I was a features photographer for one of the city papers and I was assigned to photograph an international high school spelling bee and who should be one of the finalists but this Teutonic giantess here who happened to be more or less the fantasy of every Flatbush Jewboy *I* ever grew up with, anyway. So I started popping pictures of her my ass off—September, is it all right to say 'ass' in front of the kid?"

I said, "Well, September and I have *done* ass, so you might as well *say* 'ass.'" Everyone smiled merrily at the precocious child, who was not as precocious as she sounded. The me who talked knew more than the me who knew things without saying them. The me who knew things without saying them waited in silence to see what the me who talked was going to say next. The me who is saying this right now is trying to talk and know at the same time. She's also trying to know and not know at the same time, because frankly some of the things she would find out if she knew what she was saying are kind of creepy.

"So anyway," Joe said, "I'm popping black-and-white pictures, and then I decide to pop some color pictures as well just for the hell of it, and then I get home and start developing 'em and I notice the colors aren't right, so I futz around, futz around, and what do I come up with but an entirely new color process which I then went out and patented, so I turn out to be this big lug from Flatbush who happens to have patented a process for developing color film that's pretty popular with just about everybody."

Ruella said, "I won third prize in the spelling bee and went on to become an internationally recognized fashion model, thanks to Joseph, and except for the eight years when I lived with the guru I have been with Joseph ever since the spelling bee and we have had a fabulous life together. Darling child, you really must come down and see us at the studio because you would *love* it."

So that was my first evening with Skip Hartman's friends: Joe Samuels, the self-made aesthetic Brooklyn Jewish millionaire, and Ruella Forecourt, the large but perfectly proportioned Swiss fashion model and Nietzsche enthusiast; and let us not forget September Hartman herself, the cultured, literate, independently wealthy New England WASP with posture and cooking skills.

If you are wondering what descriptive epithets I would assign to myself at that time: Mary White, obnoxious, lonely, self-loathing American orphan.

AT A CERTAIN point during the winter of our first year together, Skip Hartman and I agreed that haircutting, if nothing else, was a cultural activity we could jointly participate in. Specifically, she would cut my hair, which had not gone under the scissors since before the death of my parents. It—my hair— was big and messy and black and poured down in great impenetrable chunks over my white, skinny arms and back.

As a prelude to the haircut, we took a long shower together. Reader, one of the many advantages of wealth is good water pressure. Skip had a shower like a waterfall. She had personally painted the bathroom dark green and had painted the shower walls with realistic eucalyptus trees. She burnt mint-flavored incense when we spent time together in this, our favorite idyll. Here—even just brushing teeth together—I often felt the most intense love for Skip Hartman. Does it surprise you that I could love her at all? Love does not absolve the loved one from loving, you know.

I felt pacified and quiet that morning, sitting on the small built-in bench in the shower while Skip Hartman stood naked above me and squeezed hair conditioner from the plastic bottle onto my hair. "Your hair at this time reminds me of the wave-particle theory of light," she said, working the goo from the ends of the hair in toward my scalp. "Your hair has a certain essence of fluidity even as it could stop a bus like a brick wall."

I giggled and relaxed. "Tell me more."

She held a lock of hair close to my scalp with her left hand, while with the fingers of her right she worked to undo the tangles in outer regions of that same lock. "Once upon a time, there was a lock of Mary's hair streaming out from her head like a ray of light," she improvised, "and God saw this ray of light and was satisfied with His creation. God went on in His way being satisfied with this and the other things He had made. Then God, in His infinite capacity for noticing things, noticed how much attention certain of His other human children were paying to this lock of hair, which streamed out from Mary's head like the rays of the sun itself, only dark instead of light, some had begun to say. And God felt a little icky. Something was bugging God that He couldn't put His infinitely long finger on, at least not right away. And God meditated upon His creation, which was the same as Himself, which is to say He thought of everything at once, because He could not do otherwise. While not ceasing to think of any of His other feelings, God sort of zeroed in on His own jealousy, which was, like everything else about Him, big. But not infinite. No, not even God may feel jealous without becoming that much smaller than Himself. 'What to do, what to do about this child with magnificent hair like waves and particles at once,' God said to Himself, who was now no longer everything; specifically, He was not this hair, for had He been the hair He could not also have been jealous of the hair, or so He reasoned omnisciently. At first He considered wiping out all of humanity with an enormous flood, but then He thought better of it: 'A lot of people think highly of this child's hair. Is that any reason to kill them all? No.' Instead, God, seemingly at random, fixed on the heart of the woman named after the first month of autumn, and He filled this woman's heart with a love for the child that was frighteningly immoderate and frowned upon by most of the rest of the human community. And in this way the woman knew some small part of God's own sorrow and helplessness. The end. Time for your haircut."

The water gushing from the shower head was very hot. Skip Hartman took me gently by the temples and brought my head under the water. Steam billowed up from the shower floor. I felt mournful and soothed. I wished that she would go on making up stories about my hair until one of us died—her, probably.

Soon I was sitting in a swivel chair in the center of the book room wearing my white terry-cloth bathrobe. The book room seemed to have a knack for precipitating great onrushes of feeling. Skip stood in the doorway wearing her larger version of the same bathrobe. I swiveled left, I swiveled right, I swiveled left. Skip held a comb and scissors in one hand and a dark blue folded sheet in the other. She entered the room and did a few understated hip wiggles of the haircutters' dance. She placed the scissors and comb on the edge of a shelf. While holding one edge of the sheet in her two hands, she cast the sheet up and out across the room. The dark sheet billowed in the sunlit room with the white walls and the books. She wrapped the sheet around my neck like a cape, whereupon I could not resist saying, like the owner of a couple of capes we knew, "I want some of these old books to spread around the house. I'll sprinkle some in the backyard. I'll tile the bathroom with books. Have you got any history books for the kitchen?"

"I love to meet a fellow booklover," Skip said, a look of mischief on that face of looks. She walked toward me snipping the air with her scissors, closer and closer to my head, *snip, snip, snip*. "And what sort of haircut would we like today?"

"Well, we would like something like what we have now."

"Do we mean a big mess?"

"I guess we mean a big neatness."

"A trim?"

"Yes."

"Or how about this?" Skip said. She plunged the scissors into the nest of my hair and cut off a big hunk right up close to my scalp. A big wad of black hair the size of a cat fell to the floor. Before I could stop her she did this twice more. My hand rushed up to the side of my head, where there was now an extensive patch of hair as short as the grass on the first green of a golf course. I screamed and stood up and clawed at my neck to remove the cape. "Why did you do that?" I yelled.

"I don't know."

"You just ruined my life!"

Her face—that face of hers—grew red. Her eyes were wide open and big teardrops appeared at the bottoms of them and fell down her face. "But my darling," she said, "you have also ruined my life. I thought that was understood."

I began by hitting her face and then I moved down and started beating her sides with both fists. I pounded away at her sides, using all my strength, until I felt a terrible burning sensation in my right cheek just below my right eye. I fell back onto the floor, holding my face. It felt as if a large, burning coal were embedded in my skin. "Make it stop," I pleaded with Skip. I looked out at the room with my left eye and saw that she was gone. She came back with a paper towel and took my hands away from my face and placed the cool, wet paper towel

on my right cheek. I saw the paper towel fill up with blood in
seconds, and I understood that to make me stop punching her
she had stabbed me in the face with the scissors. She removed
the towel and placed another against my cheek, pressing hard
this time to stanch the flow of blood. "We must never hurt one
another like this again," she said.

"Did I hurt you?"

"I think you broke my ribs. Yes, you hurt me very much." She
almost started sobbing but stopped herself for the sake of the
medical emergency. "Can you see out of your right eye?"

I opened it.

"Can you see?"

I nodded.

"I was aiming for your eye, you know. I would never have
been able to forgive myself had I succeeded in blinding you."

"How about stabbing me in the face? Can you forgive yourself for that?"

"As I said, you were hurting me a great deal. I am not prepared to be a martyr."

I was relieved to hear her say that. After we returned from
the emergency room, she finished the haircut. I looked like a
boy. There was not too big of a puncture gash in my face, but
for the next several weeks it hurt if I moved around much. For
the first day or two, I sat for hours at a time on the big living
room couch with my cut face, and Skip Hartman sat beside
me with her broken ribs, and we just sat there being stunned.

Having to remain still for so long, I then accidentally discovered the pleasures of reading. I read *Pride and Prejudice*
and *Jane Eyre* (my favorites) and *Great Expectations* and
Mediocre Expectations and *James and the Giant Peach* and *The
Red and the Black* and *The Martin Luther King Story.* My heart

felt big during that time. I know it wasn't really all that big. I mean, let's face it, this Mary character is not very nice. But I can guarantee you this: she wishes she were. If she wounds the woman she loves most in all the world, if she loves her more fiercely than tenderly, it is not because she wants to do it that way, but because she does not know how else to do it. Dear reader, she cannot tell you herself, so I will tell you for her: she is trying to learn how!

I Am Not Embraced
by Everyone

WEARING MY NEW short haircut and a large square Mickey Mouse Band-Aid below my right eye, I went downtown one fine winter Monday to the place called Studio Joe. As I entered the low concrete building along the Hudson River, I could feel myself floating further adrift from the prescripted school-day life of a twelve-year-old.

Inside the building, thin, delicate people in extravagant outfits rushed about in thick heels on the gray cement floor looking desperately glamorous. They were exerting themselves toward some objective. They dressed in a certain way so as not to be nothing. You have to do everything you can to make yourself distinct from these white walls, their body shapes and outfits and manners seemed to be saying; you have to be ready at all times for that moment when you meet the person who'll carry you out of your life that is impoverished by the lack of that one intangible thing; ready to be carried into the other life that someone would carry you into if only you could meet him or her and be assured of saying or doing what you're supposed to say or do and looking how you're supposed to look, as you've always known you could, because secretly you're sure it has been willed where that can be done which has been willed, maybe.

"Yes, young man?" someone behind a tall marble embankment said to me.

"I'm here to see Joe Samuels and Ruella Forecourt."

"Of course you are."

I looked up, and saw the black boy whose pot I had stolen in the park, and felt sick.

"I'm really sorry," I said. "It was a dumb mistake."

"I have no doubt that it was," he said.

"Can you forgive me?"

"I cannot."

"I'll pay you the twenty dollars."

"You could pay me the million dollars, boy, and that would not change a thing."

I was now standing more or less directly below this person sitting behind the high marble embankment. I looked up into his face. He seemed to be trying to outwit his bulbous nose and pitted skin with lotions and overscrubbing, not yet having settled into the comfort of his ugliness. His hair was long and nappy like a partially unraveled sweater. I recognized the over-all frame of the body and the effeminate gestures of the hands, but the face seemed different. What had the face of the boy in the park looked like?

"I did meet you before in the park, right?" I asked.

"No doubt that is true, but right now let me put it to you this way: if you want to see Joe and Ruella, who is the person who needs to have been met, you or me, chicky?"

"Do you think I'm a boy or a girl?"

"Oh, I can't say that I honestly care, but I might get somebody to throw your butt out of here if you don't stop staring at me with those creepy little eyes."

"I'm just trying to figure out if you're the guy I sort of—you know, the guy who was going to sell me some pot in the park a few months ago."

"Oh, I'm the guy."

"Like I said, I'm sorry, and I'll give you the money."

"Like I said, up your butt with a broom handle."

"Listen, jerk, who the hell are you anyway? Joe and Ruella told me to come here and say hi to them; so I want to see them now."

"Yes, well, that's refreshingly spirited and insouciant and naïve to be sure. Have a seat right over there, child."

"Over where?"

"There."

"There's no place to sit down anywhere around here."

"How observant. If you walk back through the front door and sit on the curb, someone will fetch you when the special moment arrives for you to say 'Hi' to Joe and Ruella."

"Really?"

"Yes."

I sat on the curb in the long, shabby black business coat

which the boy behind the counter had looked askance at, and which I had insisted on buying in a thrift shop despite Skip's urgings. The sun was bright and the air was frosty. I looked at the seagulls hovering above the river and uttering their cold-weather survivalist cry on this Monday morning. I wondered if many children my age spent as much time as I did trying to imagine what they were supposed to be doing, how they were supposed to behave from one moment to the next in order to make themselves feel real.

A taxicab pulled up and several tall blond women got out and went into the building. Another cab pulled up and several short, dark, voluptuous Mediterranean women got out and went into the building. Another cab pulled up and two ugly Eastern European men in messy clothes who looked as if they had just crawled out of a Dumpster got out and went into the building with camera equipment. I stood up and vomited and went into the building.

The boy who may have been the boy in the park with the pot reclined at his station reading *The Village Voice*. This time he looked to me like Joseph Samuels, so basically I had no idea what the hell was going on.

"I'm back," I said.

"Yes."

"No one came to get me."

"Yes."

"You told me to wait outside and someone would come get me. That was forty minutes ago."

"I'm having a vague recollection that leaves me indifferent."

"I'm here to see—"

"I know."

"Are you related to Joe Samuels?"

"What can I do to persuade you to go away?"

"I'm related to Skip Hartman. Do you know who she is? Joe and Ruella came to our house for dinner."

"Oh, so you are September Hartman's little—yes, well, that's a whore of a different color. Oh, did I say *whore*? I meant horse."

"You're as funny as breast cancer."

Something like glee entered the rough field of the face of this boy or man who resembled Joe Samuels, except inasmuch as he was black where Joe was white, and who resembled the boy in the park, except inasmuch as he had a rough, wide face where the boy in the park had had just a face, as far as I could remember.

He put on an ear-and-mouthpiece headset and appeared to be pressing numbers on a console. "Joey," he said into the mouthpiece, "that little, ah"—he looked down at me questioningly, I made a certain unequivocal gesture, and he said—"*girl* is here to see you. The one—uh, residing at September Hartman's pied-à-terre."

Moments later, fat Joe Samuels burst through a pair of swinging high-chrome doors to our right. "This is fantastic," he said to me. "You're here just in time to see what's going on inside now. Your timing is fantastic."

The thinner, darker, younger, supercilious version of Joe looked at me now with something that was neither quite arrogance nor jealousy.

I said, "Joe Junior here made me sit out on the sidewalk for an hour."

"Oh, Joe Junior, as you call him, likes to play. Let him have his fun. He's a sweet kid," Joe Senior said.

"My name is not by any means Joe Junior. My name is Stephen Samuels," Joe Junior said haughtily.

Joe said, "Great things are afoot. Come right this way, sugar."

"My name is not by any means sugar. My name is Mary White," sugar said haughtily, and was taken by the wrist and swept further into her own life.

I remember kind of falling down a hallway and entering a white room that was filled with commotion and bright lights and silken limbs and large personalities and sophisticated camera equipment. The effect was dizzying—more than a small, traumatized, and nauseated child should be expected to understand or retain. People were taking pictures of other people against white walls and under bright lights shaded by gray umbrellas facing the wrong way. In fact, on the whole, plain people were taking pictures of pretty people, and I believe I'll stop just short of developing a theory about what sort of person stand: on which side of a fashion camera, for theories are a boy's pastime. No theories here, Jim. Just plain old observation, and pretty goddamn sloppy observation at that. You know what I'm saying?

Joe let go of my wrist and one of the blond women from the taxicab approached me, yelling, "Ruella thinks you're very special!" She was standing practically on top of me and had linked her arm in mine but had to yell to be heard over the terrifyingly impersonal dance music. "Have you read *Beyond Good and Evil* yet?" the woman, an American, yelled.

"No, but I've lived it!" I yelled.

"Ruella turned me on to Nietzsche! It's like I read Nietzsche and I go, 'This is what I've always thought about everything? But he's actually saying it?' I read it and it's like, 'Oh my *God* I *know* what you *mean!*' You *have* to read it, it's *so* amazing and

Ruella *totally* loves you. Listen I'll buy you a copy of *Beyond Good and Evil* and have it messengered, what's your address?" I told her my address, which she must have memorized because I didn't especially see her writing it down.

Joe entered my field of vision and yelled, "Mary White, this is Cindy Chenille! Ruella's training Cindy to be a model as well as an *Übermensch!*"

"Is Ruella a model or a photographer?" I asked.

"Oh, no, no, no, no, no!" Cindy Chenille said. "Ruella is very spiritual and also very sensual! It's like this: it's like she is beautiful and she is sitting in that chair in this room and the photographers take our picture in the room and the picture comes out beautiful! Do you understand?"

"No!"

Cindy Chenille strode off into a crowd of those glamorous people who were either having their pictures taken or dancing or both.

Joe led me to the director's chair in which Ruella was seated monumentally. He pressed a button on a small neat pile of black metal boxes and the music abruptly stopped. All conversation in the room stopped a moment later, as if conversation were not worthwhile without the struggle to be heard over the music. Joe pressed a skimpy black headset to the side of his large multitextured face and said, "Okay, people." His voice sounded over the speakers that had been amplifying the music. "Take a lunch break." All who had been dancing or shooting photos or meditating or carrying a bracelet left the room. Ruella and Joe and I remained alone in the enormous white room.

Joe picked up a thermos off the floor, removed the cap,

poured a pale brown liquid into a red plastic cup, and handed the cup to Ruella. "I prefer Gatorade but she likes this herbal stuff," he said.

"Several years ago I went on a spirit journey and spoke with some of the local plant life of southern New York State," Ruella said.

"The plant life'll talk to Ruella," Joe said. "Plant life clams up around me."

"You don't let the plant life get a word in edgewise, darling," Ruella said. "I asked the plants permission to harvest them for the good of myself and the people I love."

"She asked them what would be a nice drink for her to reenergize during her work, which is strenuous."

"What's your work, exactly?" I said.

"Darling, you are an intrusive little munchkin and I like you."

"Is that guy related to you?" I asked Joe.

"What guy?"

"The one who made me sit on the sidewalk."

"Oh, Stevie? He's my bastard son. He's filling in for the real receptionist, who got in a motorcycle accident, who I hope he gets back here soon skull fracture or no, because Stevie's a riot and a brilliant kid and everything, but he sort of sits out there in reception and offends the wrong people every second of every day. Kid's a bright ne'er-do-well and I blame myself."

"Who's his mother?"

"I'm not involved with the mother at this time, is the nature of these things. She's on the Coast with an upstart fragrance company. I somewhat left the two of them eighteen years ago, and six years ago the kid shows up in my living room with his whole patrimony concept that he was very convincing about, a real bright kid. I like having him around but I just don't know what to do with him, but I have a few ideas."

Skip Hartman entered the room, in brown leather. Cindy Chenille was pretty and Ruella Forecourt was magnificent, but Skip Hartman approaching with her long bare arms and leather vest and her level stride and a straw picnic basket with silver hasps overwhelmed me with scary delight. Ruella jumped up out of her chair to her full height and Joe bobbed his head vigorously. We were all happy to see Skip Hartman!

"There's no getting around the fantastic spinal carriage on you, Hartman," Joe said.

"In Skip Hartman I sense a quietude animated by a powerful life force," Ruella said.

"Skippy!" I said.

"Wary Mary!" Skip said, and bent at the waist and offered me her hair to mess up.

"She was once a model herself, you know," Joe said to me.

"Is that where all your money comes from?" I asked.

"No," she said. "All my money comes from my father, a physician who struck it rich with a medical invention."

"What did he invent?"

"A sort of crude proto-IUD. I have since aggrandized his holdings through prudent investment."

"And teaching," I said.

"No one aggrandizes through teaching," she said.

"She is so forthright," Ruella said.

"She ain't *that* forthright," I said, and while there may have been some truth to my remark, it sprang from a deep irrational mistrust of all who came close to me. What I would say now is that it's better to trust someone who is untrustworthy than not to trust anyone at all.

"Did you see my fine young man Stevie out there?" Joe asked Skip.

"I did not."

"He wasn't at the desk?"

"I saw a great many youths frolicking in the style of the age," she said, "but I did not see Stephen, and I quite think I would know him if I saw him."

Joe said, "So in essence any lunatic—I'm not impugning you here, Hartman—could walk in off the street with no one to stop him and stab Ruella in the heart."

"Joseph, you are so violent," Ruella said.

Skip put her basket down and retrieved a folding table from across the room. She put her basket on the table and removed the baguette sandwiches and the modular plastic champagne glasses and the cold bottle of champagne with the fancy orange label.

"What am I gonna do with that kid?" Joe said.

"I believe it is up to him to do something with himself," Skip said, joining the stem of a champagne glass to its vessel.

"Which brings up an interesting point," Joe said. "Namely, my Stevie's gifted at math and science, and since you're having trouble teaching the gamine here you should have my kid over every day to tutor her."

"I think I don't need another irresponsible child in my house at this time," Skip said, and popped the cork on the champagne.

I pointed to the three plastic champagne glasses Skip had put together and said, "Who's not having champagne?"

"You," Skip said.

"Oh, I see, so it's okay to have sex with me but I can't drink a teeny glass of champagne with lunch, is that it?" This wasn't a straightforward complaint so much as it was the opener for a vaudevillian routine Skip and I were working up. Her part in the routine was to blush, remove the fourth champagne glass she had been hiding in the basket, and fill it for me. "Cheers," she said.

"To my son the math and science tutor," Joe said, "because we obviously can't let him work here anymore."

Skip said, "Listen. Absolutely not."

Joe said, "So he's a little angry and smokes marijuana all day and he's a bit at loose ends which I'm not entirely innocent for since I'm his father so he does the marijuana and gets it out of his system and he's someone who's youthful for Mary here and the two of them can relax together because you know what a drag we adults can be."

"Nothing doing."

"September, he's had some tough breaks."

"Oh, I've had some tough breaks," Stephen Samuels said, ambling toward us through the white room wearing an array of loose, gauzy, beige garments that were wrapped and tucked and folded and belted in ways incomprehensible to me. "I've had a hard life. I've fallen on hard times. I'm a Dickensian urchin of the streets, where life is but a toy. Early childhood trauma, negative environmental conditioning, all the disadvantages," he said, illustrating with large elliptical motions of his right arm in the air. "Miscegenation, inversion, economic deprivation, buffeted by the winds of fate. True, I was a bright, resilient child and I rose above the odds, but then I fell back down under the odds."

"He's funny, right?" Joe said.

"Hey, *are* you the guy who tried to sell me pot in Central Park or what?"

Stephen Samuels seemed to be pondering how to answer this. "Yes. And to my credit I am the only openly homosexual marijuana dealer in the lower Central Park area. I am also unaffiliated with any of the larger marijuana cartels. I'm a self-starter and a go-getter. Marijuana is a way to both express my discontent and alleviate it. Still, I would love to quit this terrible business to somehow better serve humanity."

"See?" Joe said.

"Come here, Stephen, and let me give you a kiss," Skip said.

He approached her and kissed her on one cheek, made an unnecessarily wide arc around her face with his face, and kissed her on the other. She held his hand in one of hers and patted him on the wrist, gazing at him. "You're all grown up!"

"So give him a job."

"Oh, I can't believe this," Skip said to Joe while continuing to look at Stephen. "I don't know whether you were kidding about the marijuana or what, Stephen, but you may not sell it at or near my house or use the telephone at my house to sell it. In fact you may not sell marijuana or abet in the sale of marijuana while in my employ. I cannot believe I'm agreeing to this."

"May I smoke it outside of your house?" Stephen asked.

"That's your motherfucking business," Skip said angrily.

"Mothahfuckah!" Mary said, mock-angrily.

SO READER, I must admit, to the credit of my guardian, that I did after all receive a form of secondary education loosely based on the American high school method of one teacher per discipline. Stephen Samuels: mathematics and hard science; Joseph Samuels: fine art; Ruella Forecourt: philosophy; September Hartman: literature (less by inculcation than by osmosis). As for history: nobody at all, as befits an orphan-American.

A couple of years passed until the next event I can think of to tell you about—time enough for a healthy sapling to grow into a small tree. Not that I knew any saplings or trees. In fact, I wish I had planted a sapling when I was twelve that I could have returned to when I was fourteen and sixteen and eighteen, the way a smart young boy did in one of the books I read about people who grow up and, you know, the tree grows up with them. I am and always have been about as far from a sapling-planting mentality as a person could get. I wish there were a tree now to prove I was once twelve.

What I will say about this period of a little more than two years that I will more or less not be talking about is that nothing and nobody at that time could deliver me from my isolation from all humanity; that was mine to be kept whole by; it guarded me fiercely. I don't mean that there was not an informal mishmosh of good people in my life. I mean that I had a kind of force field around me made of tough talk and fake self-sufficiency, and nobody knew how to break through the force field. Here's how I like to imagine they could have broken through the force field: they get together and throw me a birthday party where we all eat cake; they sing me that song; then, spontaneously, every single person I know in the world comes over and hugs me and squashes me almost to death. A big group hug from all the people I know, with me at the center.

Lots of things have happened since that time—some of them good, even. My life has changed in ways I intend to tell you all about presently and that might surprise you. But I never did get that group hug. Who ever gets the total group hug? Do you?

Dirty Little Secret

OKAY, ARE YOU familiar with the Heisenberg Uncertainty Principle? This is the principle wherein an atomic physicist cannot bring her measuring rod close enough to an electron to measure it without altering the very properties of the electron she wishes to measure. Never mind that there was not so much as a single girl physicist who got her measuring rod anywhere *near* an electron in Heisenberg's day that I know of; I think my point is obvious: as it is in quantum physics, so it is in love. And that is why, instead of asking Skip Hartman where she went when she left the house without me, I tailed her. This was on a cold afternoon in the late winter of my sixteenth year.

She walked over to Fifth Avenue and down Fifth to Seventy-ninth Street. I remained half a block behind her. I say "tail," but this is just a slang term for secretly walking behind someone and did not in any way satisfy my longing to be a part of her body.

She entered a flower shop, bought a bouquet of wildflowers, went to the corner, and boarded the crosstown bus. The hardest part of running alongside the crosstown bus was running alongside it through Central Park, where it picked up a lot of speed. Luckily Skip had kept me on a strict schedule of sprinting despite a bum knee that I kept bound in a tight bandage. Still, when she got off the bus at Seventy-ninth and Broadway I was trailing her by thirty yards, gasping for breath. And thank the god of all spies for the high breeze on that day; otherwise I would not have seen the few unmistakable wisps of hair that had come partially loose from the Hartman head just before that head dropped below ground level into the Seventy-ninth Street station of the Broadway IRT. She cleared the subway turnstile and I stood halfway down the steps just out of her sight, catching my breath, shivering, underdressed for the cold, carrying no token or money, for I was not a very clever spy.

A Number One train arrived. I eased myself down the stairs, leapt the turnstile, and boarded the train in the car behind the one Skip had boarded; this way I was able to follow her and keep an even distance just by sitting still. She stayed on the train for a long time. We were carried along, each in a separate lighted vessel that trembled in the dark tunnel that ran beneath the lighted air of the planet that kept us apart from the dark and stifling cosmos.

When Skip Hartman got off the train, we were so far underground that we had to take a cavernous elevator up to the street. I did not feel I could risk not getting on the same elevator that Skip got on, so I got on it, standing behind a tall man.

She did not discover me and I was a little disappointed: shouldn't she know when the person she loved best in all the world was in the same elevator with her? The doors opened and we walked out into the street.

I could only imagine where we were, and I imagined we were in one of the suburbs of the fabled Hartman childhood: Mamaroneck, I thought, or Cos Cob. The houses of Cos Cob were much dirtier and closer together than I had expected. I had expected Cos Cob to be a seaside resort. I had expected Cos Cob to be green, or at least greenish-brown. But this place was a hilly, dirty, poor version of Manhattan. Old women walked the streets in clothes that were mismatched and worn out, their faces hardened by years of food shopping. Block after block we passed mediocre cars and peeling paint and cryptic graffiti, first Skip Hartman and, ten seconds later, I.

She went into a building in the heart of Cos Cob. The building was called Modernity Geriatric Center. I entered, and, based on the few trips I had made into Dante's *Inferno* with Skip Hartman as my guide, I knew we were in the outermost ring of Hell. Here, there was no plaint that could be heard, except of sighs, which caused the eternal air to tremble, and so on. I looked around the lobby and recognized every old person sitting in a chair with bottomed-out expectations as one of those souls in the *Inferno* who had been born before the advent of Christ and whose only sin therefore was bad luck. Because these people could not worship God aright—or whatever the equivalent sin would be nowadays, which hell if I knew what that was—they were condemned to live for the remainder of eternity without hope. Even at the age of fifteen, I knew that was the best treatment a person could hope for in either Hell or an old age home.

I slipped past the indifferent guard at the front desk and followed Skip up two flights of stairs. I walked down a corridor of
foul odors peering into each room, until I saw what I was looking for: Skip Hartman sitting on the edge of a bed and saying
to the tiny drooling white-haired person in it, "Hello, Daddy."

"Child, what month is it now?" he asked, in a little voice that
resembled hers, only an octave higher.

She smiled warmly at him. "Why, it is September, Daddy, of
course."

"So it is."

She presented him with the bouquet of wildflowers. He
grabbed it from her, embraced the stems, squeezed them to his
narrow chest, sucked in the air that was directly above the
blossoms, and squealed, "Ooooooh, September, these are
beautiful flowers."

"I'm so glad you like them, Daddy. Shall I put them in a vase
in the window where you can see them bright and splendid
with the sunlight behind them?"

"No!" he said in a panic. "Let me hold them!" He sucked in
the air above the blossoms in a paroxysm. I thought he was
going to eat them.

"Yes, hold them," she said. She reached forward with her
hand and he cowered from it. When he saw that she meant
only to touch his hair gently, he relaxed and stroked his flower
stems and let her touch his hair.

As regards hair, his head resembled that of a mature dandelion; not the full yellow dandelion, that is, but the sparse, bald-
ing white one whose hair is in danger of blowing off its head.
Skip seemed respectful of this danger as she placed the small
groupings of hair in an arrangement that could only have been
meant to satisfy her own sense of order, since her father didn't

care and the other residents and staff of the Modernity Geriatric Center could not have been expected to notice.

"Oh, September, you are touching my head," the ancient
man said softly.

"Yes, Daddy."

"Cut it out."

"Yes, Daddy." She smiled warmly again, and glanced in my
direction, and gasped. "I knew it!"

"You did?"

"Daddy, this is the girl I've been telling you so much about."

"*What* is the girl?" He was nodding over his flowers.

"Look up at her, Daddy. She is the child who asked me to
call her by the name of her dead brother. Do you remember
that story?"

"No."

"Mary, come here where he can see you."

I said, "Shit, you had a father all this time?"

"Yes, I know that I waited for too long to tell you. To introduce you to my father is a very big step for me."

I said, "Yeah, well getting screwed five times a week by a
forty-year-old is a big step for me."

Skip said, "You were on the subway. And in the elevator."

"Yeah."

"I sensed your presence keenly. I did not understand. It
troubled me. I am glad to know you were there, else I would
have thought I was going crazy."

"Yeah, well good fucking thing you aren't going crazy," I said.
"What's his name?"

"Who?"

"September, you mustn't forget me. Tell the little boy my
name."

"Hoving Harrington Hartman, I would like you to meet Mary White."

"Hoving Harrington Hartman?" I said. "That's your father's name?"

"Yes!" Hoving said.

"You people are out of your minds!"

"Come away from the doorway," Skip said. "Go to him. Go to him and touch him. He likes the physical contact."

I walked toward him. "Hoving," I said.

He stared at me as I approached. "Hoving," he said, laughing. I reached for his head.

"Get away from me, you little pecker."

I vigorously mussed the tufts of white hair, and he shrieked. A stout old Jamaican nurse marched into the room and addressed us all as children: "What is going on in here?"

"It's all right, ma'am," Skip said. "He doesn't like to be touched." The nurse left.

We took him to the Modernity courtyard, where it was lightly raining. Surrounded on all four sides by the pale-yellow brick building, the three of us held hands and strolled up and down the narrow slate passageways through the vegetation. "Rhododendron," Hoving recited. "Ivy, pachysandra, birch, clover." I thought of the long, thin, inverted-asparagus penis that I had seen hanging down between his little thighs when Skip swaddled him in diapers and thermal underwear for the walk, and his chestnut testicles in their droopy double sack.

"Crow, blue jay, seagull, starling, sparrow, cardinal, robin redbreast," he said, far away, somnambulating through some lost age of Cos Cob.

Skip said, "He used to be tall and proud and fiercely erudite."

"And so he will be again," I said gravely.

"What did you say that for?"

"I don't know. Because it sounds like something somebody would say."

"What?"

"I don't know!"

"God, this is horrible," Skip murmured. We continued to stroll gracefully as if she had not just said something worth stopping everything for.

We brought him back to his room and Skip called a car for us.

"September, what do you do now?" her father asked. "Do you teach?"

"Yes."

"And what do you do, little child?"

"I slave over a hot oven."

"Do you know what I do?"

"What?"

"I lie here."

"How extra sucky for you."

"Yes."

7

Soap as an Actual Yardstick of Civilization

ONE TUESDAY AFTERNOON in the month of June of that year, Stephen Samuels and I sat in the kitchen having our usual difficulty settling into an algebra lesson. In order to teach me about the placement of coordinates on a Cartesian grid, he had drawn on a piece of paper a pair of perpendicular lines with arrows at their ends.

"What are the arrows for?" I said.

"They're arrows, honey, don't worry about it."

"You put arrows, so I want to know what the arrows are for because of my thirst for knowledge."

"The arrows represent that the lines extend to infinity."

"And what is infinity, out of curiosity?"

"You don't know what infinity is?"

"No, so up yours."

"That which is larger than any measurable number."

"What?"

"That which is larger than any measurable number."

"I don't believe you."

"It is not germane to our topic anyway."

"I don't believe in our topic."

"How about this: could you shut your mouth you little twit because I want to just put the damn coordinates on the damn grid and be out of here and smoke myself a blunt because you are on my ultimate nerve today?"

Skip Hartman stood in the doorway saying, "Would anybody like some milk and cookies?"

"I was just teaching Ms. White here to understand the Cartesian grid."

"So I heard."

"She's a difficult pupil."

"Yes." Skip was not listening, really, and was distracted as she set two tall clear tumblers on the kitchen table, one for me and one for Stephen. She filled them with cold milk from a carton from the refrigerator. She brought a blue cylindrical tin down from a kitchen cabinet and removed the lid and presented Stephen and me with our favorite anthology of shortbreads. Stephen Samuels and I chose our shortbreads, dunked them liberally in our milks, held our shortbreads in our mouths, where we sucked the milk out of them, chewed, swallowed, and chose new shortbreads. Skip Hartman sat facing away from the table with her natural good posture that she didn't even have to think about. She tapped the smooth tabletop quickly with three of her fingernails, which were coated with clear polish and clipped short for reasons I will not go into at this time.

"September, would you stop tapping please?" Stephen said. Skip looked at him languidly and continued to tap.

"What's wrong, honey?" I said.

She looked at me like, "You know what's wrong," and also like, "Don't ask me what's wrong when you know what's wrong," and like, "Don't ever ask me what's wrong."

"The maid quit, right?" I said.

She nodded.

In the last two years we had had five housecleaners, and that morning number five had caught a glimpse of a fairly typical nine A.M. on a Tuesday in the bedroom in Skip Hartman's life with me.

"Well, I'm sure the maid was a dear girl," Stephen said, "but you cannot expect every single maid to overcome her narrow prejudices. I on the other hand know all I need to know to understand the relations between a mature woman such as yourself and a punky kid such as the little one here. What I'm saying, September, is that you pay me a beautiful amount of money to tutor the young one, and yet I find myself needful of persisting in my moonlighting career of marijuana sales amongst dangerous thugs in the park, whereas if I had just the teeniest supplement to my income for, say, cleaning a two-story apartment house on the Upper East Side once a week, I would then be able to enjoy the fine things without having to risk my neck every night."

"Oh, I don't buy that marijuana dealer crap," Skip said. "You need money to support your pot-smoking habit plain and simple. I will not give it to you and I cannot think of a thing I'd rather do less than allow you to clean my house."

"Mary, did you not see me selling marijuana in the park one day two and a half years ago?" Stephen said.

"I don't know. I guess."

Skip said, "Oh, I just don't care. You cannot clean my house. The end."

"Oh, please?"

"No."

"Oh, please please please please please?"

"Ah, the hell, I have no energy anymore for anything," Skip said, and that is how Stephen Samuels became both tutor and maid to me, though I use the latter term liberally, if not downright communistically.

On an average day in the life of Stephen Samuels, maid, he woke up at eleven A.M. in the basement apartment of his father's West Village brownstone, which he insisted on leasing for $100 a month; cooked and ate a stack of pancakes; did a half dozen bong hits; threw on a pair of skintight black leggings, a hot-pink stretch T-shirt with scooped décolletage, a black velvet blazer, and black biker boots; and wandered uptown to our kitchen to teach me about force, which equals mass times acceleration. After two hours of that, with a twenty-minute lunch break in the middle, Stephen Samuels took the can of oven cleaner out from under the sink along with a pair of chiffon-yellow rubber housecleaning gloves and a rag of old Hartman shirt. Gloves on, he directed the nozzle of the aerosol can more or less toward the center of the cavern of the oven and pressed down firmly until a quarter of the can of goo had been spent into it. And there lay the goo in the oven.

Then it was milk-and-cookies time, a time for Stephen and me to explore the nature of our friendship. Intimacy is protean, and we used our mutual devotion to soft, sodden, sugary biscuits as a springboard for meaning-making activity of inexhaustible nuance.

While Stephen and I were giggling at the table, Skip came back from wherever it was that she ever came back from and announced, "It stinks in here."

"That's the oven cleaner, honey," Stephen said.

"Well, the oven cleaner emits a penetrating odor that, I find, stinks, Stephen. When were you thinking of wiping it off?" She had stuck her head into the chamber of the oven, whence her voice came to us, muted and resounding. "Oh, this is how you purport to clean the oven? The crap is just lying here in a pile."

"We have here a very Hansel and Gretel situation at this moment in time," Stephen whispered to me, indicating Witch Hartman, who, with but one small kick in the butt, would be *in the oven.*

"This is bullshit in terms of oven-cleaning technique," she called from within the oven walls. It gave me a little thrill to hear Skip Hartman use terms like *crap* and *bullshit.* While she continued as a rule to utter phrases of classical proportions, I noticed that since the advent of me in her verbal life she had been dipping more and more often into the trough of the vernacular. Still, even the most casual or vulgar remark from her lips seemed to carry with it the force of one of the major Western thinkers, such that *bullshit!* in her mouth felt like an instance of Socratic irony or something.

Skip took up the chiffon-yellow rubber gloves that Stephen had strewn on the sink and slipped them over her hands. She wore a pale blue silk chemise and navy rayon slacks. "Considering how little you actually exerted yourself while wearing these, you managed to sweat monstrously in them," Skip said, as she wadded up a sheet of *The New York Times* and began to smear the pale, foaming goo about the five walls and two racks of the oven.

Stephen Samuels stood up from his biscuits. "I don't like the insinuation!" he said, looming directly above Skip, who knelt on the floor. She looked up at him fearfully. "You *clean* that oven, bitch." He stared down at her, eyes wide. She stared up at him. A few tears eased out from her eyes and down her face, which had turned a gentle shade of red. She said something quietly like "Oh" or "Oh no." I didn't understand what was happening. She averted her face from Stephen's, vigorously spread the oven cleaner for another minute, stopped abruptly, stood up, and walked quickly from the room, wearing the gloves.

Stephen stayed that night for dinner, which Skip Hartman cooked and served to him. He was expansive at the table. He spoke of the fierce border patrol of the American war on drugs, which, he explained, forced a local marijuana entrepreneur such as himself to rely on the domestic product, which became as a result the number-one cash crop in the entire U.S. of A. At a certain point Skip Hartman removed a wad of bills from her pants pocket, set it down in front of Stephen, and quickly left the kitchen once more.

Though she continued to pay Stephen Samuels for cleaning the house, Skip Hartman was the only person in the house over the next few months who cleaned anything. Kept the place tidy and bright, in fact. These months were a time of great closeness for Stephen and me. Once, we were running along the upstairs hallway holding hands when we happened to pass the guest bathroom, where Skip Hartman was on her knees scouring the tub. We stood and watched her lean into the work. She was facing away from us, scouring with vigor, doing violence to the mold, mildew, and soap scum. She did not pause or turn around, though she must have heard our laughter and the pitter-patter of our feet on the rug. Then I felt sad. I looked at Stephen and he looked sad. Sadness had descended upon the tableau. Skip rinsed the tub. She stood and turned and faced us. "I have no life anymore," she said. "All I ever do is clean."

After that, Skip Hartman did almost no housecleaning for an entire year. And then what happened was what happens when there is a house that is yours over which to stand vigil and you do not stand vigil: dirt and dust and foul odors crept through the walls and floor and ceiling. I don't think I had ever lived this way before. It was a bracing experience. I'm not saying that I learned anything from it, such as responsibility—hardly responsibility, or anything else.

ON A FRIDAY afternoon in the summer of my seventeenth year, Dierdre showed up on my doorstep with a little male friend who was not Harry. Dierdre had grown a foot in the last two years, while her skin had remained the same size. Now her skin was stretched so tight over her muscles and bones that you could see everything that was happening beneath it. Her pale red eyebrows had grown thinner, as had the rest of her hair. As you followed the eyebrows out toward the edges of her face they ascended and ascended, dipping only at the outermost reaches of her head as if in coy allusion to the standard shape of an eyebrow. She wore a grayish threadbare T-shirt from which she had cut away part of the neck band. No bra. Her magnificent, jutting clavicle was on display, as were her pointy breasts, thinly covered by the T-shirt, as was part of the bony concavity between those lovely little breasts.

The other person was, as I said, a little male of some kind. His body gave the impression of a lot of energy contained in a small area. He looked like a man but could also have been a boy who had aged quickly, the kind of person gifted with extraordinary bodily resiliency and health who must therefore work long and hard to damage himself where a simple night of drinking and sleep deprivation would suffice for a lesser man.

"You remember Mittler," Dierdre said. She had the cruel defiant stare from elementary school only more so, the kind of look that years of unarticulated fear and sadness work into the eyes and nose and mouth until the look is part of the hardware, part of the physical plant. The compact little man, Mittler, turned his head away, doleful.

Mittler was, you may remember, the boy who had cut me so lovingly with his pocketknife in grade school. I think I had forgotten about him without ceasing to love him. I wanted to rush into his arms and hug him and press my whole body against him, but his was a tough, sharp, unhuggable body. The best I could do was to say "Mittler!" piteously, as if I were saying the name of a puppy that had been rescued from under the ice of a frozen pond. His eyes flicked toward me and away again.

"Come in," I said. I opened the door wider, so that my visitors could see the used socks lying randomly on the floor of the entrance foyer, and the layer of dust covering the oaken banister of the staircase.

"You come out," Dierdre said. "It stinks in there."

Dierdre and I sat next to each other on the front stoop and Mittler sat behind and above and between us on the landing. I had to crane my neck to see him, which I did continuously in the hot sunlight. I was looking for vestiges of the Mittler I remembered, and I found few; the amorphous earth garments were about the extent of it. I was trying to see if the nape of his neck was what it once had been. His nape had left its mark on my consciousness—I retained a lot of affection for the two dark points of hair that grew back there on the day I tried to have sex with him in the boys' bathroom. Sitting on the stair below him, I really had to contort myself to glimpse the back of his neck. With economical head movements, he did not let me.

"Mittler's famous now, right, Mittler?"

"Fame is rot," whispered Mittler.

"Mittler's famous and brave and lives in New York City in a tent."

"Is that true, Mittler?"

"Is what true?"

"The tent."

"Sometimes I sleep in a tent and sometimes at my dad's house."

"He sleeps in a tent in Central Park!" Dierdre said. Dierdre was the most annoying person in the world. When you're ten years old, annoyingness can give you a kind of authority. When you're sixteen, you're just annoying.

"Mittler, tell her about how you fought off those guys from your tent in the middle of the night in Central Park."

"No."

While both Mittler and Dierdre were unhappy, Dierdre's unhappiness seemed false compared to that of Mittler, who could barely part his lips to speak, he was so authentically depressed.

"Did you fight off some guys, Mittler?"

"Yes he did because you see Mittler has turned his back on humanity, so he sleeps in this tent somewhere in Central Park which he won't tell me where, and he was sleeping one night when these boys who were out wilding came up and attacked the tent and they were kind of hitting him with baseball bats through the fabric of the tent and Mittler's been doing all these push-ups lately? So he comes out of the tent and takes one of the guys' baseball bats away from him and hits him with it and the other guys run away."

"Mittler, did that happen?"

"No."

"Mittler is the Central Park Tent Man from the tabloids. He has a whole belief system."

"What's your belief system, Mittler?"

"My belief system is, everything everyone else believes, I don't believe."

I liked the new misanthropic verbal style of Mittler. He had whittled down the ruminations of his early youth into these brief pronouncements, which stung and which he wouldn't even look at you while saying. He stared at a little crust of dark red sandstone on the stoop and then picked at it with his fingernail until he realized I was watching him pick at it. He stopped picking and sat there much like a stone himself. The new Mittler: vibrant, yet almost dead.

Dierdre said, "Mittler wakes at sunrise each morning and makes whalebone carvings. He doesn't eat meat. He believes in photosynthesis for all living creatures. He sleeps in a hammock suspended over broken glass. He does yoga. He doesn't need anybody. He takes no pleasure in life. He's thinking of giving up movies."

"What movies do you watch, Mittler?" I asked.

"Only Japanese movies now. Slow movies about thirst and violence and death. I'll be giving those up soon too. They pollute you. I don't want to think anymore. Thinking prevents you from living."

I was leaning back and arching up off the step I was on, trying to look up that soft, dark place, Mittler's nape. He turned his head slightly.

"Mittler doesn't believe in love," Dierdre said.

"You don't believe in love?"

"Love is banal," Mittler said. "Love is a mob religion. Millions of people love every day. How vulgar. Mobs of people loving two by two."

"Then why did you come here?" I said. He seemed to implode when I said it.

"Basically I dragged him," Dierdre said. "He needs to resolve issues."

Mittler said, " 'Basically.' Is that all you can say? Is everything 'basically' to you? You dragged me or you didn't drag me. 'Basically.' How about shut up from now on. Take a vow of silence, Dierdre."

"Well, you know, fuck you, Mittler, because I am trying to help you and no one appreciates me, and Mary, you're looking at me the whole time like I'm some ant or piece of dog doo so just fuck everybody except me who's sitting on this stoop right now."

I kept quiet because have you ever noticed how people attack each other and they are wrong, and then people defend themselves and they are also wrong?

Skip Hartman approached the stoop carrying two hand-tailored shopping bags. For a woman who was mostly restraint, she cried, "Oh, Mittler!" orgasmically, rushed to him, clung to him, and pressed his forehead to her lips. I was not jealous to see my Skippy doing something I was too chicken to do, but satisfied to be represented in the world by one so bold and clear of mind as she. She released Mittler back into the air. His skin was blotchy. He stood still and centered back into himself and, through utter stillness, got the blood back down out of the patches of his face. Skip ran a hand affectionately through Dierdre's hair and said, "Darling, you're so pretty."

We went into the kitchen, which was about the worst room of the house. "I could clean this place for you in a day," Mittler said.

Skip said, "Well, Mittler, that's very nice—"

"I don't do things because they're nice. I do things because they're useful. I need money for food."

"Oh, please, Mittler, you're sixteen and your dad has a huge house in the suburbs," Dierdre said.

"I cannot accept your offer, if offer indeed it was," Skip said, "because, though it may not look like it, I do have rather a delicate arrangement with another to clean house." Skip seemed pathetic then but I loved her anyway. I noticed with interest that I loved her even more when she did things that I found disagreeable. I was sixteen and I think it is fair to say that my ability to love was improving, even as I continued to express my love awkwardly and inconsistently at best. I nuzzled her armpit with the top of my head, as I often did in bed or while we were standing alone in the kitchen. "Could you stop that now?" she said to me.

"You're a fool," I said. "Stephen Samuels is taking advantage of you and you're letting him 'cause he's black."

"How would you know such a thing?"

"Doesn't take a forty-year-old."

"Fine. Clean the house, Mittler. What do I care? Stephen Samuels can screw himself." I loved when she lost adult perspective and behaved rashly. Who knows what kind of teenage years she had? Probably restrained and boring.

"I'll be here at eight A.M. tomorrow with my cleaning tools," Mittler said.

"Eight A.M. is not convenient for us, Mittler," Skip said.

"Eight A.M. is when I can do it." Mittler had found a wall

near the kitchen door to press his bunched-up back against à la Malcolm X in the days leading up to his assassination.

"As a housecleaner, you cannot bend the world to your will," Skip said.

"That's when I can do it."

"Then you will not do it."

"I have to leave now." He sprang up off the wall and pivoted neatly toward the door.

"Don't listen to her," I said. "Eight A.M. is fine."

Skip said, "Damn you! You can't do that!"

"Yes I can."

"All right, Mittler. Fine."

Mittler pivoted back, bowed to Skip, repivoted, and was gone.

Dierdre had sat down at the kitchen table, soaking up the scene. Skip stared at me. She said, "Dierdre, Mary and I would like to be alone."

"But I just got into the city. It's like a whole day. Where am I supposed to go?"

"You are several blocks from the Metropolitan Museum."

"*Eeew.*"

"Well, you may do what you like but you must fend for yourself."

"Can't I just stay here for a while? I won't be in you guys' way."

"Good." Skip took me harshly by the arm and led me up the stairs to our bedroom. There, she said, "You have humiliated me in front of your friends."

"Well, that's because you—"

"Wait, I'm not finished. It is hard, but I am getting used to it. Furthermore, I understand it is often my own rigidity that leads to these moments of humiliation. I am trying to learn."

"Me too," I said. "Sorry I humiliated you."

We stared at each other. There was a look of shy hopefulness in her face. This was a good moment for us. It was beautiful to be wrong together with Skip Hartman.

She attacked me with an arduous kiss. She removed my clothes and her own as fast as she could. While I stood in the center of the room, she gave my body's entire surface the vigorous Hartman rubdown. She picked me up over her shoulder as if she were a fireman risking his life to save me from a burning building. She laid me down on my side on the bed and put her hard fingers with the close-cropped nails inside of me. I loved the chaotic effect of Skip Hartman's passion on my mind. I loved the little unrelated thoughts that passed through me as she took over my body. She caressed and squeezed the various and diverse parts of me with one hand, while with the other she did something shockingly pleasurable inside me. After a while, she straddled my hip and rocked hypnotically back and forth with more and more and more pressure and speed until she practically drove me down inside the soft foam core of the mattress. All the while my mind, working on some principle of its own, formed a hazy picture of Dierdre, sitting in our kitchen, doing absolutely nothing with nowhere to go and nobody to call for her, a child at loose ends in a house of lovers.

SKIP HARTMAN DID not wish to be at home when Mittler cleaned house, so she left at 7:59 A.M. Even when she did tell me where she was going, there hovered about a Hartman departure an air of mystery. I didn't think she was necessarily lying to me, but on the other hand she could say "I'll be spending the afternoon at Lord and Taylor" and have in mind a different meaning of Lord & Taylor than the standard one. Or she could say, as she did that Saturday morning, "I will be at the green market in Union Square. The best wine and fish and corn are available at this hour, and then it's nice to linger among the vegetation for the morning, to walk down along the vegetables and inhale their vapors. People are polite at the green market. These are the same people who push at Balducci's and Fairway. People develop gentle farm manners. The average New Yorker rises to the level of the nobility of the vegetation at the open-air market in Union Square." She could say that, and its meaning would stand in the world not literally but like one of the modern poems that she loved so well. In a modern poem about the green market, the green market wouldn't be the green market, it would be death, or maybe longing. Whereas when I say, "Skip Hartman left the house and the sky was bleak," I mean only that she left and it was bleak.

I was thin and pale and dark, as I may already have told you (and I have no idea what I've already told you; *Don't look back* could be my autobiographer's motto), but I was not the languishing kind of thin and pale and dark. I was the wiry kind, as in electrical wire, with electricity running through, so it was hard for me to stay in bed past 7:30 A.M. But the anticipation of being alone in the house with Mittler was so intense that I could not move. Well, I could squirm; I could get up and do mattress trampoline exercises; I just could not leave the perimeter of the bed, at least not until Mittler rang the bell a minute after Skip left.

"Is Miss Hartman here?"

" 'Miss Hartman' is not here."

"I'll get to work then." He moved past me into the front hall with a light blue vinyl suitcase.

"What's in the suitcase?"

"Cleaning equipment."

"What kind of cleaning equipment?"

"Sponges, mostly." He stood within view of the mirror in the front hall, seeming to try not to look at himself in it. "I'm uncomfortable," he said. "I'd like to be supervised by Miss Hartman."

"Supervised how?"

"Like she would be here so you couldn't say things like 'supervised how.' "

"Mittler, you're cute!" I tried a hug. His body became a device for not being hugged. He poked me in the breast with something sharp, his fist, I guess it was.

"I'm leaving," he said.

"Don't! I'll let you alone. It'll be like I'm not even here."

Mittler shrank into a decision-making stance with his palms pressed against his thighs. "I'll start in the kitchen," he said.

I had the air conditioner in the bedroom blasting against the heat and humidity. The sky looked as if it was about to rain, which is what I meant before about the sky being bleak, in case that wasn't clear. I cowered under the fluffy duvet, except for my head, which poked out the top of the duvet so that I could read poems with it. I started to read one that goes,

> Time will say nothing but I told you so,
> Time only knows the price we have to pay;
> If I could tell you I would let you know.

I didn't like that one and started another that goes, "Two loves have I of comfort and despair." I didn't like that and tried the one that goes,

> *Lucky* and *Unlucky*
> mean the same thing, like *flammable* and *inflammable.*

Then I threw all the poetry books on the floor, because what good is poetry if it doesn't calm you down? I went all the way under the fluffy duvet and I lay under there breathing in the air I breathed out, to the rhythm of "Time will say nothing but I told you so."

Soon I got up and did some deep knee bends and some stretching and sprintwork in the bedroom and hallway. Then I did stairwork while Mittler was trying to vacuum the stairs.

"You smell like ammonia," I said on the way down.

"You have something on your shirt," I said on the way up.

He said, "Cut it out or I'm leaving."

I cooled down in the bedroom and took a shower in the rainforest environment of the bathroom and got dressed. I got undressed and put my flannel pj's back on and got under the covers and went to sleep and woke up and called Tommy.

"Hello?" Myra said.

"Myra, put Tommy on."

"Hello?" Tommy said.

"What are you doing?"

"Who is this?"

"It's me."

"Me who?"

"Mary."

"I can't horse around now. We're moving."

"What?"

"We saved up enough money to move into a nice house up north of here."

"How thrifty of you."

"I'd love to stay on the phone and be insulted but the movers are here."

"What town?"

"Marmot, the new planned and gated community. We're quite impressed with it."

"What's the phone number up there?"

"Hartman has the information."

"How come nobody told me you were moving?"

"I have to go supervise."

"You're a dick."

"Nice talking with you."

Mittler stood in the bedroom doorway with the vacuum cleaner hose in one hand and the body of the vacuum in the other. "I have to clean in here."

"Hello, Mittler." I was in my pajamas on the edge of the bed with the phone in my hand.

"I can't clean with you in here."

"So skip this room."

"Is that supposed to be funny?"

"Is what supposed to be funny?"

"Skip this room."

"Oh."

"I can't Skip the room."

"Why?"

"I gave my word."

"Oh, your *word*."

"Shut up."

"You have a *word,* and you give it."

"You don't know what you're talking about."

"Let me ask you something," I said.

"What?"

"What do you do every day?"

"Like what do you mean?"

"You wake up in your tent in Central Park and . . . ?"

"I meditate."

"What kind of meditation, transcendental?"

"No, it's my own kind of meditation which I developed. It's similar to worrying."

"Then what do you do?"

"Breakfast."

"Which is?"

"Pint of coffee."

"How do you make coffee in a tent?"

"I have a small portable camping stove that burns white gas which I have to go up to Scarsdale to get because it's illegal in the city because somebody like me with a different political philosophy might be tempted to make an explosive device and blow something up with the white gas which I haven't ever seriously considered doing. I don't make the coffee in the tent I make it on the lip of the tent."

"Oh. The *lip.*" Mittler's neck got blotchy.

"You're making it hard for me to clean the room."

"How about after the coffee?"

"I pace."

"Like back and forth in your tent?"

"Like back and forth between Fifty-ninth Street and One-hundred-tenth."

"How many times?"

"Once."

I sprang up from the bed and jumped on Mittler. He jabbed me in the breast again.

"Ow. Don't you know you're not supposed to hit a woman there?"

"You're not a woman."

"But I have tits and you poked them twice."

"Teach you to jump on me."

I jumped on him again and he hit me in the arm, hard. I mean really hard, so tears came to my eyes.

"I'm leaving. I'll call Miss Hartman so I can come back and finish when you're not here." He left.

I opened the bedroom window and leaned out to watch Mittler exit the house. He took the stairs in two long jumps, cut straight across the sidewalk, slid between two parked cars, and made a perpendicular turn to the right. Down in the street itself, he walked in a westerly direction toward the park. He was the most strictly linear walker I have ever seen. The rain began as I watched him. It was the dense kind of rain that comes down in long continuous columns rather than individual droplets. Mittler was soaked in a matter of seconds. He kept walking as if nothing different were happening in the natural world around him. He went steadily away from my house with his linear walk and his light blue valise of cleaning tools. I wondered if stoical people like him were allowed to enjoy the feeling of the rain on their faces. I thought of a song my father used to sing about an umbrella salesman:

> Pitter-patter goes the rain
> He'll mend your umbrella
> And blow out his brain.

It was eleven A.M. I was agitated and could think of nothing to do. This was standard for eleven A.M. of that period of my life. Some people would make food in this situation. I had seen people make food often enough—women, mostly—and it didn't appear to be a waste of time. I thought I could manage a grilled cheese sandwich. Because I was fearing the stretch of time between eleven A.M. and whatever came after eleven A.M., I took the most circuitous route to the kitchen, making stops in all the other rooms of the house. I also crawled on my hands and knees instead of walking upright. As I crawled along the hard brown floor from room to room, a stinky smell gathered in my nostrils. It was the smell of Mittler's cleaning fluids, of which he had left a thick, drying coat on every surface in the house, the way a dog might leave urine. As I crawled headfirst down the carpeted stairs, my eyes teared up and my nose ran and the skin on the palms of my hands first tingled and then burned. The knees of my pants became damp and the skin underneath them began to burn also.

I crawled back upstairs and changed clothes again and walked down to the kitchen on my hind legs in a pair of stiff, thick-soled hiking boots that had cost Skip Hartman $300 and that I had not used for hiking. In our household we liked good, supportive shoes, even if the hiking boots turned out to be overkill in terms of footwear to make grilled cheese in. I couldn't eat the sandwich because every time I opened my mouth it filled up with the taste of bleach and ammonia. I was angry with Mittler. I had expected more from him. As I was about to throw the grilled cheese in the garbage, Skip walked in.

"What the hell is going on here?"

"I made you a grilled cheese sandwich." It was 11:38 A.M. Her eyes and nose began to water.

"You're a child," she explained. "From now on I mustn't let you sway me in decisions better left to an adult, such as whom to hire to clean."

"Ah, but you must."

"First I hire Stephen Samuels, who cleans not at all, then I hire Mittler, who cleans too much."

"It's not Mittler's fault. I distracted him."

"Did you now?"

I know that I have tried to document the expressive activities of Skip Hartman's hair and face, but I think I have not yet spoken in particular of her nose, correct? It was a straight, medium-sized, practical nose that had the slight advantage over her hair of being an organ of both expressive *and* perceptive capacities. She tilted her head back now and vertically scrunched her nose. She seemed to be trying to sniff out events other than cleaning that had taken place in the house while she was gone. "And what exactly did you do to distract him?"

"I threatened him."

"Threatened him how?"

"Verbally."

"Mittler's fired."

"You can't do that!"

"I'm doing it."

"But you didn't even tell me Tommy and Myra are moving!"

"Oh, dear heavens. I did not tell you. I wonder why I did not tell you. That was an egregious oversight, to be sure. I suppose I don't much like your aunt and uncle."

"But they're the only people I have in the world."

"They're the only people you have in the world?"

"Yes."

"What about—"

"Yeah?"

"What about—us?"

"Us?"

"What about me?"

I could think of nothing to say. Skip's mouth hung open. Without knowing it, I think, she turned her thumbs out away from her body to show me, below the short sleeves of her lavender silk T-shirt, her taut, creamy inner forearms, and this little argument ended as many of ours did: in the kitchen, in a piteous embrace.

I Am Fucked

WE HAD MADE it to the end of another summer when Skip Hart-man glided to the curb near our house in her black high-gloss Porsche. I climbed in next to her. Skip Hartman in her brown leather driving gear, in profile in her car by the curb giving me an ominous look like a one-eyed jack, sweet indulgent reader, was at her most manly.

There was a satchel of fine luncheon meats and cheeses and fruits and fruit juices and liquors in the broad sense of the term on the buttery leather shelf behind the two seats of the Porsche. This satchel and its contents were a part of the plea-sure of the orderliness of a life with Skip Hartman. The order-liness, in turn, was a fortification against terrible events like the end of summer.

Driving out of the city, Skip said, "Stephen was very angry when I told him we had found another housecleaner."

"So?"

"He refuses to tutor you. He feels betrayed."

"He needs to learn responsibility," I said.

"The passenger seat: a center of moral authority. Joseph told me this termination has really sent Stephen into a tailspin."

"So screw him."

"I suppose that's one way to look at it."

It was a cool day in mid-September. Maybe the leaves on the trees were changing color—I didn't notice. Don't get me wrong, I wasn't making conversation with Skip Hartman or even looking at her as she drove. I was glued to the window. I just happen to have been the kind of person who, when she was looking at a landscape out a window, got distracted by her own reflection. I guess what I'm saying is, I looked at the world and saw myself. Not that I'm proud of it, or of much else that I did or said or thought or felt or was.

Toward the end of our journey we found ourselves in a dark wood. We slowed and approached a dense iron gate that was the only break for miles in a high wooden wall along the right-hand side of the bumpy road we were on. A man stepped out of a low, narrow, gray, one-story A-frame house next to the gate. He was a man of fair complexion with short blondish-orange hair who walked toward us with his mouth ajar. He wore a dark blue uniform and held a clipboard. He was older and taller and wider and lighter in color than Mittler, and didn't appear to have the odd, gentle decorousness that Mittler had, but he did have something of the Mittlerian American soldier-of-fortune can-do male way of being in the world. He appeared to be about to say something to Skip Hartman like "Name, ma'am," when Skip Hartman preempted him with "Hartman, September, and White, Mary, here to see Thomas White and Myra White."

If the man regarded the efficiency of speech and the fancy car as mockeries of himself, he was right. He looked at his clipboard. "I'm sorry but you're not on the list for today, ma'am." He was now bending over and peering into the car to see who was in the passenger seat. I stuck my tongue out at him.

"What you should be sorry about, young man," said Ms. Hartman with an imperious tone, "is the disgraceful condition of the road approaching this entrance over which you are standing guard. One is a second- or third- or fourth-class citizen until one has been granted permission to enter Marmot. This attitude of Marmot's I already do not like. Get on the telephone, please, young man—you do have a telephone in your little shed?—and call the sometimes forgetful Thomas White and ask if indeed he is expecting two lady visitors in a fancy foreign car whose shock absorbers have truly been put to the test by this approach road—which Marmot may try to disavow but whose responsibility, surely, is Marmot's."

"Yes, ma'am," said the man, the crisp American Marine politeness being strained now by the savage American Marine violence beneath it. He walked back to his little house.

I said, "God, you're a bitch. It's just a dumb job for him."

"Then he should get another dumb job, darling."

"What dumb job do you have right now?"

"Right now? Right now I have the dumb job of protecting you from idiots like him who justify their impertinence to people like you and me with some misguided concept of safeguarding gentility."

"Whatever, *darling*," I said, with my own justification for impertinence that I didn't understand but felt.

The man opened the gate for us automatically from within his narrow house and we entered Marmot. We drove along a

well-paved road for a few hundred yards through a dense for-
est of deciduous trees. The trees gave way to a small, modern
village of evenly spaced and not identical but honest and similar and comforting wooden two-story family houses. The
houses were painted in quiet varieties of gray and beige and
brown. Each house was surrounded by one or two acres of
clean, bright lawn. The shrubs were short and round and trim.
Bright flowers. Sidewalks with no people on them. No toys.
No cars. Our car in this place was like a long wet black rat sliding down the street looking for whom to eat. The front door of
one of the houses on our left flew open and Tommy came out
onto his porch in a pair of white ducks. He waved. He was
smiling. He wore black canvas sneakers and walked directly on
the bright green lawn in them, which was probably against the
law. He came down the little hill of his front lawn toward our
rat car. Skip stopped the car. Tommy waved gaily. Open-
necked red-and-white-striped short-sleeve shirt worn out over
the trousers. Skip idled. It had been a year since we'd seen
Tommy. His face had developed some fine wrinkles like abstract designs made carefully with a diamond on a sheet of
glass. Skip revved the engine. Tommy laughed. "I forgot!" he
said. "I love to leave the names at the gate but in this case I forgot. You can't park here. You have to come up into the driveway.
Preferably the nose of the car three feet from the garage door.
Fantastic!"

"Where's Myra?" I said, getting out of the car. Tommy kissed
me on the cheek for the first time ever.

"Hold this," Skip said behind me.

"What?"

"The food basket."

"What are *you* doing? *You* hold it."

She rolled her eyes.

Myra had put on fifteen pounds. It is especially gratifying to see someone you haven't seen in a long time if there has been a dramatic change in appearance: if the person has become fat or thin or shaved a beard or grown prematurely old. I loved touching Myra's body. It was a body both sturdy and soft that I wanted to ram myself against to knock from their deep hide-away some of the feelings that surely must have dwelt there. But I remembered about breaking her arm and settled for working a goodly amount of saliva onto my lips and distribut-ing it over her face with kisses. "Oh, Myra Myra Myra Myra Myra," I said, approximately. She squeezed her eyes shut. We were standing now in the new-wood-and-lacquer-smelling kitchen with lots of gray, foggy light coming in through the big windows on the street side of the house. I admired Tommy for being able to pick another house with light.

"Who wants a tour of the house?" Tommy said.

Skip said, "I do."

I said, "I don't."

"Oh, come on, Jesus, you've been here about one second and you're trying to hurt me already. Aren't you civilizing her, Hartman?"

"Not my job," Skip said, and took his arm in hers, and led him out of the room that I might commune in private with my girl relative.

"What should we do now?" I asked.

"Make something," Myra said, head down, moving her full bulk toward the refrigerator.

"What?"

"Snacks." She removed a roll of mozzarella and a jar of Span-ish olives. She had on a knee-length denim jumper and a sturdy white faded T-shirt. I wanted her to drop the glass jar on the high-gloss oaken floor or give some other sign that she loved me.

"So how do you like the new neighborhood?" I said, dancing around her while she stood and did whatever it is women do to mozzarella.

"Good."

"Do you miss the old place?"

She shrugged. Either that or she tensed up more. I strolled around the kitchen. The one accoutrement I didn't recognize from the old place was an antique field hockey mallet, if that's what you call it, that hung on the wall below the clock. The mallet was decorated with bright stripes of color. "Nice mallet," I said. I was wearing the hiking boots and tried unsuccessfully to make a scuff mark on the floor. I took off the boots and tested the slidability of the floor in my socks. It was good. I slid here and there about the kitchen while Myra shuttled from fridge to counter and back.

Skip's voice entered the kitchen through the acoustic funnel of the hallway off the kitchen. ". . . difficult," I heard her say. "This is a lovely home."

"Isn't it?" Tommy said.

They walked into the kitchen.

"Where's the food, darling?" Skip said to me.

"Myra made a spread," I said.

"Well, I don't mean Myra's little *spread*. I mean what I made for us to eat for the substantial meal of the day."

I glanced at Myra, who looked like her usual lump self. I began to develop the idea of returning to New York without Skip Hartman.

Tommy and Myra and I sat down at the kitchen table of old,

which had a sad personality, for like a dog or a child, a table is
susceptible to the vibrations of a home.

Skip stood with her back to us at the built-in counter un-
loading a three-bean salad. I thought of things around the
house that a person could use to hit and sever her spinal cord,
such as the ornamental field hockey mallet. The room was
quiet. You could hear the mozzarella sliding down people's
throats.

"Come on already, why is it so quiet in here? Somebody say
something," Tommy said.

"Where does your water come from?" Skip said, turning to
face us with the bean salad.

"Is that some kind of dirty question?" Tommy asked.

"When you turn on the tap in the kitchen sink, the water
that comes out comes from where?"

"A well."

"Where?"

"In the backyard."

"And must each homeowner have his own well in the backyard?"

"I guess. I don't know. Yeah."

"Ah."

"What do you mean, 'ah'?"

Skip had put the salad on the table and returned to the
counter to arrange the cool, damp pieces of tarragon chicken.
"I mean that you do not really need a wall and a gate with a
Special Forces commando in order to keep the poor people
out."

"So? Who cares? What are you talking about?"

"I am talking about the necessity, for living in Marmot, of
having a well. And one must suppose that when there is a well

per man, each man must buy enough land surrounding his well such that his well is, shall we say, one hundred fifty yards from his neighbor's well, because a preponderance of wells any greater than one per one hundred fifty yards would radically destabilize the water table."

"I hate when you say 'per,'" I said.

"In this way you keep the poor and lower-middle-income people out *sans* gate."

"I hate when you say 'sans.'"

"Myra, would you like a piece of tarragon chicken?"

"Yes please."

"Leg or breast?"

"Either one is fine."

"How do you keep the poor and lower-middle-income people out of your brownstone in Manhattan?" Tommy said.

"That's not the same."

"It seems similar."

"The equivalent would be if I had devised a way to keep them off the island of Manhattan altogether."

"Besides, you talk like a liberal but you live like a conservative," Tommy said.

"How would you know such a thing?"

"I've been reading up on people like you."

"Were I a liberal only insofar as I have redistributed my own wealth to you and Myra, that would surely be liberal enough."

"Let's play catch," I said.

"We don't have a ball," Tommy said.

"I have a ball in the car," I said.

"That's not a good idea," Tommy said.

"What do you mean?"

Skip said, "He means let's not make a display of ourselves in the yard because the new neighbors might not understand the friendship of the two visitors. The friendship of a mature woman with an adolescent girl can only be a form of deviancy, from the imaginary point of view of the new neighbors."

Tommy said, "Ah, come on, stop it. I go a whole three hundred and sixty-five days feeling pretty good, and then you come up here with your remarks that are designed to hurt me and make me unhappy and depressed. I'm saying lay off me because I have a toothache."

We went into the living room with the exposed beam roofing or whatever you call it and we sipped pastis, or pretended to. I excused myself to go to the bathroom. Passing the kitchen, I glanced at the clock. It was twelve-thirty in the afternoon. I removed the field hockey mallet from the wall. I crept into the hallway between the kitchen and the living room, the same hallway where Skip Hartman had been walking when she spoke the word *difficult*. I peered at them, the adults. They were sitting there: Skip Hartman on a roughly striped couch of coarse brown material, her arms spread wide over the back, one hand holding a tall, clear tumbler; Tommy with his legs crossed woman-style, thigh on thigh, a foot wagging nervously in the air; Myra balled up in another chair. I thought they were grotesque—the two people who had sold me and the one who had bought me. I went out the front door with the field hockey mallet and jogged not on the sidewalk but down in the road like Mittler toward the gate of Marmot.

I walked through the pedestrian turnstile beside the large black gate and saw the blondish-orange Marine guard getting into a beat-up small gray American car that didn't look like much but which he probably lay beneath on his back in his spare time when he was not practicing how to field-strip a muskrat or something.

"Hey!" I said.

"Ms. White, is it?" he said. He sat down in the driver's seat and started the car with the door open.

"Give me a ride to the nearest train station."

"What happened to Ms. Hartman?"

"Nothing."

"Get in."

I got in next to his big square body, which was covered by the dark uniform. An animal smell came from under the uniform like the smell of a freshly washed dog. Layered over that was a cologne smell. "What's that smell?"

"Ralph Lauren Polo. Thirty dollars a bottle, but you gotta spend money on your odor because it's connected to pheromones."

"*That's* interesting."

"What is she, your aunt or something?"

"I don't want to talk, I just want to ride."

"Fine."

It took ten minutes to get to the station in the neighboring town of Verdant. I looked out the front window while with peripheral vision I took in the man's face, especially this one small triangle of muscle below and slightly in front of his right ear that kept bulging out and going back in, bulging out and going back in, like a little straining penis under the skin of his face.

He stopped the car in the Verdant station parking lot and leaned violently in front of me to open the door on my side. I got out as the train was pulling in. The sky was deep gray. It looked as if it might rain. I backed away from his car in case he tried to shoot me. Backing steadily away with the field hockey mallet pressed along my right leg, I watched the little flexing muscle thing under the side of his face until I couldn't see it anymore. Then I watched his whole head grow dark until it became a silhouette in the shadowed darkness of the car. Then I got on the train. Then the train left the station.

WITHOUT MY KNOWLEDGE, Skip Hartman and Mittler had arranged for Mittler to be cleaning the house while we were away in the country. When I arrived home in the middle of the afternoon, Mittler was in our room, lying on the bed, naked. His body was horizontal except for his dick, which was angled up away from the base of his torso toward his chin. His hands were resting at his sides. I stood in the doorway. "Mittler, what the hell are you doing?"

He was startled. He grabbed the white comforter and threw it over himself. "None of your business," he said.

"It is my business because this is my bedroom and your penis was sticking out into the air of it."

"That was a private moment."

"You were thinking of me, weren't you?"

"Go away and let me put my clothes on."

I ran and pulled the white comforter off his body and leapt on him. He was still naked and his whole body was there for me to see plus that thing that was standing up away from his body like a small second body.

"Please don't do this to me," he said, holding my hand.

"What were you doing, really? Was that masturbation?"

"It was mental masturbation."

"Were you thinking of me?"

"Not telling."

I tried to get my clothes off while holding Mittler's hand. I took my shirt off with both hands and then went back to holding his hand. I unlaced each hiking boot with just my left hand and pulled each boot off. I got my pants off with just my left hand, and my underwear, and then I needed both hands to remove the elastic knee brace for my stress injury, and then I went back to holding his hand. I took my bra off with one hand and with my free hand held his hand, and then I started touching his body with the other hand. His body was harder and thicker than what I was used to, with hard lumps in unexpected places.

"Oh, Mittler, this is so weird for me. This is nice. I'm very excited."

"Ah."

"Mittler, I don't know how to do this. Do you know how to do this? Let's do it now. Do you know how to do this?"

"Yeah."

"Are you sure that's what you're supposed to do? Ouch. That hurts. Stop it. I said OUCH! Okay, I have an idea. All right, you go over there like that. No, turn sideways like that. Okay, you put that there and I'll put this here like this. Oh, that's much better. Oh, that feels good, Mittler."

"Ouch," he said.

"That hurts you? That feels good to me. That hurts you?"

"Let's keep doing it."

"Do you want to keep doing it? Let's keep doing it."

"I like it but it hurts. Ow, it really hurts. Let's keep going for a minute."

"Oh. Oh nice. Oh. Oh."

"OH! Stop! I think I ripped something. It feels like something tore in me."

"Oh, Mittler. Oh, I guess we had to stop because something tore, right?"

"Yeah, but let me try something. You just lie back now. You lie still and I'll go like this."

"Yeah, but is that fun for you? That's not fun for you."

"It's nice for me."

"It's nice for me too."

"It's really nice for me."

"Me too."

"Is it okay?"

"Yeah. Like that."

"Like this?"

"A little more sideways. A little more—ooh."

"Is it nice?"

"Nice."

We were quiet for a while and then that electrical pulse-shock thing happened and Mittler sounded as if he were choking and then he started asking me questions: "Was that it? Did you—you know?"

"Wait. Shut up." I didn't really mean "Shut up," I meant I needed a minute to come back into my body, but I did say "Shut up" and he heard "Shut up" and was already getting his clothes on.

"We never do this again," he said.

"What? I didn't even get to hold your dick."

"See, that's what I mean. You have no respect for me *or* my penis. I can't be with you or see you ever again because you're thoughtless. What do you think about anyway? Tell me even one thing you thought about today."

"I don't know."

"See?"

"What?"

He left.

Now listen carefully, dear reader, because I am going to give you some very important advice: don't ever have sex with a boy. He sticks you with that thing and it HURTS! And, what's worse, it feels GOOD! No, but I mean it really feels good like you wouldn't believe, which is *why* I'm saying don't do it. I am not saying that sex with a boy brings more pleasure than sex with a girl and that you should therefore favor the milder pleasure of sex with a girl. I am especially not saying that about Skip Hartman, who works my body in a way that makes me cry out sharply. She knows how to touch me with her whole body and fasten her body to my body. She lays her perimeter down on my perimeter and we fasten ourselves to each other all along the surfaces of our bodies. And this is what is especially lovely about Skip Hartman: she knows how to unfasten, too. You have to unfasten slowly and gently. Sometimes Skip and I have been fastened so deeply that even the gentlest unfastening leaves wounds in the surface of my body, and Skip knows what to do about those, too. She fills the wounds in. She will put a kiss in each wound like a poultice. She will touch my body lightly here and there like a sculptor smoothing the last bits of rough clay into the flesh of his statue of a human figure. Mittler, on the other hand, penises you and walks out.

The Louder a Lady

HOVING HARRINGTON HARTMAN arrived at our door dressed as a small Nobel Prize winner. It was a Sunday morning in late October. Skip Hartman was in the kitchen making crêpes. "Skip, it's your dad!" I yelled.

"You look fine, young man," he said. "So tall and elegant, like my daughter."

"I'm a girl."

"Yes."

"Daddy? What is going on?" Skip said. She stood in the foyer with flour on her fingertips. A thin streak of wet crêpe batter hung in her right eyebrow.

"I've decided to accept your invitation to brunch, my child," he said, in the middle range of his falsetto. Today his posture was more Hartmanesque in the Skip Hartman sense of the word. He wore a long tailored black coat. He had wire-rim spectacles and kempt hair. Someone had shaved his face.

"I see," she said. "Let me take your coat, sir." She moved to hug him.

"Don't touch me, please. Let us have a formal brunch for once."

She took his black coat in one hand and my upper arm firmly in the other and walked us swiftly into the kitchen.

"What's Daddy doing here?"

"You have gunk in your eyebrow."

"This is serious."

"How should I know?"

"You didn't orchestrate this?"

"No!"

"Sure?"

"Let go my arm, jerk."

She let go and left the kitchen and came back with Daddy. "How did you get here?" she said.

"My man drove me."

"Your man?"

"The amusing Negro boy who waves his arms about as if he were a girl."

"Stephen Samuels," we said. Skip looked at me.

"I know what you're going to say," I said, "so don't even say it."

H. H. Hartman looked less like a Nobel Prize winner now that I could see the brownish collar of his white shirt, his tapioca-stained black silk tie, and his herringbone jacket two sizes too big for him.

"Have a seat, Daddy. How do you feel about crêpes?"

"I feel about crêpes as I feel about diapers."

"Which is?"

"If I must."

He sat in a chair and put his elbows on the kitchen table. His hands were lost inside the sleeves of his jacket. "I'll give you a light back rub," I said, to get the brunch rolling.

"Get your hands off me, you creepy little shit!" he shrieked. Then, calm, indignant: "I would like a cup of milk, please."

I brought him milk in a tall glass.

"A *cup* of milk. Five fingers of milk in a *cup*."

"This is my whole childhood," Skip said, twisting her smooth Teflon crêpe pan.

I re-presented the milk in a cup. "Good mothering instincts," he said to me, "like a female cockroach." He dipped the four shriveled, oily fingers of his right hand into the milk, lifted them out, and held them above his head. Much of the milk from his fingers drained off onto the top of his head. He then tilted his face back to catch fewer than half the droplets of milk in his mouth.

"What's he doing?" I said to Skip.

"Acting like a baby. This is not a function of old age, by the way. He's always been like this."

She placed a crêpe before Hoving. The marmalade, sour cream, et cetera, et cetera, were already on the table. "Daddy," she said, "your man, as you call him. Where is he now?"

"Why, he's outside in the limo, waiting to take me back to that dreadful prison you have locked me away in."

"Mary, would you be a sport and run outside and invite our charming friend in for a word?"

I went out the door and saw the white stretch limousine with darkened windows in front of our house. The passenger window slid down with a light hum, Stephen leaned over and gave me a good long dark finger, the window slid back up, and the car took off. That was the last I was to see of Stephen Samuels for a long time.

I went back inside, conveyed Stephen's message to Skip, and was hit by a wall of ungodly stench. "What the hell is that?"

"Okay, Daddy, lie down on the floor here and let's take care of you. Did you bring extra diapers?"

"Didn't the boy bring them?"

"The boy left," I said.

"Child," he said, "do you expect me to carry a diaper wadded up in my breast pocket? Really, the level of humiliation."

He was lying face up on the kitchen floor now. Skip knelt above him and between his legs. She had removed his pants and was undoing the Velcro waistband attachments of the soiled diapers. We are talking breathtaking odor here. I couldn't look. "Honey, go upstairs and find me the biggest pair of underwear we've got," she said to me.

I dug around in Skip's underwear drawer and found a big pair of ladies' white cotton briefs from the 1950s; for what outfit or situation Skip had ever worn them I could not fathom. I of course brought them into the kitchen on top of my head. "Oh, this is just great," she said, and snatched them off my head.

Hoving, naked and freshly cleaned from the waist down, gazed at the ladies' undies in horror. "You will not put those on me."

"Well, if you're going to forget your diaper—"

"No!"

"Daddy."

"What?"

"What do you want to wear?"

"I'll wear my pants and I'll just be extra careful."

"Your pants are soiled."

Hoving began to weep. "This is terrible," he said. "I am so sorry to put you through this. A daughter should not have to see her father like this."

"It's all right, Daddy. I love you."

"Oh, September," he said, and wept. She crawled over to his head and cradled it and pushed the tears away from his eyes with her fingers.

She put a bath towel down on a kitchen chair, and he sat on it directly with his little naked buttocks. "Finish your brunch," she said, "and we'll go out and buy you some clothes and diapers afterward. Then we'll return you to the home."

"But I hate the home."

"You said you didn't mind it."

"I hate it."

"Maybe we can find you a better one."

"I hate them all."

"Well, then, where would you like to live?"

"Here with you and the little fellow."

"But Daddy, you've said many times before that you did not want to live here, don't you remember?"

"September, it is cruel of you to ask me to remember anything. I remember nothing."

"Well, Daddy, so you will live here as of now. It is a done thing."

"I don't have any say in this?" I said.

"No, you don't."

"Then he has to stop thinking I'm a boy."

"If you are nice to him, perhaps he will."

BY THE TIME the first snow fell that year I had been a blonde for several weeks. Don't worry, reader, I had it done professionally. I didn't consult the old ball and chain beforehand. I'm sure you can imagine the outbreak of ill will—some people who are pederasts are really just as uptight as you and me. No, but seriously, hair color can make a big difference in a person, especially when that hair color is blond. I mean, don't you feel that I'm talking to you differently, *dahling* reader, now that I'm recounting my life as a blonde? I'm adopting like a more voluptuous prose style—not consciously, it's just happening. For the next little while, expect me to be *sassy!*

So one night in the early part of December between the hours of eight P.M. and seven A.M., two feet of snow fell on Manhattan. Skip and I woke up, looked out the window, embraced each other, and leapt out of bed. While Skip began to dress, I ran naked in circles around her—blond up top, brunette down below—yelling, "Snow day! Snow day! Snow day!" and waving my arms. While naturally graceful, Ms. Hartman was not inclined to dance, but I made her. We did a waltz on her checkered flannel pajama shirt, which she had uncharacteristically thrown to the floor in her excitement. We held each other tight and danced over to the window and back to the bed and back to the window. She could do this thing where she hugged me from the front, aligned the heels of her palms on either side of my spine at a place that was even with my shoulder blades, locked her fingers together, and, as I was beginning to exhale, jammed her palms into my back with all the power of the leverage of her excellent posture plus the natural

inborn strength of a prizefighter. This caused the air to *whoosh*
from my mouth and set off loud crackling noises everywhere
inside my body. Sometimes it also made me laugh uncontrol-
lably, as it did that morning. Skip got me on the bed and tickled and tickled and tickled me and wouldn't let me stop
laughing until it got a little violent.

After this typical morning at home, Skip Hartman and her
blond girlfriend trudged into the blinding whiteness of Central
Park to make bas-relief angels in the snow. As we lay on our
backs laughing, whom should we run into but Mittler. Okay
not exactly "run into." He knelt forty paces away, digging for
edible roots beneath the snow, wearing a puffy blue down coat
that made him look like an astronaut digging for rocks beneath
the lunar surface. He did not see us. Skip Hartman did not see
him, for she was lying on her back with her eyes closed in a
state of ecstasy. You must understand how it was to see, across
a snowy field, after a period of months, the boy who had put
himself inside me. I don't mean just physically, I mean meta-
physically, too. Mittler had insinuated himself into my body
and remained there even as he had disappeared from the
world around it; how else can I explain that during the months
of his absence, I had often felt his fingers press into my thighs
late at night when his actual hands were miles away? I ran to
him, silent and fast.

I wonder what I knew of jealousy at the time. I am talking
about my total obliviousness to what effect my love of Mittler
would have on Skip Hartman. Could a sixteen-year-old be a
blank slate as regards jealousy? Bear in mind that I was raised
unconventionally from the age of ten by a group of oddballs,
and that whatever training in the emotions I may have received
before that time is almost entirely lost to me, except perhaps in

the form of the voice that belonged to my father, singing, for example, "I'd rather be a memory than a dream."

I tackled Mittler from behind. I grasped my favorite spot on Mittler's body—the back of his neck—and shoved his head down into the snow.

"Children," Skip said, standing above us, "what is happening here?"

Because I had forgotten she was alive, the sound of her voice startled me. Mittler wedged his hip under my legs and leveraged me off of him and spat the snow out of his mouth. He and I sat there looking at Skip. Her face was stiff, with eyes open like the eyes of a fresh, erect corpse beginning to harden in the cold. We all remained still. Skip Hartman turned her neck and looked to the north. She seemed to be remembering some vital errand. She turned her neck again and looked at us. Her beige woolen snow hat had ridden up and was perched like the cap of the court fool on the crown of her head. She pointed a gloved forefinger at the sky as if to say, "First," or "Just a moment please," or "Look at that cloud." She gazed northward once more and began to walk in the direction she was gazing, in the way that people begin to walk when they will be walking a long time. Mittler and I stood up. We watched her. While walking down a short, steep incline, Skip Hartman lost her footing and tumbled several yards to the bottom. She stood up. Clumps of snow clung unevenly to the back of her pale brown cashmere coat. She tottered stiffly and continued to walk. Reader, this is one of those moments when I wish my memory were better. What could I have thought, watching her walk away like that? Was I so ruthless in love as I am about to appear to be? Yes, I believe I was.

At the first moment that morning when nothing that I could see was Skip Hartman, I turned to Mittler. "Show me your tent," I said.

Mittler was silent for so long that I wondered if I had said "Show me your tent" or only thought it. I said it again to be sure.

"This is all wrong," he said.

"What?"

"Me thinking I should make you a pair of snowshoes."

"What?"

"I want to make you a pair of standard bearpaw snowshoes, but right away there are problems. First I'd have to find four young saplings of equal length, let's say three feet. Then I'd have to pair them off and bind the thick butt ends together with whatever material I have available, let's say raw, damp strips of deer or moose hide."

" 'Bind the thick butt ends'?"

"Then I would have to lash in a couple of wooden cross-pieces, spacing them fifteen centimeters apart, and bend and tie the remaining free ends together. Then cross-weave in more raw, damp strips of deer hide above and below the cross-pieces. This is a difficult process. The deer hide alone takes days to render into that state of rawness and dampness, plus you have to keep it warm in these arctic conditions."

" 'Render into that state'?"

"That's the thing right there. I want very much in my heart to make you the snowshoes, but you say things like '"Render into that state"?' and it hurts me. So I talk funny. So I'm just a big joke to you."

"No, Mittler."

"Snowshoes," he said, looking down at the place in the snow where my snowshoes would be if I were wearing them. "But I don't know if I can do it."

"Why?"

"First of all, you're married to Miss Hartman."

"You're such a goofball every time you say 'Miss Hartman.' "

"Second of all, you're mean and you always were and you always will be because people don't change and I'm in love with you."

"Okay, first of all—What?! Okay, first of all I'm not 'married' to Skip Hartman. I don't owe her anything. She robbed my innocence from me."

"I doubt it."

"It's true."

"So what about the other part, how you'll always be mean to me?"

"Maybe I won't, and you know something? Even mean people's fingers get cold. Mine hurt."

"Come here close to me," he said. I did. He took the two soggy gloves off my hands and stuffed them in the pockets of his puffy coat.

"You're taking my gloves *off*?"

"Trust," he said, as if he had already explained his thoughts on the subject a hundred times. He took my two red hands in one of his and shoved them gently up under his coat, under his sweater, under his other sweater, under his thermal shirt, under his T-shirt, and against his flat, hard ribs. He arranged my hands so the palms were in maximum surface contact with his warm skin. "This is what you have to do in a cold-weather survival situation is engage the bodily contact of the other per-

son for warmth." I felt his heart thrusting madly against my
palms. I was kneeling before him now.

"When are you going to show me your tent?"

"It's in a tree."

"A tree?"

"It's folded up inside a small waterproofed nylon sack that is suspended from the branch of a sycamore at approximately One-hundred-eighth Street."

"So let's get it down from the tree and open it up and go inside it and engage bodily contact of the other person for warmth."

"Due to the personnel of the Parks and Recreation Commission patrolling the area in daylight hours, I cannot open the tent at this time."

"What do you do if you get cold?"

"There are places in the tristate area like my father's house and other places that the Manhattan survivalist knows of."

"You're quite the arrogant bastard, aren't you?"

"I've got your icy hands against my chest and you're being mean again."

"I apologize. I don't always know when I'm doing it." This was true. I still don't always know when I'm doing it. Who among us is always cognizant of her own aggression? Are you? Come on, be honest, *are* you? If you are, you should write a memoir of *your* life, and you can call it *I Am Always Cognizant of My Own Aggression* by Reader Dearie.

"Would you please take me to one of those places you know about?" I said to Mittler. "Maybe one that's really nearby?"

He took me to a building on East Second Street, which had been condemned but which Mittler and several other Manhattan survivalists inhabited nonetheless. The door of the building was made of steel and badly painted the color of rust. Someone had soldered a strip of jagged metal to the bottom of the door, so when Mittler pushed the door open the piece of metal made an earsplitting screech as it scraped along the cement floor of the entrance hallway. "This is our burglar alarm," Mittler said. Two skinny and nearly identical white people regarded us from the landing of the stairs to the left of the door. They went away. We climbed two flights of stairs, walked down a decrepit hall, and stood in front of another badly painted door that was sealed with a combination padlock. Mittler undid the lock and opened the door, revealing an orange tent. The tent took up almost the whole room that contained it. It was nearly big enough to stand up in. Four people could sit inside it cross-legged on stained, tan foam-rubber squares that v ꞋꞋe not covered with cloth. Along one wall were four tightly rolled tubes of colored blankets or blanketlike material. There were two space heaters that were powered, I later learned, with electricity that the people in the building were siphoning from either the government or a large corporation, depending on who was telling you about it.

"How often do you come here?"

"I live here during the winter mostly, and during the summer I come from time to time to show solidarity. Want some tea?"

"Yes."

He squeezed water into a pot from a soft gallon-size leather canteen and pushed down over and over on the plastic pump of the fuel tank that was attached to his camping stove. He lit the stove.

"Why Scarsdale?" I said.

"What?"

"You said you had to go to Scarsdale to get the fuel because it's illegal in New York City."

"I didn't think you were listening."

"My question is why not Yonkers or Mount Vernon?"

"Because Chet who you saw for a second who was the blond guy on the stairs who is recovering from dysentery right now has a dad who doesn't talk to him who owns a camping store in Scarsdale but his sister will talk to him who works for the dad in the store and she will agree to meet him at the Scarsdale train station or sometimes at a pizza place with the dad's car with the fuel in the trunk of the car. Chet thinks he got the dysentery from being very weak from lugging the fuel from the pizza place back to the train station because it lowered his immune system plus having to go to the exact town where his father is not talking to him."

"You're opening up," I said.

Mittler left the tent. I thought that meant he was closing back down again. I was so attuned to the ways people had of closing down that sometimes when people opened up I thought they were just closing down in disguise.

"Why the tent?" I asked when he returned.

"For the orange-colored light, because the orange range of the light-frequency spectrum is the most peaceful."

"How come everyone in the world has knowledge of things like that except me?"

"Two things. Reading and living."

"I read and live."

"What do you read?"

"Poems, lately."

"Do you live the poems?"

"What kind of question is that?"

"I know you don't live them because you're not nice."

"So, I've read poems with people in them who aren't nice."

"But if you know they're not nice in the poem, you shouldn't act like them in real life. That's what I'm talking about."

"Mittler?"

"What?"

"I want to have sex with you again. Do you want to?"

"No."

I jumped on him, as was my tendency, and knocked over the camping stove and the pot of boiling water. Mittler threw me off of him and shut off the valve of the camping stove. The knee of his stiff, dark-blue jeans was darker with water. The first thing he said was, "Lucky this tent is made of flame-retardant material." The second was, "You hurt me again. This time on my leg." The floor of the tent was soaking wet. He took me to another room of the condemned building where there were no space heaters. The room was long and narrow and empty and bright, and very very cold. Mittler took off his wet pants. He stood there in his briefs, looking out the window. The skin on the side and back of his right knee was stained bright red where the boiling water had burned him after I tried to have sex with him. Also there were goose bumps on his skin. I felt that it would have been nice if I ever got to kiss the burned skin but I didn't think I was going to get to. "Do you want me to leave now and never come back?" I said.

"No."

"What do you want me to do?"

After he had looked out the window for a while longer he turned toward me and extended his muscular arms in front of his torso as if about to do a front handspring. He encircled me lightly with his arms and whispered in my ear, "You're trying to

be nice." He walked down to the other end of the room and
stood with his back against the wall in the Malcolm X position.
I paced the short width of the room near the door. It got darker.
Mittler shivered. That was how we passed the next little while.

I THINK IT might be giving reality too much credit to say that
Hoving Harrington Hartman drifted in and out of it, but when
he stood wearing one of his daughter's long, dark, masculine
aprons in the kitchen in the twilight as if prepared for my return from Mittler's condemned building and said, "I made
brownies for you to eat after a difficult day," I feared the
brownies. Who knows what he was really doing while perceiv-
ing himself to have been making brownies? He could have
cooked his own feces, for all I knew. You think I'm joking,
reader.

"Sit," he said. I sat. "Love is mysterious," he said, putting a
plate of the dark brown pastries in front of me, along with a
glass of cold milk. "Drink the milk. Milk is the mother."

I took a sip. "Have you seen Skip Hartman today?" I asked.

"Who?"

"September."

"No."

Even more than his daughter, Hoving could not be trusted
to mean what you thought he meant. He tended to get *no* and
yes mixed up. He sat down across the table from me with a cup
of hot water and sighed. He grasped a large brownie and
jammed the entire thing into his mouth. It took him a while to
moisten and soften it with his saliva and, with his tongue and
the roof of his mouth, press it down to a shape and size he
could start to chew. During this time he stared at me and I listened to the air whistling in and out of his nostrils. Once he

started chewing, he tried to smile at me with his misshapen teeth, of which there were about half the number that his daughter had, but by all counts she had an unusually high number. With half the brownie down his gullet he said again, "Love is mysterious. As you get older, your understanding increases, but so does the amount of pain you must endure, so it may seem as if you are standing still." Hoving gagged and spat a small spheroid gob of wet brownie onto the kitchen floor. "Go on," he said, "have a brownie."

"How do I know it's really a brownie?"

"Flour, egg, milk, bittersweet chocolate, sugar, vanilla, baking soda, walnuts, salt. Have one."

"Not hungry."

"Today you are defeated by love. You are listless. Tomorrow, you will understand something that you do not understand today, and the pain will be less. You will kiss and feel pleasure again. For now, have a brownie."

"Don't want to."

"I see that you are too sad to eat a brownie. Go to your room."

I went.

FOR THE NEXT five nights Skip Hartman slept away from home and did not return in the day. I called Joe and Ruella and Tommy and Myra and everyone I knew to ask if they had heard from her. They all said they had not and I thought they were lying.

I was afraid to leave the house. I believed Skip Hartman was waiting around the corner for me to leave. When I left she would come in and change the locks on the front door and put all my things on the sidewalk. She would fold all my things—

my T-shirts and pants and things—into perfectly square piles and place them on the sidewalk, and she would line up my shoes along the wrought-iron fence on the sidewalk next to the clothes. She would place my books—the books she had given me, the important books she thought I needed to own, though she owned most of them in first edition—in two piles: one pile of novels, one pile of poems. The novel pile would be Charlotte Brontë and Emily Brontë and Jane Austen and Nathaniel Hawthorne and Marguerite Duras. The poem pile would be William Carlos Williams and William Shakespeare and William Matthews and Wallace Stevens and Sharon Olds and W. H. Auden and Marianne Moore and Mary Oliver and Elizabeth Bishop. The books would all be wrapped in see-through plastic against the weather. So would all the clothes and the shoes. I thought of everything in the world that I owned. A moment later, I was done thinking of everything in the world that I owned. Could you own a person? I knew you could sell a person. Could you give a person away? What is the difference between losing a person and giving a person away? You could be sitting in your house not thinking of anything, I thought, and some people whom you thought you couldn't lose could come up to you in your house and say, "Darling, we are going out for the evening," and you could say, "Bye," and you could give them a kiss, and unbeknownst to you, you are giving those people away with that kiss.

I did not leave the house for five days. I did not like Hoving Harrington Hartman and I avoided him, except when I was out of my mind with boredom, and then I would visit him in his bed in the living room, where he liked to remain, chattering to himself for most of the daylight hours. He had a remarkable sense of smell which, Skip claimed, made him the gifted gynecologist he once had been. The noises Hoving made when he smelled beautiful things were like the noises other people make when someone does a nice thing to them sexually. I brought him a head of red leaf lettuce. He sat up in bed and sniffed it carefully. He peeled back a few leaves and sniffed beneath them. "This is what death will smell like," he said.

Skip returned and pretended she did not know what she knew about Mittler and me, which meant that she walked around looking hard and fragile like a porcelain vase. She hardly spoke to me. I spread my books and clothes around all the rooms of the house. I hid some of my books behind her books. I made her read to me in the book room in the afternoon. I tried to sit in her lap when she read but she pushed me off. When she grabbed my body and pulled it toward her body each night in bed, it could not have been something she did of her own will.

As for Mittler, he and I played a complicated game over the next several months that went like this: I waited for him to contact me, and he did not contact me.

In the middle of March on the first warm morning of the year, I went down to the condemned building on East Second Street and tried the badly painted steel door. It was locked. I stood by the door in the sunlight. Clear water dripped from the roofs and fire escapes of all the buildings on the block. I stood for an hour in my running shoes. My toes went numb. I jogged up the block and back. Chet, the boy with dysentery, came walking down the street in mottled brown clothing. He was bone-thin. He smelled like molasses and horse manure.

"Chet," I said.

"You're making a face. Do I know you?"

"I'm Mittler's friend."

"Mittler doesn't have friends."

"How come you smell so bad?"

"It's the dysentery. I can't change my clothes."

"Does Mittler still live here?"

"Maybe."

"Is he in there now?"

"Maybe."

"I love him."

"The louder a lady proclaims her love, the more carefully you must inspect your pubic hair for crab lice after she leaves your mattress."

"Who said that?"

Chet swiveled his head as if to locate the person who said it. He had fine, light hair that clung to his chalky scalp and neck.

"Could you check if Mittler's in there?"

I think what was happening now was Chet was swooning. The skin on his face, a little viridian to begin with, turned green. His eyelids fluttered—have you noticed it's the boys of the world who are naturally gifted with long eyelashes? He fell against the wall, which thumped a short gust of air from him. He leaned in a little twilight of dysentery. The way he practiced it, dysentery looked calm and voluptuous. The wall of the building was covered with guerrilla posters. The ambiguous poster Chet leaned on showed a man who, as best I could tell, had two anuses.

I put my hand in Chet's damp, sticky pants pocket and retrieved a key. I draped one of Chet's wan arms over my shoulders and opened the shrieking door of the condemned building. A person appeared on the landing who was basically the female Chet. The female Chet may or may not have had dysentery but resembled Chet and had, for all intents and purposes, the same hair as Chet and the same unwashed body as Chet enshrouded in the same limp garments as Chet's. I said, "I am helping Chet."

"Put him on the bottom stair," she directed from the landing. I did, and there we all were for a moment: Chet crumpled on the bottom stair; lady Chet in the dim light on the top stair, hands on hips, ethereal and thin; and I, wondering how much energy it would take to get past lady Chet. I moved first, slowly. The girl stared at me, swaying slightly; her eyes did not protrude so much as her face receded on all sides of her eyes. I stopped one stair below her. "No guests unaccompanied by a resident," she recited, as if in a trance.

"I want to see Mittler."

"Not here."

"I want to leave him a note."

"No guests unaccompanied."

"So accompany me."

"But Chet," the girl said sadly, pointing to the crumpled body.

"I have to go past you now."

"Don't."

I went past her. She didn't move. I continued on up the stairs. She shrieked, less like a girl than a door.

I walked down the hallway toward the room that contained Mittler's orange tent. I almost did not see the shadow at my side. Then I felt my ribs being crushed. My head bounced against something hard—the wall. I thought of my parents and I saw them out on the highway being crushed by a truck. They were small and innocent. I saw them, the woman and the man, and then I did not see them and I could not remember them. Now something was trying to flatten my windpipe against the wall, like the windpipes of the children who went to the planet that existed in only two dimensions in A *Wrinkle in Time,* a book that was read to me once a long time ago by Jane Building, the first teacher I had after my parents died. I brought my knee up fast and got Mittler right in the testes. He let go my throat. I stood against the wall gasping for air while he lay on the floor curled up in a tight ball like a sow bug. He was not breathing, but the name of God kept oozing out his mouth in a soft whisper.

After a while he sat up and said, "I made you a hat."

"Oh, no, you did? What kind of a hat?"

"Well, a Gore-Tex rain hat. A cap, I would say. But now your hair's a different color so I don't know."

My hair was half-and-half hair at that point. "I hate my hair."

"Me too. The cap is blue. The hat. It's waterproof and has a brim to keep the water off your face."

"I like the water on my face."

"How was I supposed to know that? Ah, shit, I screwed up." He looked disconsolate.

"Mittler, you're funny."

"Are you being mean again?"

"Oh, no. Oh, no." I felt fiercely tender toward him because he had attacked me in the hall and because of the hat. I wanted to touch him but I knew he wouldn't want me to. "Maybe I don't really want the water on my face," I said.

"Would you like to see the hat now?"

"Yes."

The air in his tent had a fresh citrus smell that was a tribute to Mittler's scrupulous cleanliness. "Did you make orange-flavored tea?" I said.

"I'm not ever making tea when you're around."

"What's that smell?"

"This is the nontoxic orange pekoe air freshener which does not deplete the ozone."

"What's the ozone?"

"What have you been, raised by dogs?"

"I think you know who I've been raised by."

"Now you're making *me* mean."

"Fine, I'll leave." Walking away down Second Street, I heard my name. I turned around. Mittler was leaning out a window holding the hat. "Your hat!"

"Throw it down!"

"Come up and get it!"

"Take back what you said!"

"I take it back!"

Mittler was making tea when I returned. "Just stay away from the damned stove."

I wanted to express my gratitude for the tea. I know a lot of people can express gratitude by talking, and in this way the recipient of the gratitude does not feel violated by the gratitude. But there is a certain kind of gratitude that I feel that is like an electrical current that makes it impossible for me to speak, and it becomes almost mandatory that I move quickly through space and hug someone or scream or bite or kick or tackle someone or fuck them. Instead, I squatted in the corner of Mittler's tent, shaking. I didn't ask to see the hat, even. Reader, this is one of those times when I wish you or I could reach back in time and give a pat on the back to that frantic little teenage girl for being *so* careful with that teenage boy's feelings.

He gave me the tea. It was chamomile. He said it would calm me down because Mittler was an observant friend and kind and considerate. Chamomile tea is some kind of unnatural abomination. Whoever invented chamomile must really have been out of ideas. It is tea made from powdered cat vomit, I think.

Mittler gave me the hat. It was a baseball cap, dark blue, a little boxy, rough-hewn. I put it on. I was still shaking.

"Do you need more tea?"

"No thank you."

My ribs ached and the left side of my head throbbed where he had bounced it off the wall. I could not control my heart or lungs. He adjusted the brim of the cap on my head. When he did this, I did not reach up and touch his hand. "It looks cute on you. I wish I could have made a little bit better of a hat."

"It's nice."

"Do you want to go to Staten Island? I know a skiff there that we could take out into the harbor and harvest oysters which are a natural food resource of the area."

I shook my head. I was frozen to the spot.

"You're perspiring heavily," he said. "I'll take the hat off you." He took it off. "May I mop your brow with a clean chamois cloth?" he said. I nodded. He wiped my face with the soft cloth. "Your neck is very—what?—white and, uh, damp. Should I daub your neck as well?" I nodded. He daubed my neck. "You have thermal underwear on?" he said. I nodded. "It's not like I'm saying 'take off your pants,' but it's just I notice you're sweating so maybe you should—oh, God, I know this doesn't sound right—undress a little."

He helped me with my jacket and boots and pants and thermal underwear. He said, "Now I'm seeing that you're sweating but also shaking and I'm thinking I could ask you to lie on the floor and then with certain techniques I've learned in workshops and books I could realign the polarity of the energy field of your body, so is that something I could ask you to do, lie on the floor and I polarize?" I nodded. "Do you want me to help you lie on the floor?" I nodded. He held the back of my head the way you hold the heads of newborn babies, which will virtually fall off if you don't hold them. I lay on the floor and he held his arms out over my body like someone playing a zombie in a movie. He moved his two parallel arms low down along the length of my body. "You're very very very tense," he said. He placed a hand on my forehead and one on my belly. Inside my mouth was my bloody tongue. His hands made a small circular motion in my flesh. "You're resisting. I can feel it," he said. He made the circles for a while longer and suddenly got to his feet. "Ah, shit, I can't do this. I don't know what I'm doing." He was very upset. "You're a mess," he said. "Look at your hair." He picked some of my hair up off the tent floor and held it in his hand to scorn it. He gathered all my loose hair up into his hands. He touched my head with his fingers. He was not polarizing me anymore, he was touching me. He touched my mouth with his fingers, and then with his mouth, and that was our first kiss. I fell into a Chetlike swoon, and I cannot remember exactly what happened next.

Hours later, not having emerged fully from the swoon, I could not figure out my place in the world. By place in the world I mean whose house I was supposed to stay at now.

Once I was wide awake, I figured it out. In fact, it turned out to be not that hard to figure out. I chose the place with the luxury furniture.

WHILE SLEEPING ON the luxury furniture over the next few weeks, I often dreamt of Mittler. In my dreams he was someone who only crushed me. No tea, no hats, no polarity massage. Just crushing me in the hallway. I cherished him for it. If someone loves you only as a thing to be crushed, who's to say that's not loving?

Each morning during that period, Skip had some new set of comments or questions. "I can see why it is that you feel such a strong affinity for an American male," she said one morning.

"Why?"

"You are practically one yourself."

"What's that supposed to mean?"

"It means that it is the legacy and birthright of the American male to love a person, all the while wishing that person were someone else."

"What makes you an expert on the subject?"

"It is a form of self-deception, you know."

"What is?"

"Never mind."

On another morning she said, "Your actions do not destroy me. I will survive this. You will see, and you will be grateful. I trust you."

"What if I leave you for him?"

"I'll still trust you."

On another morning she actually said, "What has he got that I haven't got?"

"A penis."

"Seriously."

"He's surprising."

"Surprising."

"He's devoted to me but he's also his own man."

"I hate when you don't have the faintest idea what you're talking about. You don't know what *own* means. You don't know what *man* means."

"He gives me nice things and makes me feel good. Then, when I want to go, he lets me go. If you love something, set it free. If it comes back to you it is yours. If it doesn't come back, it never was."

"Oh, please God tell me she did not just say that. I thought we had pulled you out of the public schools before you'd been exposed to that horrifying aphorism."

"Well, he's surprising, which you still didn't answer."

"Please. He is surprising in exactly the same bland way all young men are surprising."

"How would you know?"

"I experimented. And I paid the price for it, as you will."

"What's that supposed to mean?"

"You'll see."

"You're not scaring me, you know."

"Fine."

"Anyway, Mittler's not just surprising. He's also exciting."

"Well, that's different. I see your point there. Exciting. I cannot compete with that. God forbid twenty-four hours should pass in which someone has not excited you. You must be made to feel unrelenting pleasure all day every day. One must devote one's energies to providing constant stimulation for you. One must give up one's very life so that all experience for you will be one long coitus."

My Body Writes Checks
My Mind Can't Cash

THE FIELD HOCKEY mallet I stole from Uncle Tommy got him into a little bit of trouble. I mean his attitude toward the field hockey mallet theft did. He thought he wasn't well liked in Marmot, and while that was true, he also thought Marmot had broken into his house as one single Marmot entity and stolen his decorative field hockey mallet from the wall of his kitchen. "Marmot thinks it can play with the head of its electronics repairman," was the way he put it on the phone to Skip Hartman, who in turn put it that way to me. But Tommy was not the rube or dupe that Marmot expected him to be. He would not be subjugated, or even friendly. He painted his front door and shutters bright red. He channeled his energy. He slept all day and roamed the streets of Marmot at night on foot, unshaven in his cape. He antagonized the local boys who worked at the Marmot Food Mart. He rarely opened his downtown repair shop for business, and people whose broken stereos he had in the shop could not get them back from him, and that was their own damn fault for being complicit in the mallet abscondence. He was fined for the red door and he did not pay the fine and he did not repaint the door. He became a prominent citizen. In the middle of May, two officers of the law came to the red door. He punched one of them and went to jail where he was treated, not so nicely, for his hurt hand.

Skip Hartman drove up to bail him out. She made me go with her. We reached the gate and the squared-off young man with the small wad of phallic muscle in his lower face refused to let us through. Skip handed him five twenty-dollar bills and he let us through. We stopped by the house to ask Myra for directions to the police station. Myra had not bailed Tommy out herself because she had been out shopping when Tommy punched the officer, and when he had tried to call her from the police station he kept getting the machine, as they say.

We knocked on the front door, which Marmot had now whitewashed. No answer. We went around back and found Myra in a long folding chair on the deck.

I said, "Myra, what the hell are you doing?"

"Thinking about my garden."

"Hi, it's me, your niece."

"Hi."

"Tommy's in jail." I watched her face, and there I saw the same look of generalized perturbation that I had seen on the day the grounds manager caught Paul and me sleeping in a hole in the first green. Then the look disappeared, not into the air but down into that body that was so full of bad feeling I wondered when it was going to burst.

"I knew he was gone for a long time. He likes to wander around," she said.

"Myra, did you just hear me? I said he's in jail."

"I know."

"Are you an automaton?" One tear leaked out of her body, followed by another.

Skip said, "He remarked that he has been trying to call you on the telephone from jail."

Myra looked at her.

"Have you heard the phone ring?"

"Yes."

"Why didn't you answer it?"

"I don't like to answer the phone."

I looked down at the place in the yard where the garden ought to have been. The soil was gray and dry and covered in spots with clover and grass. A few long brown stalks of things lay on their sides.

"You haven't been gardening."

"I've been thinking of it."

Skip said, "Tell her we must go to the police station to post bail on her husband."

I said, "Who do I look like, Doctor Dolittle? You tell her."

"Myra, can you tell us how to get to the police station by car?" Skip said.

Nothing.

"IT'S THE SOLEMNITY I hate," Skip Hartman said that evening in the White living room.

"Yeah, the solemnity," Tommy said.

"Solemnity!" I said.

"So they jailed you because you punched an officer. Fine. But the worst part of it is the way they attempted to infantilize you."

"No, actually being strip-searched was the worst part," Tommy said.

I said, "I think the worst part in all this would be being Myra, right, My-my?" She looked at me. I said, "Say something, say something."

"I'll get some finger food," she said.

"That's not what I meant! I meant respond to the situation, you fucking piece of meat!" (I can see now that perhaps I was being too hard on her.)

"Right back," she said, meaning, I'll be right back. She walked toward the kitchen. I leapt up and blocked her way. I put my hands on her shoulders and leaned into her. Her shoulders felt bulky and firm. She had a naturally low center of gravity and kept moving forward. I slid backward in my socks on the polished oaken floor of the living room.

"Say something say something say something say something."

Myra paused and scowled at me. I mean that her eyebrows went up and the ends of her mouth went down so that her lips formed two pale pink crescents that sandwiched a black crescent. Her face lost suppleness and looked like a hard plastic child's Halloween mask. Myra fell on the floor and twitched. Her eyes closed and she was still. Tommy screamed and rushed to her. Skip Hartman called an ambulance. The ambulance took Myra to the Marmot Medical Center, where she was treated for a stroke.

Reader, now don't be cruel and think, How can you tell the difference between Myra before a stroke and Myra after a stroke? The difference was that she needed someone to take care of her in the most basic way, which Tommy could not do. He could not do it because during his assault trial he lost control and slapped the prosecuting attorney. The judge indicted him on the spot for assault and declared a mistrial. For the next four months Tommy lived in the Marmot town jail. Skip Hartman moved up to Marmot to care for Myra White.

SKIP HARTMAN'S MOVE was a boon to me in terms of not having to sneak rendezvous with Mittler. Still, if her move seemed to say to me, "You don't have to sneak rendezvous with Mittler," it also seemed to say, "However, you will pay a price." But her move, being a move and not, say, a tearstained five-page letter written to me in anguish on her first night alone with my thrombotic aunt in Marmot, did not specify what that price would be. After all, there were prices everywhere, and I was an adolescent without fiscal savvy. Even now I am in capitalism but not of it.

Mittler offered me love that was tender and hard and angry and fair. With the advent of the warm weather, he folded up his indoor tent and suspended a hammock from hooks he had secured in the crumbling walls of the room in the condemned building. He made me sleep with him in the hammock. It was not at all comfortable.

"Why do I have to sleep with you in the hammock?"

"Because."

"Because why?"

He answered me not with a word but a look; no, not even a look, unless looking away counts as a look.

I lay in the hammock at night but rarely slept in it, so when I came home in the morning, I turned on the AC, collapsed into the soft white duvet, slept for four hours, woke up, slowly washed the dried boy–girl fluid and grime from my body, and made huevos rancheros, a hearty meal for a young woman. I wished there were a way to make huevos rancheros elsewhere than the kitchen, which was a fright, for Hoving Hartman loved to cook but not to clean. He also loved to eat food in all the rooms of the house, but not to clean.

Hoving's body itself was a disaster. Neither of us liked when I changed his diapers, so I tended to save it up for a few days at a time. Once, in the middle of summer, I smelled him in the upstairs hallway and charged at him with a fresh pair.

He said, "Get away from me, you little bratty boy. You poked me last time."

"I'm not a boy."

"Yes you are and stop trying to deny it."

I did what I should have done long ago. I lifted up my T-shirt and showed him my breasts.

"Holy criminy!" We stood in the dark hallway on the long, thin Persian rug. He stared dutifully. I kept my shirt aloft a long while so those breasts would imprint on his old man's brain.

"May I touch them?"

"Yeah, but only for like a second."

In his brief tactile encounter with my breasts he was grave and clinical, as a man would be who had touched women for a living. "Thank you," he said when he was done.

"Thank you," I said.

"You may now change me if you like." I did change him there in the hallway and showed his bottom and his privates the same respect he had shown my breasts. His face looked contemplative, mildly pleased, as he lay back on the floor with his knees up and his legs spread. In this way I did not mind changing him so much and we developed a way of relating to one another that was suited to the task.

I felt less certain of myself in the problem area of his mouth. It, too, emitted an odor. It was one of those places in the world—like El Salvador—in which I knew atrocities were being committed but I was hesitant to find out what they were. Some bleeding went on in there that I caught glimpses of from time to time. He had, as I believe I have previously documented, several fuzzy gray-brown teeth of his own. These were attached to his bloody gums and could not have been detached without the use of force. But I would now like to introduce into the record some other teeth of his that were more architectural in nature. These could be attached and detached by him at will and by me, eventually, with some cajoling. It was not just the bleeding and the odor that convinced me to make my first oral intervention in Hoving. One day after my nap and my shower, I tiptoed into the war zone of the kitchen to fetch my huevos and I saw him at the kitchen table lipping a thing that I at first mistook for the rib cage of a chicken, but which I then realized was his set of false teeth. He held them up to his mouth on the tips of his oily little fingers, not lipping only but sucking, too, the cheesy-soft matter from the crevices of them. I am not willing to state categorically that I saw one thick segmented strand of this pink-faint goo struggle up from its lodging and wiggle for dear life as Hoving brought his wet, open mouth down over it, but I'm saying that's what I thought I saw. I ran to the cabinet under the sink, took out a pair of rubber dishwashing gloves, slipped them on, grabbed the teeth from his hands, and okay I think it's fair to say that I raced around the house screaming, *"Eeeeew! Eeeeew!"* until I could locate the minty acid wash and drop his awful teeth into it.

I came back downstairs and I was very mad at him. "Grandpa," I said, "could you please not ever do that? It's really disgusting and you could probably poison yourself or something."

"Child, am I your grandfather?" he asked.

"No. I don't know why I called you that. It just came out of my mouth."

"Do you have a grandfather?"

"I don't know."

"Come here, sweet girl," he said, and opened his arms to me. I went into them, and put my cheek on his shoulder, and felt indescribably unhappy.

I PASSED THE road test for my driver's license by the width of the hairs on my chinny-chin-chin. Skip bought me a car for my seventeenth-and-a-half birthday. Two days later I smashed it and she bought me a new one and I smashed that and she bought me another and I used it to drive Hoving up to Marmot on Labor Day.

I don't know why I hate the end of August so much. If each year at that time I could smash the car just enough to get into a monthlong coma without any major bone breaks or contusions, I think I'd appreciate the vacation from consciousness. I navigated the car up the driveway. I did not sec the weed trimmer until after I had heard the front wheel crush it, and by then it wasn't a weed trimmer anymore.

Hoving raced ahead of me up the flagstones with his side-to-side bowlegged wobble-walk and knocked on the door. Skip Hartman shouted, "It's open!" from deep within. We found her on the threshold of the living room and the deck. "Daddy," she said, in a tone as if chastising him for not allowing himself to have been driven up for a visit sooner. She placed her hands on his shoulders, bent forward, and gave him a kiss on his forehead. Me, she stared at.

"Hi, Skip."

She nodded.

"It was a long car ride."

She looked at me.

"My back is kind of hurty-ow-y."

"Upper back or lower?"

"Middle."

"Hm."

"What have you to nibble on?" Hoving said.

"Your teeth," I said.

"Ha, ha, ha, ha, ha, ha, the lad is funny."

"I thought we were past that 'lad' crap."

"I'll prepare snacks when I've finished feeding Myra," Skip said.

I said to Skip, "So I was wondering if you could align my back by that hugging thing you do."

"I could not."

I went out to the deck to watch Skip feed Myra.

"Did you bring fresh diapers for him?" she asked.

"Who do you think's been changing him for the last few months?"

"The suffering must be fantastic."

"You know, all you have to do is forbid me to be in love with him. Did you ever think of that?"

"It had not occurred to me."

"So, forbid me."

"No, I mean it had not occurred to me that you were in love with him. Please excuse me." She dropped a spoonful of stewed carrots onto the wooden surface of the deck, stood up, and walked into the house.

Myra reclined in the chair in the same position she had been in when we came up to bail out Tommy. She was wrapped in a brown woolen army blanket. The sun shone directly down upon her. She stared out at the birch and maple and pine trees beyond the yard. I sat in the small folding bridge chair Skip had been sitting in to feed her. She turned her head slowly to look at me. Taking full advantage of her psychomotor retardation, I gazed into her eyes for longer than she would ever have let me before the stroke. For the first time, I saw how quick she was inside that slow body. I saw urgency in those eyes. I thought I almost saw the words she might bring into existence on behalf of her own feelings, if she were a woman who knew what she felt, and for the moment, because of her eyes' eloquence, I suspected she was such a woman after all.

I picked up the spoon from the floor of the deck and wiped it off on my ancient T-shirt. I dipped the spoon into the shallow porcelain bowl and brought it toward her mouth with stew on it, chanting the age-old pun, *"Choo-choo-choo-choo."* She bit on the spoon with the crushing jaw strength of a snapping turtle. She would not release the spoon. I looked out at the trees and wondered what part of the house Skip Hartman had gone to and what she was thinking now.

"I'm hungry," Myra said.

"What?"

"You are d. You are d. You are day. You are daydreaming."

I removed the spoon from her mouth and filled it and said again, *"Choo-choo-choo-choo."*

Myra said, "D."

"What?"

"Doe."

"What?"

"Don't."

"Don't feed you? You said you were hungry."

"Don't."

"Don't what?"

"Don't ch."

"*What?*"

"Don't *choo-choo.*"

"Oh. Oops."

I finished feeding this new invalid and self-assertive Myra and went inside. The doorbell was ringing. I answered it. Hoving stood there in a shirt and tie and suitcoat and no other clothing. A big, sturdy fellow in his fifties was holding Hoving by the back of his collar—more or less where the scruff of his neck would be if he had one. The big man looked like a fatter, older, more upstanding version of the man at the gate of Marmot.

Hoving's face looked vacant and sad. The other man's face looked disciplined in its principles.

"Who are you?" the man said to me.

I said, "Who are you?"

"I'm John Hand. This man came out of this house and wandered into my yard, where he shouldn't be. I also don't know how he got in because there's a fence."

"Oh, naughty!" I slapped Hoving's hand. "By the way, are you related to the guy at the gate?"

"Johnny? He's my son. Now, who are you?"

"That's my grandpa. I'll take him now, thank you."

"Are you related to Tommy White?"

"My mommy's not home. I'm not supposed to talk to strangers."

"Do you have any idea what this—this man did?"

"Grandpa, what did you do?"

"Well, my child, I was out for a lovely barefoot stroll in the backyard. I do so enjoy the sensation of stiff grasses in the soft skin between my toes. Too, the varieties of olfactory sensation in this part of the country at this time of the year allow me to dream fondly of days finer than the present one. In the vicinity of this gentleman's home, I smelt a septic tank running high, which caused a sympathetic stirring in my own bowels. And child, you know how I loathe the sensation of fecal matter clinging to my skin, and the subsequent dermal irritation. I was able to discard my trousers and nappies in the nick of time for a pleasant open-air defecation. I so enjoy a lovely stroll in the country."

"Oh, Grandpa, you sure are aware of those sensations. Grandpa likes to play that edge between emeritus professor and disgusting senile fart. It's funny, right?"

"No." John Hand stood blocking the sky, hands on hips.

Skip Hartman emerged from a room somewhere and took up a position next to me. Her eyes were red, and the splotchy red and beige skin on her face hung more loosely on the bone than I had remembered. Still, the erect posture and broad shoulders and the expansive breadth of clavicle that Skip introduced to our side of the doorway would be, I sensed, a more than adequate balance to the bulk and indignation this man was weighing in with on his side. "What goes on here?" she asked.

"Who are you?" John Hand said.

Skip said, "Who are you?"

"I am John Hand, a village elder."

"Elder than what?"

"Is this your father?"

"Yes."

"He shat in my yard so please keep him inside this damn house. Nothing personal."

"You say 'elder,' but the word 'vigilante' springs to mind."

"You're out of line, lady. Is this your daughter?"

"Why?"

"Is it?"

"I don't have to tell you anything."

"Then I'll tell you something. This is not the kind of household we want in Marmot. Tommy White is a troublemaker, and I don't think this is your daughter, and we prefer if the children of the community are not exposed to any lesbian or other homosexual type of activity."

"Did you say 'lesbian'?"

"Yes, ma'am, I did."

"That is quite interesting, for you see, this young chap here is not a lesbian, nor could he and I in any way be construed as engaging in lesbian or other homosexual type of activity. In that regard, sir, I commend to your attention the perfectly formed penis that hangs—and sometimes does not hang, if you follow my meaning, sir—between the boy's legs. Paul, undo your trousers for the gentleman."

John Hand stared open-mouthed at the crotch of my pants, which I unzipped. "Oh no," he said, and turned around and started to walk away down the flagstones. "Oh no, no, no, this will not do."

Skip and Hoving walked inside the house together, and I

finished the gesture of taking the talked-about penis out of my
pants. There it was, reader, hanging out for all the world to see,
only no one was looking; not John Hand, not Skip Hartman,
not even me. So like the fellow said, was it really there?

AFTER WE LOCKED Hoving in the guest room of Tommy's house,
Skip and I put Myra in the car and drove down to the Marmot
courthouse, where they were holding the prisoner. The courthouse and the police station took up an entire block of downtown Marmot across the street from the Town Square. The
Town Square was a prim hunk of wilderness with a pond, a
gazebo, tall shade trees, and hillocks and meadows. The courthouse and the police station shared a wide, elongated rectan-
gle of flat green crew-cut lawn. They were fraternal twin brick
buildings of three stories, each with a wide marblesque staircase that led up to a row of white Ionic columns.

I pushed Myra's wheelchair up the ramp along the side of
the courthouse steps. The ramp marred the grandeur of the
steps and seemed out of keeping with Marmot's civic intentions. A gaudy chandelier hung from the ceiling of the main
hall of the courthouse. A uniformed officer greeted us and led
us to the back of the main hall. We took an elevator down a
floor and walked (or rolled) along a low-ceilinged corridor lit
with fluorescent bulbs.

"Where are we?" Skip asked.

"We're on our way to the holding facility."

Wheeling Myra, I leaned forward and whispered in her ear,
"Facility."

She gradually craned her neck around to look at me. "Fa-ci-
li-ty," I said, and nodded at her authoritatively. She rolled her
eyes.

We entered a yellow concrete room with no windows. Another man in uniform who had big red hands waved in front of each of our bodies an electronic object that looked like half the handlebars of a girl's bicycle. He left and came back with Tommy, and my heart filled with admiration. If there was someone who could make despair into a visual style, it was he. He stood several feet into the room and glanced at the three of us. He looked down at his feet and waved: that was his greeting. His body listed to one side but his head remained vertical, as if his ear were pressed to an invisible door behind which a secret conversation was taking place. He had applied gobs of pomade to his light hair to darken it and bring forward the shape of his skull. His face was shaved. Dark, livid rings marked the perimeters of the skeletal holes that accommodated his eyes. Already a thin man, he had lost ten or fifteen pounds. His personal jail uniform of khaki pants and a pale blue work shirt was neatly pressed and loose on his body. A small yellow Walkman was clipped to the waistband of the pants. The sleeves of the shirt were rolled halfway up his arms with a sharply creased fold in the cuff. He wore brown plastic sandals and gray cotton socks.

"As you know, Myra, I have a lot of problems finding shoes that fit me well," he said, looking at his feet still. The man with the red hands stood behind him and in front of the closed door of the yellow room. Skip and I sat in molded plastic chairs. I held one of the handles of Myra's wheelchair and casually moved her back and forth as if rocking a baby to sleep in its carriage. Tommy said, "My right foot is bigger than my left and my heels are very narrow whereas the toes at the front end of my foot are very wide. My feet were swelling up for some reason and they were blistering up along the knuckle of the toe in

my usual shoes, so the town government issued me these sandals, which is why I'm wearing them. Plus I listen to a lot of
Bach now so I don't move around much anyway.

"Sometimes I'm listening to the Suites for Unaccompanied
Cello on my headphones in my cell in the middle of the day,
and I feel like I can hear Pablo Casals talking to me. Sometimes he's just saying 'Unhhh' and sometimes he speaks in
complete sentences like 'All is not well' or 'Everything won't
turn out fine.' I have a toothache but I'm not telling anyone
about it. It doesn't hurt that much, it's just that sometimes it
makes one whole side of my head hurt. They have a bargain
toothpaste here at the jail that I don't think is effective. Plus I
forget to brush because of the Bach. The Bach doesn't make
me feel better but it helps to pass the time because there's one
hour of TV a day and it's always during a bad show. I can play
the Bach whenever I want but I'm trying to be careful so the
batteries don't run down. Could you bring me fresh batteries?"
he asked, looking at his sandals.

"I'm so glad you've discovered Bach," Skip said.

Tommy rushed forward, reached under and behind the
armpits of Myra, pulled her toward him, and hugged her hard
and long. "My sweetheart is in a coma or something," he whispered. "Can you hear me?" Myra's mouth hung open and she
seemed to be staring at a blank area of the yellow wall. I did
not understand what governed her ability to speak and move at
some times and not others, but I sensed in Myra at this moment a conscious decision; I sensed whim, whimsy even. Yes,
her mouth hung open and a trickle of drool spilled over the
bottom lip, but were not the corners of her mouth upturning in
the slightest? Perhaps I was not the only person in the world
who registered the correctness of the pairing of this woman

with this ailment. Could it be that a certain muted and immobilized girl was playing it up a little, was discovering, for the first time in her life, the pleasures of theater?

Tommy released Myra. Skip said, "I shall bring you the batteries you need. Double A?"

"I don't want *you* to bring them. I want her to bring them. The invalid. She brings them or it's no good. You bring them," he said, pointing at Myra, "or nothing will ever be good."

"F," Myra said. Oh, I thought I knew what two words were coming and I hoped she'd be able to produce them.

"Foo," Myra said.

"What, honey?"

"Food." (Oh well.)

"Oh, you want to know how the prison food is!" Tommy said. "Everybody, *this* is my wife. The gal I married is in her coma or whatever, but she can still ask after my well-being. God, I love you, honey." He embraced her again.

"That's not what she was doing," I said.

"What?"

"You think everything everyone says in the world is about you. She's hungry. She wants food."

"How the hell do you know?"

"Because, you selfish idiot. Who even cares if you're in jail? I'm glad you're in jail."

Tommy lunged anemically at me and the guard caught him. He said, "Okay, fine, Myra, maybe you are hungry. I don't give a damn about any of you people anyway. You can let me go now, I won't go near them," he said to the guard, who was hugging him from behind. The guard let go. Tommy placed the earphones in his ears and pressed the PLAY button on the Walkman that was clipped to his waistband. He went and stood facing one corner of the yellow cement room and waved his right arm from side to side across his torso with flowing undulations of his wrist, as if moving the bow of a cello.

Skip drove Tommy's big sedan back to the house. I sat in back with Myra. Midway on the ride home, Myra spoke my name. I turned to her. Her hand came slowly up toward my face and poked me in the eye. Maybe she was trying to remove a stray eyelash.

I Fail

ON THE TUESDAY after Labor Day I woke up at dawn and entered Myra's room. She lay with open eyes in her dark, half-empty bed. I kissed her cheek. Then I went into the room where Hoving groggily reclined, scooped him up, put him in my car before he knew what was happening, and left Marmot without a word to Skip Hartman.

It was a rainy day. If nothing else, I came away from this visit with a new mental picture of Skip Hartman's hair. The new hair was without its previous machinelike segmentation, reader. The new hair not only touched her shoulders but cascaded over her shoulders. It had a curl and a wave. Many strands of the new hair fell about her shoulders on their own, away from the central body of the hair. Many of the strands of the new hair were gray against the sort of manila field of the rest of her hair. She was forty-two years old. She was a mature woman with gray hair who did not need someone like me who was a child and a fool who caused her grief. If I could not witness such a monumental change in the hair of someone I loved while it was happening, I might as well be dead. In the car on the Taconic State Parkway, my face imitated the sky.

Hoving said, "I am not accustomed to traveling in my bedclothes. Now that Labor Day has passed I like a pair of dark worsted wool slacks and a button-down poplin open at the collar."

"Did you notice her hair?"

"My daughter's hair has been graying for some time. It's inhumane to force a man to travel in his pajamas."

"So change."

"Change me," he said with a beatific smile.

I slammed on the brakes and lost control of the car on the wet, oily road and skidded and turned into the skid and came to a stop on the grassy shoulder. I got out, opened the back door on the passenger side, opened the front door on the same side, lifted little Hoving Harrington out, and placed him in the backseat. I removed his overnight bag from the trunk, took off his red flannel pajamas, changed his diaper, and put the fresh clothes on him. I stood outside the car in the grass and leaned in, manipulating his body. Drops of water hit my back through my frayed T-shirt. I noticed Hoving's large speckled head and the thin, isolated clumps of white hair that made his head resemble the head of an old dandelion. *Look at the old, pale dandelion and the bright young dandelion side by side,* a voice came back to me. *It is lovely to try to hold the two in your mind as one, for they are the same flower. See how the wind comes to kill the old dandelion. It is the very death of the old dandelion that spreads the seeds that make the new dandelion. See how the old dandelion willingly allows itself to be destroyed by the wind to honor and uphold the next generation of dandelions.*

We beat the morning rush-hour traffic into the city and I called Skip Hartman on the phone.

"Skippy," I said.

"What?"

"Your hair changed."

"What?"

"Your hair is different."

"Different from what?"

"I just wanted you to know I noticed."

"I see."

"Skippy?"

"What?"

"I love you."

She did not respond.

I said, "You don't have to feed Myra baby food."

"What?"

"Myra can chew really hard."

"Yes. Good-bye, Mary."

"Wait!"

"What do you want?"

"The sun came out in the city. Is it still raining there?"

"Good-bye." She hung up.

I was in a state of agitation. I changed into my pink Lycra-spandex exercise unitard with the white stripe down the side and left the house. I jogged over to Second Avenue and took a right, heading downtown. The unitard made me feel snug inside my own body and I knew that Mittler, whom I was going to visit, would not approve of its color. Mittler favored clothing that was loose and natural and free and brown; he did not want to startle the animals of Central Park. Mittler was the animal I wanted to startle, or so I imagine I thought, but who knows if, at the age of seventeen, I thought anything at all?

When I reached Second Street I took a left and sprinted until I came to the condemned building. Chet stood out front, looking robust in a clean shirt. The sun shone on his back from the east.

"Hey, Chetty, looking good."

"September is a good month for me."

"How's the dysentery?"

"I'm getting a solid turd."

"Nice."

"It holds together."

"Have you seen Mittler?"

"That I cannot say."

"Oh, for Christ's sake, say."

"Why?"

"Fuck."

"He's not here."

"Can I wait here with you?"

"It's funny."

"What?"

"People want to stick together. It's bad luck."

"Bad luck?"

"Well, think of shit. Shit is lucky, compared to people. Sticking together is not a whole lifelong project for shit. *I* want my shit to stick together in nice firm little groups, but that's me imposing my needs on the shit. The shit itself doesn't care. The shit doesn't give a shit." This he found very funny and leaned against the wall laughing between two graffiti messages, one saying, NO POLICE and the other, BEWARE OF MUG-

GERS—DON'T GET CAUGHT ALONE. After a while he sat down and fell asleep on a mound of sand on the sidewalk.

Chet's friend who looked like Chet came out of the building. I said hello.

"How they hanging?" she said.

"Seen Mittler?"

"He's been in the park the last few nights."

"Central Park?"

"What'd you think I meant, Tompkins?"

"Is Chet all right?" We looked down at Chet.

"Chet's going to die."

I ran up to Tenth Street on Avenue B. On Tenth I ran over to Fifth Avenue. I ran up Fifth, and when I got to Central Park I borrowed a kid's skateboard that kind of was just there in the grass where the kid wasn't paying attention to it. This skateboard I used to get me up to 108th Street near the tree from which Mittler hung a minimum necessary amount of outdoor supplies with a strong fishing line. Coming over a hill on foot, I saw him in profile at the base of a tulip tree. The shape of Mittler's head in the northern woods of Central Park in the late morning with the sun coming almost straight down onto his hair reminded me of the noble head shapes of our early hunting-and-gathering biped forefathers.

"Hi, cutie," I said.

"I've been anxiously awaiting your return from Marmot. Don't call me cutie. I don't want to know what happened in Marmot."

"Okay."

"So don't tell me what happened there."

"Okay."

"I think it's best if I don't hear about it."

"Okay."

"Okay." He nodded. "I'm scouting out this tree."

"For what?"

"So that I can scout it out."

"But what do you scout it out *for*?"

"You just look at it and touch it and think about it."

"Then what?"

"Then nothing."

"I think I have ankle cancer. Can you get that? Look at this thing. What is this thing?"

"I have a poem," he blurted.

"What kind of poem?"

"Well, it's a non-rhyming poem about trees. Just a regular poem. And in a way it's also about you. Oh, and also it's written by, um, me."

"You wrote a poem about me?"

"In a way."

"Mittler, I can't stand you. Can I see it?"

He looked away and handed me a piece of paper with a handwritten poem on it. This is the poem:

Poem Praising the Trees of Manhattan

I see all the trees of Manhattan lined up in a row.

The paper birch, whose white bark is good to start a fire,
The tulip tree, who is tall and fashioned by geometry,
The Japanese maple, who is a delicate tree with red hair,
The pear tree of West Eleventh Street, who blossoms white and
    sweet for five days in March to make me want to die,

The sugar maple, whose leaf is the logo of Parks Commissioner
    Henry Stern, an eccentric,

The oak tree, who has an indecent relationship to squirrels,
The tamarack, who oozes semen all year like me only not
    ashamed,
The juniper, medium-sized and proud like me only not ashamed,

The poplar, who appears in great Western works of art I haven't
    seen or read,
The sycamore, who is in that Grace Paley story you read me in
    the hammock that time,
The magnolia, home to unhappy starlings,
The rhododendron—don't understand him, can't relate to him,

The ailanthus, thrives in disturbed sites, enjoys violence,
The butternut, light and soft and weak and neglected,
The mimosa, snubbed me once when I needed her, just like
    something you would do,
The giant sequoia, who isn't even here as you are often not here
    even when you are here.

You are water and sun for the trees of Manhattan,
I am afraid of you,
Afraid of you,
Raid of you,
Aid of you,
Of you,
View,
You,
ooh.

Sincerely, Mittler

We strolled a long time through the woods of northern Manhattan holding hands. I spoke to Mittler of how I loved his
poem. I asked him not to be afraid of me. He denied my re-

quest. He told me my exercise suit was hideous. I asked him to look at my ankle and tell me if he thought there was any cancer on it. He said I should lean against a tree which he identified as a lollygag pine or something. Bending slightly, he lifted my foot up to his face and inspected the ankle in question. "I don't know what the hell it is but it's definitely not cancer. I think we should make our bed by this tree, which will protect us."

"You want to sleep in Central Park?"

"I do it all the time."

"I don't. How do you know the tree will protect us?"

"It's a feeling."

"What's the feeling?"

"Like a dark voice."

We had walked and talked a long time. The sun that had been shining on the top of Mittler's hunting-and-gathering head now shone on the side of his head and his left ear as he faced north and gazed adoringly at the tree. I waited by the tree while he retrieved his tent and other things from the other benevolent tree. Two big black boys my age walked by along a path. One of them was bald and the other had long braids. They stared at me. I was scared. Mittler came back and I told him I didn't want to sleep in Central Park. He said the tree would protect me and he would too. He constructed his small, low, unobtrusive tent that you could not sit up in. He gathered fallen white birch bark and wood and made a fire. He cooked lentils, which he had soaked the previous night under a rock at Sixty-seventh Street. To the lentils he added garlic and carrots and diced celery and zucchini and basil and salt and pepper and, toward the end, a tomato. His resourcefulness was a comfort to me, even as I realized how helpless I would be with no one to feed me. We ate and I burned my tongue, which ruined the meal. The sun had set and the sky was deep violet. We slid into his little tube tent. It was so close in there that I breathed in the air he breathed out, and vice versa. Our bodies were pressed together. I felt bloated and gassy, while he was getting excited. There wasn't room for us to get our clothes off so he made two quick openings in our clothes and fucked me. I had to pee, which hurt. Also, because we were so tight in there, he scraped my neck with his face hairs. I started to feel scared, as if he were stabbing me over and over with that penis. But I was also excited and wanted him to keep doing it. Mittler was pretty good at control, but you know how boys are at that age, reader. His body quaked and his penis got extra stiff and large just to tantalize me before he burst and yelled and went slack. He lay on top of me. I know how dreamy and delicate any-one—even a boy—feels after that explosion. I wanted to be sweet with him the way he usually tried to be with me after sex—except when he was all freaked out and had to leave— but I was also mad at him for having sex with me when I had to pee and for getting me all excited, so I made him keep thrusting even though he said doing that made the skin all over his body feel funny in a bad way. I made him keep doing it and doing it and nothing happened and then we were both mad at each other. Then I made him escort me out of the tent to pee. We went back into the tent and fell asleep pressed up against each other, mad.

I woke up in the middle of the night having to pee again. I asked him to come out with me again. He said no. I said pretty please and he said no. I asked him if he had a flashlight. He told me I wouldn't need a flashlight because it was New York City, that I should look up at the sky when I got outside the tent and I'd see that it was not black as it would be in nature but pale red like the skin surrounding a wound that could not properly heal. I walked outside and gazed up at the soft pink glow and found it soothing. Gazing at the sky, I peed standing up in my special way. I walked back to the tent and felt a sharp discomfort in the bottom of my left foot. Every time I tried to place my foot on the ground the discomfort grew worse. I hopped the last few yards to the tent and felt the bottom of my foot with my hand. It was wet. I looked at my fingers and the wetness was dark or black. I touched the bottom of my foot again and now I felt the sharp discomfort on two of my fingers as well. I told Mittler and he said, "Wait here." He raced off skillfully along the dark, uneven ground. He came back several minutes later with a kerosene lamp. He lit the lamp and together we looked at the bottom of my left foot. A long sliver of green glass stuck up out of it, surrounded by thick red blood. He pulled gently at the glass. It sort of kept coming out of my foot. It wasn't so much a sliver as a wide piece of jagged glass, much of which had been inside the flesh of my foot. When it was all the way out, a lot more blood pumped up out of the cut and onto Mittler and the lip of Mittler's tent and the ground. He inspected the opening in my foot and removed some little shards. He took off his T-shirt and wrapped it around the foot and raced off along the ground again, not tumbling or falling or stepping on glass himself. He came back with a first-aid kit. "Where do you get all this stuff?"

"Trees."

He cleaned the wound and injected my foot with a local anesthetic. He sewed the bottom of my foot like the best girl in home ec class.

"How do you know how to do all this stuff?"

"I read books."

"So do I."

"Then you must know how to do stuff too."

"I know how to recite a poem by heart."

"My poem?" he said, and stopped sewing me, and looked up at me hopefully with his mouth open.

"No, silly, I just read your poem once a few hours ago. How could I have memorized it?"

"Oh." He sewed more flesh and was sad. When finished he said, "We should try to get some sleep now."

"Here?"

"Yes."

"I am not sleeping in a broken glass jungle with a hurt foot. I want soft pillows or I'm breaking off the relationship."

"Well, isn't that just typical. The same day I give you my best poem you're *breaking off the relationship* just because something sharp went in your foot."

"Take me home."

He did. On piggyback. At first he ran but I told him that the bouncing hurt my foot, so then he walked swiftly, quietly, and smoothly. At three A.M. on this hot summer morning, Mittler carried me up the stone steps to the door of my house. He was strong and quiet and handsome and wet.

"I'll just check on Hoving and we can go to sleep," I said, unlocking the top lock.

"I am honor bound not to sleep in this house."

"You are an asshole chickenshit."

"I am already acting against a principle I hold dear."

"What principle?"

"No adultery."

"How about the principle of not leaving someone alone with a hurt foot?"

"Come to my house."

"Asshole."

I looked in on the old man, who sat in bed silently mouthing words, his arms stretched out along his small legs, palms up as if in supplication.

I went to the bedroom of the erstwhile couple and opened the drawer where Skip kept roughly $10,000 in walking-around money. I grabbed a stack of twenties and joined Mittler on the street, where we had a moral struggle about whether to take a cab, which I won.

At his condemned house I told Mittler I couldn't sleep in his hammock with him because my foot needed not to be touching anything. He gathered rectangular naked foam-rubber mats from around the building and laid them down on the floor of his room, one adjacent to the next, creating a soft place for two people to sleep. I told him I did not want him sleeping next to me because he might inadvertently kick my foot in his sleep, plus I needed to be alone without anyone touching me so he should just get up into his damn hammock. He did. We lay in the semidark, I on my adjacent foam-rubber rectangles, he in his hammock above me, not sleeping. I watched the rhombuses of pale light move across the ceiling as the cars and trucks passed on Houston Street.

An hour into our silence Mittler blurted, "You're not grateful I cared for you with my survival skills."

I told him, using the term *dipshit*, that he was the whole reason I *had* a cut foot, and so much for our having been protected by his stupid tree, et cetera. He intimated that the tree was maybe trying to teach me a lesson and I asked him what sort of lesson and he said it was for the tree to teach and me to learn. I said that yes, in fact he was right, that indeed the lesson was not to spend time with him, Mittler, again, ever, and I hopped down the stairs of Mittler's condemned building.

Chetty lay asleep on the soft, damp bed of sand that was piled up against the building on the sidewalk. The sun, which just now rose over the borough of Queens, cast a few rays of orange light on the bottoms of Chetty's dirty, naked, east-facing feet. I hopped down to Houston Street and caught a cab home.

HOME WAS NOT the comfy place it once had been. The house smelled bad. Cockroaches and mice strolled the floors and countertops of the kitchen. Dust was general over the rugs, the stairs, the hallways and books. It had been dirty before, but the dirt had not been embedded in the infrastructure as it was now. Outside my window the air grew cold and dark, and trees whose names I did not know gave up their leaves.

It was all I could do to prevent a mold from consuming the skin and mouth of the old man. I rarely left the house. I thought of the two people I loved best moving over the surface of the earth. I thought of all the things they did and said and were. I hated the stupid way I flitted from one to the other, causing harm in my inimitable carefree manner. I wished to be certain of anything. I spent days at a time in bed reading books. I read *The Children's Hour* and *Tea and Sympathy* and *Woodworking for Morons* and *The Cake Bible* and *Prolegomena* and *Tales of Love* and *A Lover's Discourse* and *Seven Types of Ambiguity* and *Amongst Women* and *The Long Lavender Look* and *Berlin Stories* and *The High Peaks Trail Guide* and *Divorce Talk* and *On Death and Dying* and *Civilization and Its Discontents* and *Playing and Reality* and *Decline and Fall of the Roman Empire*, by Gibbon. I don't know Gibbon's first name. Few people do, but everyone knows that you have to say "Gibbon" after you say *"Decline and Fall of the Roman Empire."* That is not something you learn from books but from living with people who read them.

I didn't run, reader, I didn't sprint. I didn't bounce on the bed. I didn't punch or tackle anyone, or take a walk. I wiped the skin of Hoving with a warm, soapy cloth, and succumbed to lethargy, and was seventeen.

In the middle of December, Tommy got out of jail and Skip Hartman moved back to New York City. First thing she did: hired a cleaning service. Second thing: bought calf-length flower-print skirts and pretty clips for her thick gray hair that now hung halfway down her back. She announced that she did not wish to sleep in the bed that I was sleeping in. I volunteered to move in with Hoving, whom I liked. I set up a cot in the living room, shut off the lights, undressed, and inserted my naked body into a sleeping bag on top of the cot in much the same way as I remembered the slick, bare glans of Mittler's penis, grown soft, sliding back into the clothlike sheath of his foreskin after he made love to me.

Hoving screamed. "What is it?" I asked.

"I cannot tolerate the darkness," he said, half reclining on his seven pillows, for he did not ever lie down that I knew of. "I must be able to look down and see my own body in the middle of the night, else how do I know it is there?"

I turned on the light and dozed off.

"Yes, my pretty, yes, my pretty ones, you shall not go hungry," I heard him say several hours later.

The radiator in the living room was going full blast. I was covered in sweat. "Who you talking to?" I asked, not entirely awake.

"The mice in my bed."

I jumped up and ran to him. His legs were parted on the white sheet. With his left hand, he pointed down at the area of his crotch where, in the palm of his right hand, he held his thin, elongated old man's penis and testicles before him carefully, like delicate pets.

I said, "Those are the mice?"

"Yes. They're hungry. Would you be so kind as to buy them a lump of cheese, dear girl? You see I've forgotten my wallet."

"I would love to but I only have a nickel, which my mother gave me to buy pencils and things for school."

"Yes, I quite see your predicament," he said sadly.

"Are they good friends?"

"Beg pardon?"

"The mice. Do they treat you well?"

"Yes, yes. They're lovely."

"They *are* lovely. Do they give you trouble, ever?"

"Oh, sometimes they create quite a lot of mischief but just now they are being very gentle."

"You don't ever sleep, do you?"

"Not a wink."

I WAS TRYING to be really nice to Skip Hartman because I loved her and I thought, foolishly, that she was mad at me. What I mean is that I knew I had wounded her in her heart, and I just assumed that everyone responded to such wounds as I did—with intense, violent anger.

Since I slept poorly in Hoving's room, I went down to the kitchen at four o'clock one morning shortly after Skip's return and baked the angel food cake with butter-cream frosting that I had read about in *The Cake Bible*. Later that morning at the breakfast table, after the three of us had eaten the cake, Skip Hartman touched one of her hands with the other. I said, "Why don't you touch my hand?"

"I think you know why. We must determine, my dear girl, what you will do and where you will live, now that your eighteenth birthday is approaching and you do not love me in the way that I wish to be loved."

"But I think I'm starting to again."

She gave me a look.

"You could try just enduring me," I said.

"Yes, that is one of the possibilities I am considering."

"That's what people used to do in the nineteenth century."

"How would you know?"

"I read it."

"Where?"

"I forget."

"Husbands also used to lock their wives in insane asylums, as did for example Charles Dickens," she said.

"I prefer the enduring thing. We endure each other because we love each other and romantic love is difficult and good and enduring."

"Ah, she has become a philosopher of love. I am eating cake with Socrates."

I walked out of the kitchen and up to the room from which I had been displaced—my room—and closed the door and wedged a straight-backed wooden chair beneath the doorknob. I opened the French windows and paced the room. I wished for the cold wind to come blowing down the littered avenues of my thoughts and sweep away the garbage. After several hours I sat down on the bed to compose an original love poem for Skip Hartman.

Just as I was done writing the first draft of the poem, Skip knocked on the door, and when I didn't answer she banged on the door, then pounded on the door, then shouted through the door, "Open this fucking door!" While she was doing that, I was not making major structural changes to the poem, I was mainly copying it out in a clean hand, because the visual presentation of a poem is important, especially as I would be giving the poem to the woman who had taught me penmanship. I removed the chair. She came in and said, "It's freezing in here!" and closed the windows. I handed her the poem, which was basically the same poem Mittler had written to me only without the references to trees.

She read it.

"How could you have written this?"

"Because I love you."

"No. What I mean is that I think you did not write this. You didn't write this."

"Yes, that's what I was doing while you were pounding on the door."

"No. You plagiarized."

I could not speak. As far as I know—which is not very far in such matters—this was the first time in my life that I could not think of something to say to Skip Hartman. I believed that I understood the predicament of Myra: how can one speak when a lie is untenable and the truth is unbearable?

"That boy Mittler wrote you a love poem and you thought, 'Oh, I'll just change a few words and give it to the old hag. She won't know the difference.'"

"That's not fair. I wasn't thinking 'old hag.'"

"Yes, you are right. It is not fair of me to say that when you speak to yourself of me you say 'old hag.' How terribly unfair of me to say that. My dear, sweet, wild girl," she said, as the teardrops came quickly one after the other from her eyes, "what have I done to you from the very moment of our acquaintance that has not been unfair? Perhaps nothing. You must leave this house. That you must do so—" she stopped talking for a moment. "That you must do so is as obvious as it is awful. You mustn't waste a moment more of your precious life in this house. Please. Today you must leave. You must leave within the hour. I will go out of the room now. Whatever you wish to take from this house belongs to you. Once you have left, do not come back. I will pack you a dinner."

I wore my hiking boots and a warm coat on my back—one of the big black woolen men's coats that Skip hated. I stuffed a backpack with half a dozen pairs of underwear, two extra bras, a pair of sneakers, some T-shirts, $10,000 in cash, and a paperback copy of *Pride and Prejudice*, which I was rereading at the time. I went into the kitchen and saw the tongue sandwich wrapped in plastic on the kitchen counter. I wanted to know where the woman was who had made the sandwich. I tried to think of her. I tried to form the words of whole sentences she had ever said to me in order to carry her out of the house in my mouth. I thought of *You are introducing me to aspects of myself that I hadn't an inkling existed before I met you*, and I thought of *Touch the bottoms of my feet lightly with your fingers, please*, and *How humiliated I am to love a child*, and I thought of "*I think of it with wonder now, the glass of mucus that stood on the table in front of my father all weekend*," and "*and he was always quietly arrayed*," and, of course, *You mustn't waste a moment more of your precious life in this house*. But all the words she had said changed when I said them. A word her narrow lips had formed perfectly in the air got sloppy on its way across the thick little swamp of my lips. And so instead of what she said, I thought of what she looked like. I stood next to the kitchen counter touching the plastic wrap on the tongue sandwich with my bare fingers. The new wrinkles in Skip Hartman's face were most satisfying for me to picture. In my mind I saw the small, soft gathering of skin along the line of her jaw and underneath her chin. I saw the radial grooves in the skin at the outer sides of her eyes. I saw the tiny vertical wrinkles that connected the base of her nose to the top of her mouth and resembled the negative image of a skyful of thin bolts of lightning as seen from far away at night. I compared and contrasted the virile, taut tummy of the robust woman I had met in her middle thirties with the larger, wider, softer, puffy belly of the sad, gray-haired lady who had just made me a sandwich. And then I thought of the supreme instance of the skin of her silken white-and-blue breasts swooping down to the rough, bunched-up red-brown skin of her unsuckled nipples. And then I did not know why I had begun to think of those breasts; I knew only that I wanted them here now in the kitchen, so much that it made me tremble, and I knew that I would not have them or hold them or taste them ever again in my life because of having been rash, duplicitous, and young.

I crossed the threshold of the house and entered the world. A fierce, cold wind blew from east to west down in the street. The air had grown dark and dropped below freezing. I walked into the wind. When I had gone ten feet down the block I heard the tiny sound of the voice of Hoving Harrington Hartman push through the wind. "My child!" he called to me. "I am hungry! Would you fix me a bowl of soup?" I did not turn around. I continued to walk away from him. "Yes, of course," he said. "You are young and you must enjoy this spirited time of your life," he called, his voice almost inaudible now. I did not answer him.

THIS WAS A wicked cold night, and bleak. By bleak I now mean that the sky offered nothing in the way of comfort, and my mind responded to the sky's nothing with nothing of its own. I walked down Lexington Avenue and shivered. I could have checked into a hotel but what then? For someone who continued to keep all people at bay with my perpetually rejuvenating force field of hatred and suspicion, I was oddly unsuited to being alone. I did not know how to be alone.

I ducked into Grand Central Station to warm up. It was late, and a few derelicts and homeless folks—probably without $10,000 in their pockets—loitered around the enormous room whose ceiling was a comfortingly intelligible miniature of a sky that was in reality chaotic and brutal. I sat on the marble steps near the Vanderbilt exit and tried hard to think about a lot of things at once, kind of like what I'm doing now in the comfort of my own home, as they say. Reader, I have found that living is like memoir writing: when I want most urgently to understand my life, I am least able to do so; later, when it doesn't matter so much, everything becomes clear for a brief interval; later still, I hardly remember what it was I had wanted so desperately to understand.

On the marble steps, I recalled Skip Hartman's remark that everything she had ever done to me was unfair. That was not true. While it may have been unfair of her to have *bought* me at the age of eleven, it was decidedly fair of her to have *rescued* me at the age of eleven. And as it was with Skip's buying and rescuing, so it was with my loving and hating: I am someone who, for better and for worse, doubles up, emotionally and otherwise.

By tapping his nightstick on the stair next to my thigh, a uniformed police officer communicated to me that I could not sit on the marble steps any longer. In full knowledge that I would somehow manage to hurt the boy who was my destination, I walked down through the bitter cold to East Second Street.

I saw myself as a runaway train hurtling out of Grand Central Station on its way to a wreck, and carrying one passenger, a little woman who stood in the window waving frantically; was she waving for help, was she waving for everyone to get out of the way, or was she just waving hello?

12 *Unrelenting Pleasure*

SHIVERING, DISTRAUGHT, I walked down to Mittler's building, found him in, and frantically assaulted his arms and lips and head with a series of compliments. "Stop it," he said. "How's your foot?"

"What's that supposed to mean?" I was standing inside his orange tent, the top of my head grazing its soft ceiling.

"Sit down," he said.

I sat and offered him half the tongue sandwich Skip Hartman had made me. He dissolved powdered fruit-and-vitamin mix in a quart of water and served me in a collapsible tin cup. We listened to each other chew and swallow.

"Skip kicked me out," I said.

He said nothing. We fell asleep on opposite sides of the tent.

In the morning, Mittler made us tea and showed me his new

device. "You can puncture any part of your body with this. Well, not any part, but any part you can fit in between here and here." This thing looked as if a small sewing machine had mated with a gun.

"What's the point?"

"The point is I'm going to puncture my mouth."

"Puncture your mouth? That's like making a hole in a hole."

"I mean my lip."

"Which lip?"

He pointed to a place on his upper lip that, were he to sneer, would fold upward.

"Why would you do that?"

"To have an actual wound in a place that's kind of already wounded anyway."

"Your lip is wounded?"

"My mouth."

"What do you mean?"

"I mean that I can never say what I mean."

"So a hole in your lip is going to fix that?"

"No!"

"What then?"

"It'll just look cool and kind of wounded."

"It'll look like a moth is eating your face."

"No, it's a tiny hole, and you put something through it like a small gold ring."

"Oh, you mean you're going to pierce your lip. Why the hell didn't you say so?"

"See what I mean?"

It was true that Mittler, despite the forcefulness of his ideas, spoke awkwardly. He became graceful and found peace in tasks that required physical technique. And so I felt pleasure in sipping the tea he had made and in watching him oil and load his lip-ring gun; pleasure but not happiness, for pleasure is just pleasure and not a balsam against disappointment, separation, grief.

"Merry Christmas, guys," someone said. It was Chetty. He had been hiding under an army blanket at the back of the tent, and was syringe-thin.

"It's Christmas?" Mittler and I said.

"Wow, I can't believe that bitch threw me out on Christmas Eve!"

"The little orphling was abandoned on Christmas Eve?" Chetty asked. "Mildred and I have come to cheer everybody up. Oh, Mildred! You may come in!" Mildred entered, nearly as thin as Chet, topless, wearing a long Indian print skirt. Thick tufts of light brown hair grew from under her arms. Her breasts were much like those of a boy. "I present to you Mildred Wanwood," Chetty said. Mildred curtsied shyly. "Mildred likes to stand alone outside someone's private dwelling and wait to be asked in. She can't shake off the loneliness of property ownership. She grew up in Englewood Cliffs. Mildred, give the children their toys."

Mildred reached into a bright Guatemalan satchel. I started to cry and spilled my tea. "What's the matter?" Mildred said.

"It's Christmas and you're giving me a present," I said.

"Aw, shut up, you little twat," Chetty said gently, and stroked my hair with his dirty fingers. "Of course you get a present. Everyone here gets one. Besides, Mittler loves you. Besides that, you amuse us."

Mildred held out a small sheet of white paper perforated into segments that looked like postage stamps, only half the size and without pictures on them. Mittler put the gun on the ground, carefully tore off four squares of the paper, and handed one to each of us. Mildred undulated down into a sitting position next to Chetty at the back of the tent. "Do you know what this is?" she asked me. She was excited like a thin puppy.

Chetty said, "I bet she doesn't know. She was raised by Republicans."

"Put it in your mouth but don't swallow it," Mildred said.

I looked at Mittler, who balanced his square on the tip of his index finger. "Couldn't hurt at this point," he said, and popped it in his mouth.

Chetty and Mildred looked at each other and stuck out their tongues. Chetty placed his square on Mildred's tongue and Mildred placed her square on Chetty's tongue. "Merry Christmas," they said. They leaned close and touched cracked lips. Mittler raised his eyebrows at me.

"What's gonna happen?" I asked.

"Stuff that's never happened before," Mildred said.

"Make it new," Chetty said.

I put the square in my mouth.

Mildred and Chetty helped one another to their bony feet. "We'll be back. We're going dancing in the snow."

"There is no snow," I said.

"She's so literal," Chetty said, and left with Mildred.

"Now what do we do?" I asked Mittler.

"I'm going to puncture my mouth."

"What about me?"

"You want your mouth punctured?"

"No."

"Then wait."

"I've been waiting my whole life. I'm sick of it."

"So read."

"Reading *is* waiting."

I opened up *Pride and Prejudice*. I love, love, *love* Jane Austen's understatement. "Dirty stockings and a face glowing with the warmth of exercise," only Jane could have said. I haven't seen a picture, but that Jane must have been ferociously plain. Only someone with—I don't know—let's say two radically different-sized nostrils would be careful to write such symmetrical sentences as she did. On the other hand, it is the luxury of the gorgeous to write sentences that look and sound and are amorphous and shitty. Witness the present account.

As Elizabeth Bennett reached Pemberley Wood, I became aware of each atom that composed my face vibrating in a fixed position and told Mittler about it. He moaned. He was curled up in a tight ball on the floor, grimacing. I asked him what he was doing.

"Holding myself in."

I wished he hadn't said that because my atoms broke away from their fixed positions and my face kind of went out all over the tent. "Mittler, what was on those little white squares?"

"Atoms."

"Did you make a hole in your head yet?"

"No."

"Why not?"

"Because then a giant universal being would stick a straw in my head and suck out my brain."

"Could we talk about something more normal, please?"

"Go ahead."

"Okay, first I have to wrap this towel around my face." I wrapped a towel tightly around my skull in the face area and couldn't breathe so I unwrapped it. Then I jammed my fists into my eye sockets. That seemed to help some.

"So, Mittler."

"Yeah?"

"How was school today?"

"Good."

"What did you learn?"

"Fractals."

"What are fractals?"

"They're when all things in the universe get smaller and smaller and smaller and smaller until everything is nothing and vice versa."

"Maybe we should have sex."

"No!"

"What should we do?"

"Put my sleeping bag on top of me and then jump up and down on it."

I did that for a few minutes.

"Oh, that's much better," he said. "You want me to do it to you?"

"Yeah, but walk, don't jump."

He walked on my legs and butt and back with his soft padded feet. Mittler's a good walker.

"Maybe we should kiss a little," he said, pointing the gun at me.

"What are you going to do if I say no, pierce my navel?"

For a time, then, we sat side by side and kissed in a pleasant, soothing fashion. Because my eyes were closed, I didn't see Mittler bring the gun to our mouths, but I heard a soft pop and felt a pinprick in my top lip. As I tried to jerk my head away he grabbed the back of my head and held it in place.

"Don't move," he said. His words came out distorted, and when he spoke I felt a sharp pain in my lip.

"Huh?" I felt the pain when I spoke, too.

"Stay still."

"What happened?" I said, or tried to say, but something prevented me from making the w and p sounds.

"I locked us together."

"What?"

"We are wearing one lip ring between the two of us," he said, but because it sounded as if he were saying "Ee are airing un lyring eating the ooh uh us," and because an hour ago I had eaten a piece of paper with very strong LSD on it for the first time ever, I didn't have a clear sense of what was happening.

Mittler leaned back, pulling me down over him; that was the easiest way for him to reach the hand mirror in the corner of the tent by the door. He held up the mirror so I could see how we were connected.

I said, "Great. Did you do this on purpose?"

"I don't know. Maybe. I guess."

"Now I can't leave you without ripping your face open."

"So how is that different from before?"

Mittler lay on his back and I lay facedown on him. I did not allow my face to rest fully on his face because the lip ring would have sliced into our upper gums. I held my head so that the tips of our noses were lightly touching and my hair, hanging down, enclosed the top and side perimeters of his face. He rotated his body clockwise until he lay on his right side and I lay on my left. We remained face-to-face, tripping on acid, and helped each other learn to talk. We took turns saying things because we did not yet know how to speak at the same time. We practiced English word pronunciation. We timed our breathing so that he would not inhale my exhalations and vice versa, but then sometimes we laughed so hard that we coughed into each other's mouths. We rested. I repeatedly felt a kind of ultra-sensation begin on the bottoms of my feet, surge up my body, and shoot out the top of my head, as if a giant pastry chef were pressing me out with a low-voltage rolling pin.

Time passed. The tent walls grew dim and we saw elongated shadows of football-player-sized cats and dogs hanging low in the sky above Houston Street and whipping each other with flexible bamboo rods.

"You're squeezing my pelvic bone very hard," Mittler said.

This was the most fun I could remember having, ever.

In the morning, Mildred and Chetty came back to the tent with dilated pupils. They put fresh squares of LSD-soaked paper in our mouths. They did not ask how or why a single gold ring had punctured one of each of our lips, nor did they seem to notice that that was the case.

Mildred said, "I can't stand it, I can't stand it!" and raced around and around the tent screaming. She tore a clump or two of hair from her head before Chetty reached her and, holding her with his frail arms, pinned her even frailer ones down to her sides. "I'm standing it, I'm standing it," Mildred said.

They left. Mittler closed his eyes and began to age very quickly. His skull and all the bones of his arms and legs shrank while his skin remained the same size. All the ripe boy skin drooped off his little frame. He looked very unhappy and he didn't have to tell me I was the cause of his unhappiness. His upper lip became so droopy that he was able to stand up and move around the tent while staying attached to me by a long, limp putty-length of lip. He did a little soft-shoe dance and his long-lipped grin communicated a thousand regrets. He sang me this song:

> "A fine romance with you, bitch, is
> A long tap dance in Hell, which is
> Better than a metal-toe kick in the teeth.
> I like it when you're on top
> But not when I'm underneath.

> "A fine romance, with no fucking,
> A fine romance. With this lip ring,
> If we tried to fuck you would rip off my face.
> To love is to self-erase.
> I'd rather be sprayed with Mace.

> "A fine romance, my good woman,
> My gal with a dick with a foreskin hood, woman.
> You never give the poems I write you a chance.
> You steal them for Miss Fancy Pants.
> This is a fine romance."

"Mittler cut it out, you're giving me the creeps."
"What?"
"Stop singing!"
"Who's singing? I was asleep."
"So who was singing?"

"I don't know. I dreamt I was a diseased elm tree."

"Mittler, can you really go to sleep on this drug? I'm so tired but I can't sleep."

"There's a trick to it. First, relax your tongue."

"What do you mean?"

"I mean shut up."

"Oh."

"Also, let your tongue lean against the inside wall of your mouth."

"Okay, then what?"

"Well, if you're saying 'Okay, then what?' you're not doing it. Are you doing it now?"

"Yes."

"If you're saying 'Yes' then you're not—"

"Mittler!"

"Okay, after you relax your tongue, count backward from a million."

"One million, nine hundred ninety-nine thousand nine hundred and ninety-nine, nine hundred ninety-nine thousand nine hundred and ninety-eight, nine hundred ninety-nine thousand nine hundred and ninety-seven, nine hundred ninety-nine thousand nine hundred and ninety-six, nine hundred ninety-nine thousand nine hundred and ninety-five, nine hundred ninety-nine thousand nine hundred and ninety-four, nine hundred ninety-nine thousand nine hundred and ninety-three—"

"Count in your head."

"I am counting in my head."

"Count in the part of your head that isn't your mouth."

I was down in the mid-nine hundred thousands when Paul entered the room. He was imperially thin and arrayed in paja-mas of light. I rolled onto my back to look at him, dragging

Mittler, who, asleep, had become a loose, soft, malleable fillet. Lying on my back, I gazed directly into the wide-open nostrils of yore, the gently veined inner nostrils of my twin baby brother, just as I remembered them. There above me was the familiar sneer of the face of my kin, the overall cruelty; there was the tall forehead, the translucent, squeezable gullet, the skull-encrusted brain; and there, the enormous sadness of his own diminutive self, attached like a misguided deer tick to the gross but bloodless body of infinity.

"You!" he said, pointing a bony finger of light.

I lay accused.

"You have forgotten me," he said.

"No I haven't. You've forgotten me."

"Don't be an idiot."

"Don't you."

"Admit that you have not thought of me even once in years," Paul said.

"I think of you all the time, just not consciously."

"You never think of me."

"You already said that."

"I taught you how to think, and you forgot."

"I don't want to think like you and you can't make me."

"You killed me. Now honor me."

"How?"

"Honor me."

"Do all dead people just repeat themselves?"

"That is the job of the dead."

"Oh, Christ."

"Perfect example."

"How am I supposed to honor you?"

"Kill him, just like you killed me."

Dread surged into my body like a stronger drug than the one
I had voluntarily taken. "No." I started to cry.

"Make the harder choice, as I taught you. Kill the boy you're
sleeping with. Kill kill kill kill kill kill kill kill kill kill kill kill kill
kill kill kill kill kill kill."

I screamed, and the abrupt change in the shape of my
mouth woke Mittler. "Okay, honey, you're having a bad trip."
Paul stood above us shaking his head.

"What's a bad trip?"

"It's when you see something you shouldn't have to see."

"What should I do?"

Mittler held my head in place against his and rolled us one
over the other until he could reach his camping stove and collapsible cooking pot. "I'll make us mugwort tea."

"Okay."

Paul walked out of the tent, staring at me, bearing the tedious nostalgia that only someone who had once been alive
could feel.

We drank the tea all morning and into the afternoon, and
had to pee. "Why don't we run a catheter from my bladder directly into your bladder," I said. He said ha ha ha and wondered if I would give the sarcasm a rest for just one moment of
one day of my entire life. We went to the receptacle that
served as a toilet in Mittler's building. It's hard not to get
splashed by urine, reader, if the person whose lip your lip is
stuck to is peeing into a bucket. We needed several days to figure out how not to get splashed, and the same amount of time
to figure out how to eat without hurting one another's mouths.
In fact, anything other than lying still required at least several
days' practice, and even after that, careful planning and coop-
erative execution. We lay still for much of the time. I read to

him from *Pride and Prejudice*. He read to me from the diaries of John Muir. We found it helpful to continue taking LSD once or twice a day.

CHILDHOOD FRIENDS DIERDRE and Harry showed up, slumming for drugs. Harry had obtained an American motorcycle and an electric guitar and was fat. The guitar, because Harry was fat and also tall, seemed distant, resting high up near his neck. Harry himself seemed distant, literally and figuratively above us, semi-interested at most in the weather down there, least interested of all in his girlfriend, Dierdre. Harry at rest in the center of the Mittlerian tent with leather pockets full of beef jerky and apple-mint sucking candies was like a lazy Susan of record-breaking size around which no diner could comfortably maneuver. When Harry sat around the tent, Mittler and I had to sit on the tip of a foot or hand belonging to him, or at the distant edge of one of the fatty extensions of his person. Thin, tiny Dierdre sat curled in the aerie of his lap. We passed squares of drugged paper up to Dierdre and she tossed the paper farther up toward his mouth. To watch Dierdre do this was like watching a little girl throw a paper airplane through the doorway of a cathedral.

Dierdre didn't seem to be doing so well. This was evident in the state of her freckles. No freckle had changed shape or size or position or color; she did not possess more freckles or fewer freckles, and yet each freckle had been—*sullied* is the word I want to use. I do not recall observing any other sign of her discontent than those downgraded freckles. Her sternum was its bony, pale self, as was the rippled skin stretched across her upper ribs, as were the lovely nipples pointing faithfully forward beneath her white scoop-neck T-shirt. Her same obnoxious talk did not betray an increased dissatisfaction with life. Just the freckles.

"It's usually so clean in here," Dierdre said. "What happened? You don't wash anymore? You don't do laundry?"

"No," Mittler and I said, our upper lips forming a small tent above our lower lips.

"Maybe you should hire a cleaning lady," she said. "Maybe Skip Hartman could clean for you."

"Very funny," we said, because one of the methods we had developed for not tearing each other's mouths open was to think the same thoughts and say the same words at the same time.

"What's funny to me," Dierdre continued, in the same vein, "is how you're like this idealist guy, Mittler, with your shared lip ring and your housing rights and your East Village squatter community, but you can't clean your room. You two look ridiculous, by the way, and you smell bad."

I said, "You are so fucking—"

"—obnoxious," Mittler said. "You have not changed—" he said.

"—in the least," I said. "You are no different—" I added.

"—than you were in the sixth grade," he completed. "Obnoxious—" he said.

"—right out of the womb," I said.

"An obnoxious seed," he said.

"A burden on your parents," I said.

"And on all who know you," he said.

"Unwanted," I said.

"Unloved," he said. "And yet spoiled—" he said.

"—rotten," I said.

Dierdre didn't just cry. She wailed. She stood up and ran out of the tent. We heard her footsteps going down the stairs. We heard the loud screech of the metal door scraping open against the concrete floor, another screech, and a slam. We had vanquished Dierdre. We had pummeled her, pulverized her. We took more LSD.

"Look, it's the two-headed monster," Harry pronounced from atop the Parnassian height of his body.

Mittler said, "Wow, we were really mean. How the hell'd that happen?"

"Our hostility—" I said.

"—is greater than the sum of its parts," he said.

Harry said, "Dierdre got raped."

"What?"

"She got raped and she's fragile and you two just broke her," he said, as if reciting something he'd rehearsed many times and didn't care about. This was a different Harry from the one I remembered, if what I remembered makes any difference. This one was articulate and bored. He still had that same head on him—curly thin yellowed beard, gray skin, bags under the eyes—only the entire head itself had expanded to the size of a pumpkin. "Dierdre got raped in a cabin on an island off the coast of Maine. It was her own damn fault. I can't love her anymore. Don't know how to tell her."

"Cruel giant," Mittler said.

I said, "Tell us what happened."

"Oh, her and me were riding up the coast on my Harley at the end of the summer and we got in a big fight and she told me to go away and die so I left her in the parking lot of this bar on the Maine coast. She went in the bar and there was this skinny little drunk boy who talked to her and she worked that kind of reverse charm on him, you know? Where she says

mean things to you for an hour nonstop until you feel so bat-
tered you just want to hug her really tight?" Harry said, as if all
this were the oldest and most uninteresting thing a person
could ever waste his time saying. "So she sour-talks him into
letting her stay at his shack—all these people have shacks up
there and they marry their sisters and whatnot—only she says
he has to not touch her the whole night or else her big
boyfriend who rides a Harley will beat the crap out of him and
probably dismember his dick—by which she meant me, like
I'm gonna really tangle with some inbred New England serial
killer–looking guy over *her*.

"So the guy lets her stay at his shack and she wakes up at ten
A.M. and the guy is standing in the doorway of his shack, he's
been awake for hours, out hunting beaver skins or lobsters or
whatever they hunt up there, and he presents her with beaver-
skin gifts or whatever, and some flowers, and says no girl ever
made him treat her like a lady and it makes him feel real classy
and would she like to take a ride out to a deserted island on his
outboard."

Harry's eyes were half closed and I honestly thought he was
going to fall asleep in the middle of his own story.

"So the forest-geek boy takes my girl out to this island and I
guess she's thinking, Here's a boy who's real nice to me and
treats me like a lady, unlike that fat fuck of a Harley-riding
boyfriend, who practically ignores me every second. So they
come up onto the beach, she gets out of the boat, and he
punches her really hard in the face, over and over, and takes
her to a shack and does stuff—" Mittler and I saw a big pulse
work its way up the huge body of Harry and come out his
mouth as a small, high noise, a prolonged squeak. "'Eeeeeeee
does stuff to my nice girl that she won't even say what he did

cause it was so bad and she won't ever be all right, you know? The guy left her in the shack and he didn't care what happened. She crawled down to the beach and the Coast Guard saw her. That guy, he hurt her for all time, you know?" Harry was so big and sad now. This giant person being sad in our tent, shaking, squealing softly with unhappiness. "He hurt her all the way for the whole thing until she lies down and dies somewhere, guys. How can that happen? Now my whole life sucks too 'cause I love her and I don't even want to anymore. I can't help it. You know, guys? Everything is bad now forever and I hate her and I'm gonna marry her."

Harry sighed. His mass resettled. He quieted. Only a slight tremor of his flesh persisted, causing the orange cloth walls of the tent to billow. Mittler and I caressed his flanks, soothing him.

"You guys are nice," he said, sounding indifferent again.

"Play us a song on your guitar," Mittler said.

"Don't feel like it."

"Try," Mittler said.

Harry fiddled with the guitar strap, which, wrapped around his neck, looked like a piece of dental floss wrapped around a sequoia. He lowered the guitar to the height of his voluminous breasts. He removed a small electric amp from an inside pocket of his leather jacket, plugged it in, and strummed. He sighed again, played some chords, and mumbled some words off-key that sounded like "Living on the streets with all the petty people" and "You used to get juiced in the head" and "You used to be so abused" and "You used to ride on the chrome horse with your boy who's fat" and "You got some secrets to conceeeec-uhl" and a bunch of other things I couldn't make out.

Dierdre, who must have been drawn toward the sound of her own life being sung by the one who knew it best, returned to us. There was a thick red line running horizontally across her face—her mouth—with the shape of which she was trying to tell us something about how she felt. She felt bad. And by pressing her lips together she was saying she would try to keep all that badness contained inside her in our presence, and by the way she held her shoulders so stiffly and carefully she was asking us to be very gentle with her, and we were. Harry sat in a grand, glazed stupor. Mittler and I picked up Dierdre and held her in our arms as one would hold a small child who has fallen from her bicycle. We raised her up above our heads and laid her to sleep on the soft, rounded shelf of flesh where Harry's breast ended and his belly began.

The sky outside the window outside the tent had been dark for hours. Mittler and I ate a bedtime snack of LSD and with our hands we described garish-colored, violent paintings in the air before falling asleep.

Sometime in the night, I looked up and saw Dierdre darkly glowing, her small body a collapsed firmament. For a while I lay with dozing Mittler in the lowest foothills of Harry and gazed up at Dierdre's twinkling freckles. Then I undertook a journey to her. Out of a large T-shirt, I fashioned a frontal pouch in which to carry the sleeping body of Mittler while I climbed the lower slopes of Harry. I attached a rope to Harry's thigh and climbed up his leg. I trekked his hip and the lunar arc of his belly. Somewhere in the middle of the night, I cast off from the edge of Harry's breast and made my ascent of the body of Dierdre, one of the roughs, a cosmos: for days, I traveled those degraded heavens. I roamed the unhappy constellations of her limbs. I traversed deserts of scar tissue, barren and desolate. I stopped to rest and drink at great salt lakes of sweat. When I approached a terrible bright freckle, I positioned Mittler in front of my eyes, making of his head an eclipse from behind which to look without going blind. I reached my destination, the abandoned planet of her cunt. There I found ravages. I went spelunking in a strip-mined outer crevice of her labia. I scaled and descended the steep, wasted folds. Holding the length of Mittler's body perpendicular to my own, I thus maintained my balance on the soft and treacherous footing of the ridge high over the abyss of her vagina. I had arrived at the point in the journey, reader, where the traveler wishes she had not left home. I regretted my terrible decision to take this trip. I was afraid I would lose myself in the place where she had been made to die. I woke Mittler and made him carry me away from the dark red cavern that held in the memory of its walls more violence than time and forgetting could erode. Mittler carried me safely back to the tent floor and I fell asleep, shivering, sad, feeling the most gentle tenderness toward Dierdre and doubting I could make my feelings the least bit useful to her.

A FEW DAYS after Dierdre and Harry left the tent, we discovered that Harry had left behind all the beef jerky and apple-mint sucking candies he had been holding in the pockets of his pants, shirt, and jacket, which was a considerable amount of food. It was early or mid- or late January. Mittler and I, who had not eaten solid food since Christmas Eve, ate beef jerky and apple-mint sucking candies for the next twenty-four hours, and drank our usual mugs of herbal tea. We were both by now growing acne and skin rashes. It could be said that acne and skin rashes covered one fifth of the collective surface of our two bodies, though an accurate estimate at that time was thoroughly impossible and is now even more so. Only the upper lip, lip wound, and lip ring area of our bodies did we maintain in a state of scrupulous cleanliness. Our interest in corporal maintenance of any kind dropped off sharply beyond the immediate lip area. In fact, for reasons we did not have the mental coherency to question, our bodies had become to us, at best, life-support systems for our upper lips.

Stephen Samuels, my former friend and math tutor and maid, arrived wearing a comically exaggerated scowl meant to show his attitude toward our lifestyle. Stephen was trim and well-rested and wore a navy four-button worsted wool suit, the jacket of which he held prissily folded over his left forearm while he sat down on a rolled sleeping bag. The complexion of his face was clear and smooth. His posture and movements seemed designed to say, "I find everything in my immediate vicinity distasteful, but for the sake of my dear, dear friends I am willing to endure my own discomfort, though God knows you in particular, Mary, have been nothing if not disloyal to me on a Mata Harian scale."

Mittler and I sat up and faced him, insofar as it was possible to face anyone but each other.

"How come *you* look so good?" I asked him.

"Oh, I have my own small upstart company now, thank you."

"What's your company?"

"It's a little thing I like to call Mountebank, Incorporated."

Mittler said, "What product or service do you offer?"

"Marketing consultation."

"What do you market?"

"I market ideas about marketing."

"What do the people you market your ideas to market?"

"Packages."

"What's in the packages?"

"Things and ideas of things."

"What kinds of things?"

"Oh, sweetheart, that is so unimportant. I train my clients to train their market how to feel toward the packages my clients' ideas come in, but this is really quite a bore to discuss with you two as I see that you have no idea what I'm talking about, and are your pupils crazy dilated or did someone replace your eyeballs with black marbles?"

"Marbles," we said.

"Oh, the little Pushmi-Pullyu is tripping its brains out. Isn't that just *darling*."

I said, "How did you know we were here?"

"I ran into those two friends of yours, the forlorn hipsters, those children who, between the two of them, form the number ten."

"Dierdre and Harry?"

"I suppose."

"Dierdre got raped."

"No wonder she looked so hideous."

"Stephen, you are cold."

"With my fragile emotional makeup I cannot afford to be hot," he said. "I have alerted my quondam father of your whereabouts. He may come for a visit. He may also inform Ms. September Hartman so her head doesn't get worried."

"I don't care about her head. She kicked me out!" I said.

"On Christmas Eve!" Mittler said.

"Yes, well, being what I am, I find the situations you get yourself into quite amusing, Mary. You allowed yourself to be sold by one Caucasian to another Caucasian, and now you have more or less shackled yourself intentionally to this boy. These are types of situations that I as a twentieth-century Negro feel disinclined to get myself involved in."

"We resent what you're saying," we said.

"Yes, of course you do," Stephen said. "This is such a hetero thing you're doing here. You would never catch a couple of homos doing this. You would never catch a man doing this without a woman. It's very vagina-y in here. You've even got an herbal-vaginal tea brewing on the stove."

Stephen Samuels looked at his watch, said that he had a meeting with some people about a canine mint breath-freshener concept, and excused himself.

NIETZSCHEAN FASHION MODEL Ruella Forecourt arrived not long after with her husband, Joe Samuels. Joe, usually chatty, seemed cowed that afternoon. Ruella spoke a great deal, the heaviness of her Swiss-German accent advancing and retreating with the passion of her feelings on a given subject. She told us the story about the day Friedrich Nietzsche saw a man whipping his little dray horse too often and too hard on a street outside his apartment in Turin. Nietzsche ran out into the street and embraced the forlorn, bleeding horse about the neck, and the horse began speaking to Nietzsche in fluent German. At this point, Nietzsche crossed the invisible border between philosophy and madness, *without a return ticket,* as Ruella put it. On the afternoon when Ruella visited us, I felt that she existed to embody the topic of conversation between Nietzsche and the horse.

"Oh, darlings," she said, "the light in here is perfectly lurid."

"Lurid," Joe agreed, nodding vigorously.

"I would love to shoot stills of you in situ. The little Siamese twins. Of course you would have to be naked, and my dear boy you would have to grab her here like so."

"I don't grab her there," Mittler said.

"We don't ever get naked," I said.

"Why my dears, could you possibly mean that you two do not enjoy sexual congress?"

"Congress, the executive and judicial branches," I said.

"But you must let me shoot nudes of you."

"No nudes," we said.

"I have of course told you about my pornography project?" she said. "I intend to assemble a complete visual typology of dominant and submissive sexual positions for women. Of those positions I will then create a sign language on the model of the American Sign Language for the deaf. Either a given position will be assigned an arbitrary letter value—for example, *woman sits backward on supine man's penis* will be the letter *a*—or a position will function as an ideogram—for example, *woman reclining alone, legs casually spread, bracing herself on her elbows, gently touching the sides of her own hips* would represent *water* or *peace*. Once I have created my Alphabet of Female Sexual Positions, I will then write feminist treatises using this alphabet, and I hope others will do so as well. And that is my project and you are lovely children that I would like to include in your peculiar tent."

"Nope," we said.

"I'm financing the project," Joe said proudly. That was Joe's first feckless chink in Ruella's wall of speech.

I said, "No hard documentation, please."

"Or soft," Mittler said. "How much does the project cost?" he asked Joe.

"Much more than you'd think," Joe said, "and she's reaping all the profit."

"How come?"

"Because I love her."

"Also because Joseph and I agree that I must not be subjugated by him. Yes, because you see the white man may subjugate the African-American man and the white man may subjugate the indigenous American man and the white man may subjugate the South American man and the white man may subjugate the Caribbean man and the white man may subjugate the Chinese man and the white man may subjugate the European man but—oh, darling, who is that thin boy I am thinking of?"

Joe said, "How the hell should I know, dear?"

"Dear, you mustn't say 'hell' to me. The thin lovely martyr boy, the one who said the beautiful thing I want to tell the children."

"John Lennon," Joe said.

"Yes, children, the white man may subjugate all the other men and even himself but you see the little fellow John Lennon who died so dreadfully also said to us that the woman is the nigger of the world," a phrase which in Ruella's mouth sounded like *Deh voomon eess deh neegah uff de veldt.* "One must at all costs avoid to be subjugated," she said.

Mittler said, "But you're subjugating Joe."

"No, darling, I am *using* Joe."

"That's worse."

"Oh, no, darling, it is better. It is good to use, and even more so, it is good to be used. I myself wake up in the morning and I cannot wait for the first person to use me today. Oh, it is beautiful to be used *and* it is fun to be used. In the woman's life it is the supreme achievement to be used and the man must learn to honor the woman by using her properly. The man also must learn to be used by the woman and to enjoy it because it is lovely. For me personally I am sometimes so impatient for someone to use me that I give up waiting and use myself."

MILDRED, THE GIRLFRIEND of Chetty, who when her feathers were not too ruffled behaved like a mother hen, had been hen enough one day to shoplift a pair of flexible narrow-necked toothbrushes and bring them back to us at the roost. That night, Mittler and I carried the new toothbrushes and a tube of toothpaste into a small room where a smooth white porcelain bowl of water rested on the floor. Above the porcelain bowl, Mittler and I stood side by side, as much as that was possible. First I and then Mittler squeezed the tube and laid the bright green toothpaste down along the tops of the bristles of our toothbrushes. We angled our heads away from each other as far as we could without hurting ourselves, and opened our mouths wide. Our two mouths, connected and opened as they were, resembled a symbol for infinity in which the two adjacent loops were filled in with black ink. We brushed. While brushing, Mittler brought up the topic of, "Is this working out for you?"

"Is what working out?"

"Our arrangement."

"I haven't thought about it."

"Think about it."

"Okay."

"No, I mean right now."

"I just did."

"And?"

"I'm saying, it's okay."

"Just okay?"

"Well, it's nice. It's fun. I mean I think sometime I'll want to, you know, go outside again, go for a run, ride a bus. I've been thinking of getting a dog," I said, shoving the bristles back and forth along the tops of my lower right molars.

"I don't want you to buy a dog. People with dogs are liars. Like the person will trip on the sidewalk and blame it on the dog."

"How about ride a bus?"

"What about how nicely we're attached to each other?"

"I just said, it's fun."

"But I want to always be this way with you."

"Literally?"

"Yeah, I think so. Do you?"

We rinsed and spat.

"Sure," I said. "I guess."

HARRY RETURNED TO the tent at noon one day. He had Hoving Harrington Hartman in his hands. "He wanted to see you," Harry said.

"This revolting Cyclops brought me here against my will," Hoving said.

Harry placed the little man in the center of the tent and left. Hoving had shrunken since I saw him, and his stained and wrinkled black wool coat brushed against the floor of the tent. The sky outside the building outside the tent was clear. The sun, because this was winter in lower Manhattan, occupied the area of the sky south of Houston Street and shone directly through the window outside our tent, making the tent walls especially orange and bright. "I'm in Hell," Hoving said in a voice that was a high-pitched, cracked variation of the voice of the woman I loved most in the world. "I had often wondered if this would happen. I tried to be decent in all my individual dealings with people. I did not ever behave in a lascivious manner in my private gynecological practice, though on several occasions I was quite tempted to do so. While it is true that the proto-intrauterine device that I invented caused severe health complications in some of the women who used it, it is also true that I neither intended nor foresaw those complications and, furthermore, that each woman who sued received a substantial out-of-court settlement. Should I have sold all my stock shares in my own invention and given away not only all of my proceeds but all of the proceeds of my proceeds? Apparently so. Ah, my legs ache, just as in life. I suppose I should not be surprised that Hell is a continuation of old age in perpetuity."

"You're not in Hell, you're in the East Village," we said.

I said, "Look, Grandpa, it's me."

Hoving squinted at us. "Is that my darling grandchild? But my dear, I am confused. You were kind to me on earth. Why are you in Hell? You treated me gently and reminded me of my mama. Has someone killed you?"

"Shut up, Grandpa, you're scaring me."

"Oh, yes, now I remember. You're an insolent creep. I'm glad you're dead."

Mittler said, "Please have a seat, sir. I'll fix you some tea."

Hoving stared at Mittler and said to me, "My precious, who is this falsely polite little gargoyle you've extruded from your face?"

"That's Mittler. You've met him, remember?"

"I remember nothing. My grandchild, if you are the Devil and you have made yourself a two-headed monster to scare me, cut it out."

Mittler said, "Do you think Harry gave him a hit of acid?"

"No, he's just paranoid and senile, which is kind of the same as being on LSD except when you come down, you're dead."

Hoving became frantic and leapt at us and tried to pull our heads apart, but we were stronger and had often practiced how to keep them together in such an event. We each used a hand to restrain Hoving, while using the other to stabilize our heads. "I'm hungry," Hoving said.

"We'll have to give him beef jerky," I said.

Hoving said, "I adore beef jerky."

Hoving sat on the floor of the tent with his legs splayed out in front of him, nibbling on the tip of the beef stick. He gazed at nothing. An invisible hood seemed to have descended over his eyes. He had that pouty, almost catatonically blank look of contentment that five-year-olds get after they've cried a long time and then been appeased with food. Though his body had shrunken, his face had remained the same size, which made it look huge. It was tinted orange in the tent-filtered sunlight. His eyebrows were thick and pale. His forehead was so tall and featured with wrinkles that the total front of his head looked like two faces, one on top of the other.

Mittler said, "How old is he anyway?"

"Ninety," Hoving said dreamily.

"Don't believe him," I said. "He has no idea how old he is."

Hoving looked at me. "I know exactly how old I am. You think because I am frightened of damnation that I am not in my right mind. Well, let me tell you something, girlie. This boy is wasting his love on you, and he knows it, and he should snap out of it, and so should you. You belong with my daughter. Instead, you left her, fool."

"She kicked me out! On Christmas Eve!"

"That is crap. You kicked yourself out. Thank you for the beef jerky." Hoving stood up and left the tent.

TO BE SEVENTEEN and eating LSD every day for three months in a filthy squat in New York City while stapled to your boyfriend's face is to be seventeen. Eventually, one must either die or turn eighteen. The latter befell me.

The following morning I woke up at three o'clock, which is generally the time of day when a person sneaks away from the one who loves her beyond reason. I unclasped the lip ring, slid it up out of my lip, and clasped it again, leaving it inside Mittler. I stood up slowly. This was like being released from the gravitational field of the planet you've been living on for three months. I thought I would rise up into the air and dissipate like a cloud. I hugged myself for a few minutes while staring at Mittler, who did not wake up. To weigh myself down, I put on all the clothes I had arrived in, though the weather was much warmer now than it had been then. Already wearing my own black wool overcoat, I put on Mittler's puffy, hooded down jacket that resembled a dark blue space suit, which I thought would help protect me from the thin air beyond the immediate atmosphere of him. I started out of the tent and then, reader, I did something I would not have done when I was seventeen: I thought of how much he would miss his jacket, and took it off. I have long understood that it is not nice to be cruel, but I am still learning how to tell the difference between nice behavior and cruel behavior.

I started out of the tent again and remembered the $10,000 in hundreds I had stashed in one of the blanket rolls shortly after my arrival. I checked the blanket roll and found nothing. I went down the hall to the room where Mildred and Chetty were sleeping, woke Chetty, and asked him for the money.

Chetty said, "Oh, sorry, we bought a motorcycle with most of it and spent the rest on nice clothes and fancy dinners. I've got twenty bucks I could give you."

"Okay."

He gave me two dirty little tens. I floated down the stairs and out into the world.

LISTEN: AFTER DETACHING myself from that boy, I wandered Manhattan and the Bronx for hours and hours. I wanted to go home, and when I spoke the word *home* to myself, I pictured my bedroom with the white comforter and the large French windows; I pictured Skip Hartman standing with her back to me, looking out the French windows. I wanted to go home to Skip Hartman. She was the one I loved most. Mittler may have been the gentler soul, but Ms. Hartman, who owned me, knew how to tolerate my fierce separateness. She knew how to tolerate my hatred of her. My hatred helped her; we understood that about each other. The one thing that she did not know how to tolerate in me was my wish to be with Mittler. I had now succeeded in exhausting that wish.

I wondered if I could return to her. I pictured her standing with her back to me, looking out the French windows. The question was, Does she turn around or does she not turn around? Does she turn around? *Once you have left,* she had said on Christmas Eve, *do not come back.* She does not turn around. I could not return to her.

Nor could I now, with twenty dollars in my pocket, check into a hotel.

Several hours after nightfall, I boarded a train and rode it to Verdant, New York. The Verdant train station, which also serves Marmot, is a place you can look at late at night and think of all the nice things that happen there, if you are inclined to think that way. I mean that you could get off the train and watch the three other passengers climb into their cars and drive away, and then you could stand by yourself in the dark, desolate little parking lot and—if you are of a certain cast of mind—you could mentally populate that parking lot with families of children greeting their dads as the dads arrive from the city after a day of work in a clean office, and you could imagine a lot of good cheer imbuing such a reunion, which happens every fucking evening.

As I was retying my hiking boots before undertaking the walk to Marmot, that gray, beat-up American car swung into the deserted parking lot. The big former Marine Corps fellow, whose name I decidedly cannot remember now, stopped his car beside me. As far as noticeability of pectorals, this man was on a par with the best and brightest *Playboy* centerfold. In his navy pea coat and white dress shirt, whose top three buttons were unfastened, he displayed a taut, striated cleavage. I saw in his future the kind of physiological corruption and decay that only such exaggerated good health can hint at. Places on his body were muscular that shouldn't have been, his skull and fingers, for example. In chichi multicultural combat training programs sponsored by the U.S. government, this man had learned eight different systems of sticking hard parts of his body into soft parts of other people's bodies in order to incapacitate or damage them, and he was offering me a ride into the dark woods. I declined.

I left the parking lot and walked along a tree-bordered road dimly illumined by streetlamps. The man stayed still in his car in the parking lot. I was relieved to think he was waiting for the next train. Then his car crept out of the parking lot and followed me slowly along the road. Then it pulled up alongside me. He rolled down the window. I continued to walk and he drove his car next to me and looked at me. He made ambiguous comments, sort of innocent-slash-deeply-noninnocent comments such as "Those are nice pants. Are you of Scottish ancestry? Hop in, I won't hurt you."

I just want to say quickly here before I get to the ghastly part that these two phenomena are connected, that one could not exist without the other: the violent, frustrated ex-Marine sadist in his car following the solitary girl late at night, and the cheerful family greeting Dad as he steps off the 5:23 out of Manhattan. They go together like a horse and carriage.

I refused his initial offers of a ride, but not because I thought accepting would make it any more likely that he'd do something bad to me; I knew he'd do something bad independent of what I accepted or did not accept. No, I refused as a kind of hopeful planning gesture: I thought I might need, in my future life, if indeed there would be such, the memory of having resisted. And when I accepted his seventh offer of a ride, I did so on the principle that whatever bad thing he was going to do to me would be over with sooner than if I did not accept. Actually, I have no idea why I accepted. He shoved open the passenger side door of his car and I climbed in next to him.

He said, "Where are you going?"

I said, "Where do you think I'm going, dipshit?" There was no principle behind this remark. In fact, this remark can now be declared purely counterproductive.

He said, "I've got a cassette player back at the guardhouse. Do you like music?"

"No."

"What kind of music do you like?"

"Songs that specifically express hatred toward people who work in guardhouses."

"Sing me one."

> "Whistle while you work.
> Hitler is a jerk.
> Eenie-meenie,
> Bit his peenie.
> Now it doesn't work."

He hit the brakes hard, threw the stick shift into neutral, and applauded so vigorously that he could have crushed the skull of a newborn baby each time he slammed one of his palms with the other.

He started to drive again. "Come on," he said. "Tell me something about yourself."

"I like flowers and trees."

"What else?"

"I just got out of a very intense relationship so I'm feeling kind of fragile."

"Who were you in the relationship with?"

"Someone kind of like you only much smarter and nicer."

"Why'd you break up with him?"

"As I said, he was kind of like you."

"Who has the nicer body, him or me?"

"Him."

"Who's stronger, brute strengthwise?"

"Would you shut the fuck up? I hate you."

He reached inside his coat pocket and pulled out a long knife whose molded handle doubled as brass knuckles. He held the knife between his left hand and the steering wheel as he drove. The little jaw muscle that looked like a small erect penis sheathed under the thin skin of his face began to twitch rapidly. I went to punch him hard in the right ear to break some of the small, delicate bones of his hearing mechanism, but he blocked my punch with his right forearm. He slammed on the brakes again, grabbed me by the wrist with his right hand, and sliced open my palm. "Stay put and don't insult me. It really hurts when you insult me."

When we arrived at the guardhouse by the Marmot entrance gate he said, "Reach inside the glove compartment and pass me that roll of duct tape."

"What do you need duct tape for?"

He punched my arm and I gave him the duct tape. He held me by the wrist and dragged me across the stick shift and out the driver's door of his car. He shoved me ahead of him into the deserted guardhouse. The guardhouse was about seven feet by seven feet. He pressed me face first against one of the walls and began trying to yank down my pants.

"Can I just say one thing?" I asked.

"What?"

"You won't be able to do it. Your dick will be limp."

He uttered a long sort of sigh of frustration and said, "Then

I'll just have to kill you." He made it sound as if it would be a very unsatisfying consolation for him. "Come on," he said, "just cooperate."

"Oh, okay," I said. I turned around slowly and caressed his face and kneed him in the testicles as hard as I could.

He punched me in the chest and I sat down on the floor and couldn't breathe. At around the time he punched me I thought I heard the quiet engine of a European car, but I knew I was hearing what I wished to hear.

"You okay?" the man asked, squatting in front of me. "Come on, be a sport here, won't you?" He rammed his shoulder into my torso, as if he were a football player and I a tackling dummy. He unzipped my pants, pulled down my thermal underwear, and stared in wonder and dread at my naked crotch. That was when Skip Hartman entered the small guardhouse. "Mr. Hand," she said. "Please stand up and turn around." He stood me up and held my throat firmly in his fingers. I could not breathe. He turned his head to look at Skip, pointed the knife at her, and said, "Stay right there."

"Come to me," she said.

"What?"

"Come and make love to me. Mary is a child. I am a woman. I know how to love you. I know what you want. I know how to make you feel good."

"If you try to trick me I'll slit your fucking throat," he said.

"Fair enough. Now make love to me."

He gave my throat one last good-luck squeeze and released me. I fell on the floor. I still could not breathe. He went to Skip Hartman, and she embraced him in the same way that she had often embraced me to realign my back when it was sore. I watched the veins stand out on the skin of her bare forearms that pressed into his back. She was embracing him with all her might. He could not move. "Hey," he croaked, "you're suffocating me. Hey." I looked at her blank, open-eyed face over his shoulder as she continued to make her arms into a single boa-constrictor sort of appendage and squeezed the hell out of his torso. After a minute, his body went limp. She laid him gently facedown on the floor, pressed one knee into his spine, took the roll of duct tape from the little shelf where he had placed it, and wrapped the tape around his hands behind his back. She taped his feet together and turned his head to the side and placed a piece of tape over his mouth. He stirred then. She lifted him up and sat him in the swivel chair of the guard-house. He was awake now, and I sensed that he could still have head-butted Skip Hartman and picked up his knife and cut out her entrails, but he didn't seem to want to. She bound his torso and his thighs to the chair. His face looked peaceful and sad like the face of a child who has just been thrown a loving birthday party but who has failed to receive that one red fire truck that would have made this the perfect day.

"Put a piece of tape over his nose," I said, sitting on the floor, dressed, bruised.

"Why?"

"To kill him."

The man did not look at me. He slouched in the chair. Skip stared out the window of the guardhouse with an expression of mild satisfaction, as if she were admiring what an excellent job she had done of parking her car.

"I'll drive you to the house and give you a glass of wine," she said to me. She pressed the button that opened the iron gate. She made a small circle of her thumb and forefinger as if making the "okay" sign and flicked the top of the man's ear with her forefinger. We left the guardhouse and got in the car and drove into Marmot.

No lights were on in Tommy's house. She drove the car up the driveway and stopped. "Did he hurt you?" she said.

"I don't know." My body had gone numb and I could hardly think or speak. She stood up out of the car and left the door open. She walked rigidly across the wet grass toward the front door, and lost her footing and fell down, and stood up again. She stood still for a moment and looked around in a daze, as if she didn't know where she was.

She let us into the house. It was empty: no people, no furniture. "Tommy and Myra sold the house," she said. "For now, they are living in my house in the city. I drove up tonight to be here for the closing tomorrow morning. I have handled the sale of the house because of course I am the only one who knows how to handle these sorts of things without screwing them up. I'm not sure why I decided to drive up tonight instead of tomorrow morning. I had a presentiment. I had a—um. Wine?"

We walked into the kitchen and Skip turned on the light. We stood in the bright, bare kitchen. Her arms and legs were vibrating. She went to a cabinet and removed one of two bottles of Bordeaux. She opened her purse and pulled out a wineglass. "I expected to be alone and did not bring a second glass. I hope you do not mind sharing?"

Her words themselves were a kind of crystal wineglass on a high shelf: sharp and elegant and clear but far away; I could not reach them. She turned off the kitchen light.

"Walk with me, dear, to the living room and we shall sit on the floor together and share wine from this glass."

We sat in the living room. Faint light from the moon and the neighbors' electric lamps came through the sliding glass door at the back of the house. Skip Hartman uncorked the wine with the corkscrew of her Salvation Army knife, poured the red wine into the glass, and, ever the gentleman, offered me the first sip. I stared at it. "Don't want?" she said. "Very well." She drained the glass, poured another, offered that; I declined; she drained it again, poured another, drained that.

"Go back and kill him," I said.

"No."

"Call the police."

"He is the police."

She poured another glass of wine and drank it. The bottle was empty. She stood up and held out her hand. "Come with me. I can't touch you?" She withdrew her hand. "Come with me. Stay by my side." I stood. We went to the kitchen. She walked with more fluidity now. In the dark kitchen, she retrieved the other bottle of Bordeaux. We walked back to the living room.

"Everything is fine," she said, "when you are by my side." She reached out and tried to stroke my hair but I punched her hand. She stood next to me and watched me in the dim light of the room. A while later, she asked if I would ever let her touch me again.

"Maybe," I said.

"When?"

"Now."

"Where?"

"On the cheek."

"How?"

"With one finger, for three seconds."

She did just as I said. We sat down. For the record, I was eventually able to express my gratitude to Skip Hartman for rescuing me, and I believe I expressed it in ways considerate and tender and even erotically satisfying for all concerned, but that night I was too freaked out to express much of anything beyond my extreme freaked-outedness.

Skip opened the new bottle of wine, poured herself a glass, and drank it.

"Where'd you learn to fight?" I said.

"I did not learn."

"How did you beat him?"

"I think it is a question of urgency of intent: I was fighting for the love of my life, while he was fighting for a lousy fuck."

"You have to go back and kill him or he's gonna come after us."

"No he won't."

"Yes he will."

"You saw him sitting subdued in the chair?"

"Yeah. He looked weird. Quiet."

"He gave up very quickly and easily, and once he had given up, I believe he was happy, is the way it occurs to me to describe it. What I think I mean is that a kind of peace obtains in the heart of this man now that he has been forcibly prevented from committing his terrible deed. It is over, you see. No more struggle. There may be in his heart some disappointment over not having gotten away with it, but from the beginning of such an endeavor as his, the rapist sees getting away with it as only one of several possibilities of completion, and not necessarily the one most to be desired. In fact, *getting away with it* is hardly to be considered a mode of completion at all, now, is it? *Getting away with it* is, frankly, nothing more than an extended period of uncertainty during which the rapist must wonder continuously, *Did I get away with it?* That is, as I say, hardly the state of affairs of completion. That is the state of affairs of *on-goingness*. Furthermore, it must be said that only someone with the sturdiest emotional makeup should consider *getting away with it* as a realistic goal for rape. And perhaps it need not be added that the rapist almost by definition is not made of the sturdiest emotional stuff."

"You oughtta know."

"Yes, that also need not be added and yet you have seen fit to add it. I oughtta know. I oughtta know and I do know. I do know because I oughtta know. I always do what I oughtta do. Where was I? Oh, yes, I believe I was saying that *getting away with it* requires extraordinary mental stamina against doubt and self-hatred; *getting away with it* calls upon inexhaustible reserves of patience. *Getting away with it* is the most attenuated form of delayed reward I can think of. In terms of attenuation I rank it above getting a Ph.D. in comparative literature, or even having an interest-bearing savings account at a neighborhood bank. *Getting caught,* by contrast, is easy, simple, quick, and gratifying."

"Skippy, you're drunk."

"It is so nice."

"I've eaten LSD every day since I last saw you."

"Is that your special way of telling me you've missed me?"

"Yes."

"And have I missed you?"

"Terribly."

13 *Seven Types of Ambiguity*

"WHAT ARE YOU doing?" Myra said to me. She was standing on the threshold of the book room of our comfortable brownstone on the Upper East Side of Manhattan. I sat inside the book room at the rosewood desk. It was a Sunday morning in springtime.

"I'm writing my memoirs. Want to read them?"

"Don't think I'd understand them."

"Of course you would, honey. You are a groovy, self-knowing woman."

"Maybe some other time. I just wanted to tell you I'm going down to clean the kitchen and make blueberry pancakes. They'll be ready in half an hour."

"Come here and let me kiss you," I said.

Myra blushed and backed away from the threshold. I got up

out of my chair and approached her and she kept backing away. I caught her halfway down the hall and gave her a light, dry kiss on the cheek. She pawed at her cheek as if to wipe off the kiss, and went downstairs.

Reader, isn't it totally cool how Myra bounced back from that stroke? She even used it to sort of grind out a couple of new little personality traits. I wouldn't dare say that Myra was a new woman—you're not going to get any of that kind of crap here as we draw toward the end of this account. Still, Myra is modest proof of a girl's ability to progress. "Modest proof indeed," you might say, but I say Myra is an inherently incremental chick, and I have been rewarded by waiting a very very very long time for her to accomplish the smallest change. Though I certainly do not deserve it, I hope you have been able to find it in your heart to wait similarly for me.

I went back to my memoirs and became lost in writing until I heard the distinctive rhythm of the Hartman footsteps, back and forth, back and forth, on the floor of the upstairs hallway. "Skip, is that you?" I called.

"Yes. Is that you, Mary?"

"Yes, Skip. I'm in here writing my memoirs."

"And how is it going so far?"

"I'm starting with recent events and working my way back."

"I see." She came to the doorway. She wore a long navy-blue skirt with a red and yellow dragonfly/dung beetle/cockroach print. Beige silk shell. White athletic socks.

"I'm writing in the third person for greater objectivity. You know, like when I refer to myself I say 'she' instead of 'I,' " I said.

"Yes, dear, I know what the third person is."

"Are you just going to be snide from now on?"

"I'm not *just* going to be snide. Would you read me what you've written so far?"

"Ahem. 'Two women sat on the bare oak floor of the empty house in the suburbs, one of them getting drunk on red wine, the other numbed by trauma and fear; one of them tall and slender and graceful and educated, the other short and wiry and wild and fearful and sad; one of them older and doting and heartsick and crazy for love, the other younger and contrary and inconsistent and capricious and mercurial and loving; one of them sad and defeated and tamed and subdued and re-silient and resigned and tortured and guilty and doubtful and world-weary and decent and sick and kind, the other sad and abrasive and unrealistic and defiled and subdued and volatile and ephemeral and weak and sick and sad and abused and grateᶠ··l and shocking; one of them with nice posture, the other not so much.' What do you think?"

"Grown tired of a career in plagiarism?"

"Does that mean you like it?"

"It's very touching."

"Shit. Just say you like it."

"I like it."

"You're lying."

"Aunt Myra has made pancakes for breakfast. Why don't you join us all in the kitchen."

"I can't. I'm writing."

"Whatever." She cocked her head sideways, looked down, and held her two hands out in front of her shoulders, palms facing me in the universal *whatever* body posture. I looked at her long, slender fingers and the creases in her palms. I thought of other things she had done with those hands: held a glass of wine; patted her father on the head; manipulated the steering wheel of a car; taped the mouth of that rapist guy; turned the pages of a book; gently touched my bare shoulder. She was halfway down the stairs when I caught up with her and stopped her and took her hand in mine. Her face turned splotchy red and she brushed a lock of smooth gray hair from her eyes and it fell back into her eyes. I removed a bobby pin from where it had been nestled in the side of her head and re-placed it, pinning back the stray lock she had just tried to brush away. We went down to breakfast together. So much for writing my memoirs.

Everyone was in the kitchen—my whole bouillabaisse of a family. There was Myra, walking toward the kitchen counter to address her blueberry pancakes. She had returned to her same way of walking that involved no shoulder movement. Her body still had the look of being a more concentrated mass than other people's bodies: one of her arms would weigh more than one of someone else's arms of equal size.

"Hoving and I are having bagels and lox," Tommy said defi-antly. He was in an excellent mood.

"The boy is keen on bagels and lox," Hoving said. "He's been to prison so why not let him have what he wants." Hoving wore the old cape that belonged to Tommy, the one that was black on the outside and red on the inside. On Hoving's body it drooped and was filthy with food stains and dried drippings of God knows what origin. Hoving wore his clothes with a senile, old-money stainedness that Tommy would not dare aspire to, a filth-style that no doubt disgusted Tommy even as it thrilled him.

Skip and I sat down at the table in the kitchen. With a metal spatula, Myra placed blueberry pancakes on our plates and on her own. Tommy and his new best friend, Hoving, shared a conversation on bagel technique. Skip leaned over and whispered in my ear, "Guess who is now the exclusive changer of Hoving's diapers."

"No!" I whispered.

Tommy said, "I hate secrecy between women."

Hoving said, "Young man, now that the bagel has been lightly toasted, you must spread a thin layer of cream cheese, thus. Do you see the way I am grasping the knife?"

"Myra, look at the way he's grasping the knife," Tommy said. "This is a professional medical practitioner with many years' surgical experience, spreading the cream cheese in retirement."

"Myra, these pancakes are exquisite," Skip said.

I said, "The elderly white-haired man was saucy and irrelevant and dirty and kind; his young male companion was handsome and freckled and self-regarding. The old man was churlish and nonsensical and sweetly paternal and drooling; the young man was languid and vicious and obtuse and amused; the young man's taciturn wife's pancakes had been pronounced exquisite."

"Hartman, what's she doing?" Tommy asked.

"Our young woman seems to have become a play-by-play announcer of her own life. She's dictating her autobiography live, as it were."

"Who's she dictating it to?"

"To the general populace of the kitchen. To no one in particular. To the air."

"She's dictating her memoir to the air," I sang in an operatic soprano. "She's dictating her memoir to the air, she's dictating her meh-heh-heh-heh-heh-heh-heh-mwah tooooooo theeeeee aiyah!"

"Well, we're going to move out soon anyway, which you can put in your memoir," Tommy said. "Myra, honey, when you're done with your pancakes I think we should go apartment hunting. Maybe in Brooklyn. What was that middle-income neighborhood near the park with all the black people where the real estate is still cheap? Do you think black people would tolerate us in the neighborhood or do I look too much like I'm from Darien? Would someone please answer me?"

"Isn't the boy gloriously straightforward and simple?" Hoving said. "He's like a fool in a Shakespearean tragedy."

Reader, I think it happened when I closed my eyes and was wishing Tommy away. A utensil dropped onto a plate. A plate dropped onto the floor and shattered. I opened my eyes. Hoving's chin was on the table and his eyes were closed. Skip was yelling, "Hoving!" Tommy yelled his name too. Myra picked up the phone and pressed the emergency number and spoke our address softly to the person on the other end. We moved the table to the side of the room and put Hoving's body on the ground as if we were all about to change his diapers. Skip knelt above him and exhaled into his mouth and pressed down on his chest with the palm of one hand over the palm of the other hand, and exhaled into his mouth again and put her ear to his mouth to listen for breath. She repeated these movements for the next five minutes. Hoving was dead.

She sat cross-legged over him and held his head in her lap. His neck was bent at a sharp angle and I worried she was hurting him. She caressed his forehead, saying, "My sweet boy, my sweetheart, my nice man." I stood above Skip and touched her hard, orderly head and told her I loved Hoving. She said, "He was a good little father."

"He was an exemplary man," Tommy said, and touched the hem of his cape.

"Hoving," Myra said.

The ambulance arrived.

IN THE MONTHS following Hoving's funeral, Tommy and Myra moved out of the house. September Hartman and I became a pair of thin, sullen, lonely spinsters such as you might find sighing and puttering around the attics and hearths of nineteenth-century novels devoted principally to spirited young men. She and I slept in the same bed but rarely touched. We woke up grumpy and tried to give or receive comfort, often without success.

"I never thought I would say this, but without that man in my life I do not know what to do with myself," Skip said one morning before dawn, lying next to me.

"Yeah," I said.

"What do you mean, 'yeah'?"

"Don't snap at me."

"I was not aware that I was snapping."

"Well, you were."

"Then I am sorry."

"I'm sorry too."

"What are you sorry about?"

"I'm sorry you don't know what to do with yourself without Hoving."

"Well, that's very kind of you."

"Don't talk to me like I'm a stranger. It gives me the creeps."

"Come here, darling," she said. I rolled on my side to face

her. Softly, she kissed a few different spots on my face, and that was nice. "I had thought," she said, "that my life for the next while would be given over to caring for my little brood: Hoving, you, even those people, your aunt and uncle, Myra and Thomas. And now—"

"And now there's just me, and I'm not so good at being cared for."

"Say something nice to me," she said.

" 'Now slides the silent meteor on, and leaves / A shining furrow, as thy thoughts in me,' " I said.

A few tears dribbled out of Skip's eyes, which she shut, and she rested her head on my shoulder and fell asleep for another hour. I lay awake, looking at her and looking out the window and wondering if adulthood meant letting someone you love lie on your arm in the morning when you want to get up and get out of the house, plus your arm is going numb.

When she woke up she said, "I dreamt we were playing that running game we played when you were a child."

"What running game?"

"The one you called Going Away and Coming Back."

"You mean where I sprinted around the block and you timed me?"

"Yes."

"So what happened in the dream?"

"You sprinted around the block and I timed you."

"What was my time?"

"Three months."

"No, seriously."

"I don't know."

"How old was I?"

"My age."

"How old were you?"

"Same age as you. I mean we were both my current age, but you were also a small child, younger than when I met you."

"Huh. Weird."

"Is that something you would be interested in doing?"

"You mean being an adult and being a child at the same time?"

"She is a comedian. I am in bed now with Richard Pryor."

"Sprinting? Sure, I'd give it a try."

On the way out to the street, Skip noticed the postcard on the low table in the entrance foyer. She picked it up and read it and winced. "This is for you," she said.

"Yeah, I've seen it." It had been written and sent to me by Mittler and it said, "I'm not dead, you know."

"Why did you leave it there?"

"I couldn't figure out what to do with it. I didn't want to save it and I didn't want to throw it away."

"You wanted me to see it."

"How do you know?"

"All right, forget it, forget it."

In subsequent years I have, by the way, received a number of postcards from Mittler, with messages on them such as "Not dead" and "Not dead yet" and "Still not dead," lately post-marked in Montana.

We stood together on the stoop of the building. Summer had come and the air was warm. The sky that morning was filling up with tall, dark clouds.

"Quickly, it's going to rain," she said, holding the stopwatch in the air. I went down to the sidewalk and waited. "Ready?" she said. "Go!" I stood still. "And the difficulty is?"

"You're supposed to start with 'Runners take your marks.'"

"Yes, of course. Runners take your marks." I squatted and leaned forward and pressed my fingertips to the sidewalk. "Set." I stuck my butt up in the air. She let me remain in that position for a good ten seconds.

"I feel silly," I said.

"Go!"

I shot out low along the sidewalk, my best start in years. On about the fifth step I felt something go *pop!* in my right calf, followed by a searing pain and a shower of raindrops from the sky. I fell on the ground and clutched my calf. Skip ran to me and carried me in out of the rain.

Half an hour later, during the dramatic summer rainstorm, we were sitting on the dark-blue linen-upholstered couch in the living room, formerly Hoving's bedroom. My right leg was draped across her lap, along with an ice pack, which she held to my calf, and an old hardcover copy of Gray's *Anatomy,* which she scrutinized. Incidentally, this is a position we have duplicated many times since that morning. We often read books like this: I hold my book cradled in my arms and she rests her book on my ankles, which are in turn resting upon her thighs. We are efficient readers in this position. I read the most number of words with the greatest comprehension while my legs are casually, absently, touching her legs. This alignment of our bodies makes reading easy, convenient, and fun.

"You seem to have pulled your tibialis posterior," she said on that morning.

"I think you should get a job," I said.

"And what makes you think I do not have a job?"

"I don't see you going off to work every day."

"And what if I were to say that you are my job?"

"I'd say that's not enough. You yourself said a few hours ago that you don't know what to do with yourself."

"Oh, don't quote me. I hate when you quote me."

"You could teach."

"Teach."

"Teach."

"Absolutely out of the question."

"Why, because seven years ago you seduced an eleven-year-old on the job?"

"Yes."

"Bullshit."

"Don't say 'bullshit' in an argument with me. The naughty word has no special argument-winning powers with me."

"Both of us need jobs," I said.

"Your job should be to get a high school diploma."

"And yours?"

"I think I would like to be the mother of your child."

"Holy shit."

"There she goes again, bringing the naughty word into the conversation."

"No, do you really want to?"

"Yes."

"How would we do it?"

"Don't tell me I forgot to teach you about the birds and bees."

"Wow. I'm, like, blown away here."

"Think about it."

"I am. I'm thinking about it like crazy."

"But I will not raise a child in an unstable family environment. Therefore, if you decide that child-rearing is something you would like to do, you must tell me a few things for certain," Skip Hartman said to me.

"Such as?"

"Will you ever go back to Mittler?"

"No."

"How can you be sure?"

"I'm sure."

"Will you stay with me until I die?" she asked.

"Yes," I said.

"And will you love me?"

"Yes."

Reader, that's it, basically. I mean, basically, that's it. That's all she wrote, so to speak. Thank you very much for your interest and indulgence. Okay, wait, there's one more thing. That conversation I just reported to you? For once in my life I am certain beyond an unreasonable doubt that what I have transcribed is exactly what was spoken on that occasion. I will give it again to make it stick:

"Will you love me?" I asked.

"Yes," she said.

"And will you stay with me until I die?"

MATTHEW SHARPE is the author of *Stories from the Tube*. He has published stories in *Zoetrope, Harper's, American Letters and Commentary, Witness, The Quarterly,* and *Fiction.* He lives in New York.

A C K N O W L E D G M E N T S

Many thanks to Currer Bell, Gabriel Brownstein, E. Shaskan Bumas, Alexis Hurley, Roland Kelts, Becky Kramer, Nora Krug, Neil Levi, Franco Moretti, Bruce Morrow, Beth Pearson, Daniel Rembert, Sergio Santos, Oona Schmid, Carole Sharpe, Myron Sharpe, Susanna Sharpe, Jacqueline Steiner, Robert "Bob" Sullivan, and Amy Zalman.

Special thanks to editor Bruce Tracy, agent Jennifer Hengen, and publicist Brian McLendon, who have made so much out of *Nothing*.

Printed in the United States
by Baker & Taylor Publisher Services